"As a former Army wife, I have such a heart for the families who serve our nation just as much as their active duty spouses do. Wives who have to alternatively run the show and hand over the reins. Children who can't quite grasp where Dad is. I'm glad to see Sharon Gerdes has this same heart. Thank you, Sharon, for writing this amazing story! Well written and evocative."

—Jaxine Daniels, Author, Best Military Romance

"Sharon's novel, *Back in Six Weeks*, is intriguing and engaging. Sharon draws the reader into the world of a mother, who is experiencing postpartum psychosis and dealing with the aftermath. Her novel is an important contribution to literature that addresses mental health issues related to childbearing."

—Jennifer Hentz Moyer, Mental Health Advocate, Author of *A Mother's Climb Out of Darkness*

"An engaging narrative about a woman's struggles with postpartum psychosis. Gerdes' storytelling ability brought her characters to life and is a must read for anyone interested in perinatal mood disorders."

—Susan Benjamin Feingold, Psy.D., Clinical Psychologist, Author of *Happy Endings, New Beginnings: Navigating Postpartum Disorders*

"As a working mom, I was immersed in Kate's struggles. As a military spouse, I identified with her pain. This powerful novel is one helluva great read!"

—Jennifer Lovett, Author of thriller romances with Veteran's issues, Air Force Veteran & Wife, Communicator

Praise for *Back in Six Weeks*

"In *Back in Six Weeks*, Gerdes bravely illuminates postpartum psychosis, a subject that has long been darkened by stigma and profound misunderstanding. The first-person perspective draws the reader directly into the confused mental state of agitation, panic, and distortion of reality. It is powerful, honest and extremely absorbing."

—Karen Kleiman, MSW,
Founder, The Postpartum Stress Center,
Author of *Therapy and the Postpartum Woman*

"*Back in Six Weeks* was riveting, compelling, and heartfelt. I couldn't put it down. Every health provider who works with moms should read it so they know what postpartum psychosis is and what it feels like to the mom experiencing it. What a phenomenal story!"

—Diane Sanford, Ph.D.,
Co-author *Life Will Never Be the Same:
The Real Mom's Postpartum Survival Guide*

"Gerdes has written that rare piece: a fictional story of postpartum psychosis with a ring of truth. In it, a woman's relatively mild case of postpartum psychosis shatters her psyche and strains her marriage. This book includes an important but often overlooked aspect of the postpartum psychosis experience—the 'post-recovery recovery.'"

—Teresa Twomey, JD, Author of
Understanding Postpartum Psychosis: A Temporary Madness

"*Back in Six Weeks* accurately depicts the demands placed on our military families as a result of constant deployments. Inspired by true events, Gerdes gives us a personal look at the life of an Air Force wife during the Cold War."

—Joe Kinego, Colonel, USAF Retired,
SR-71 pilot and squadron commander

"Sharon Gerdes has given us a gift in her novel *Back in Six Weeks*. Her ability to write a fictional account of the complexities of maternal mental illness is remarkable. She has captured the man's emotional reactions, the couple's relationship, the difficulties in their workplaces, as well as an authentic voice of the traumatized woman. Bravo!"

—Jane I. Honikman, M.S.,
Co-founder Postpartum Education for Parents,
Founder Postpartum Support International

"*Back in Six Weeks* is brilliant. It is a very emotion-inducing story. So many things in the book will ring bells for women who have been through similar situations."

—Mary Jo Beug, Author,
Postpartum Mood Disorder Survivor

"After years of hiding her shameful memories of postpartum psychosis, Sharon Gerdes could no longer tolerate the silence. With the help of the ancient tool of storytelling, she allowed her mind to move toward those awful weeks. The longer she wrote, the stronger she felt. No longer constrained by the veil of shame, she turned her formidable fiction writing skill into an excellent novel to help raise public awareness of postpartum psychosis as well as to help women who have experienced it."

—Jerry Waxler, M.S., Author of
Memoir Revolution: A Social Shift that Uses Your Story to Heal, Connect, and Inspire

"Captivating and real. As a clinician, to gain insight into the thought process of Kate as she experiences a postpartum psychosis was disarming and invaluable."

—Lita Simanis, LCSW, Coordinator, Pregnancy and Postpartum Mood & Anxiety Disorder Program,
Alexian Brothers Hospital Network

Back in Six Weeks

Sharon Gerdes

SKG Press
Monument, Colorado
2014

SKG Press
www.SharonGerdes.com

Cover & Interior Design: Angela Werner, Höhne-Werner Design
Cover photo: Julia Vering & Cathy Bowers
Author photo: Johnny Wilson, Wilson Photography
Scripture quotations are taken from *The Living Bible* copyright ©1971. Used by permission of Tyndale House Publishers, Inc., Carol Stream, Illinois 60188. All rights reserved.

Printed in the United States of America

ISBN-13: 978-0-9904679-0-8

Dedication

I'd like to dedicate this book to my mother, Bernadine Vering. She was proud that I was writing about my struggles as a mother, and I'm very sad that she passed before she could see the final book in print. A professor of psychology once told me—women who have a strong mother, a mother who teaches them to believe in themselves, have a better chance of recovery from perinatal mood disorders. I haven't seen the science, but in my heart I believe that is true.

I'd also like to dedicate this book to the other women in my "tribe," as one postpartum survivor called us. Most of us are survivors, and have triumphed over our challenges. Sadly, too many mothers commit suicide or other acts which cause them to spend years in mental hospitals or in prison. As I've heard their stories, I feel very fortunate. Thanks to all those working in the field of postpartum mental health.

Lastly, I'd like to thank all the family, neighbors, and church members who helped me during a difficult time. My teeny baby grew to be a man that I'm proud to call my son. He followed in his father's footsteps and served our country proudly. My happiest Mother's Day was when he called to say that he was safely back in the States after a tour of duty in Afghanistan.

Revelation 2:10 *You will be persecuted for 'ten days'.*

1.

June 21, 1980 – Day 1

"Now. Push. Hard!"

One push. That's all it took. In less than sixty seconds, a tiny red human with skinny, flailing arms and legs—and unmistakable boy parts—emerged. Not the little blond girl that Mike and I had been dreaming about for so many years. Not our baby Angela. I collapsed back on the bed, numb. Too exhausted to voice the rage that seethed inside me. How could they have thought this was false labor? How dare they tell me to go to sleep and quit bothering them? Could such a tiny baby live? At the moment, I wasn't even sure I cared.

"Waaaa!" My tiny preemie protested. A strong, angry cry.

My baby! Of course I wanted him to live. So what if he wasn't a girl. He was a Wahlberg, Mike's son, Jason's little brother, and my precious baby. The soft jabs and kicks these past three months had come from his tiny limbs.

Dr. Turner swaddled my son in a blanket. "I'm the only doctor on duty, and I need to stabilize him."

My chest pounded. "Stabilize—"

He cradled my baby in his arms and left without another word. Freckle-faced nurse Judy touched my shoulder. "I'll be back." Then she rushed to follow.

I lay there, bleeding, blaming. It had all happened so fast. I could barely absorb the reality. He wasn't due for another six weeks.

Judy hurried back into the room. "I'm so sorry, Kate. We don't normally deliver on the ward. Colonel Reeves insisted it was only Braxton Hicks contractions. Then I heard your scream." She swabbed my arm with a stinky antiseptic, jabbed me with a needle, and inserted an IV tube.

Dr. Turner popped back, a surgical mask slung below his neck. "We're doing everything possible to save your son, Mrs. Wahlberg. We'll know more in an hour."

Everything possible? Dreams of booties and baby buntings now dangled. I closed my eyes and sent up a silent Hail Mary.

The doctor administered a few quick stitches, where he had cut my episiotomy. I winced at each sharp sting.

"We didn't want any pressure on the baby's brain. Preemies are extremely fragile at this stage," he explained. "We'll get you something for the pain, and to help you sleep."

Then he hurried back to the nursery before I could utter a word.

Just seven days ago, Mike kissed me goodbye and headed for Okinawa. My swollen ankles told me something wasn't right with the pregnancy. I should have seen a civilian doctor, gotten a second opinion. But I couldn't upset Mike before he flew overseas. I'd been an Air Force wife long enough to know: the mission comes first.

The drama of the past week had been overwhelming—three trips to the base hospital emergency room, juggling work deadlines and mommy duties, shuffling my toddler Jason between day care and neighbors. I'd had it all under control. Then the dam broke.

Judy returned. I struggled to sit up. "I want to see my baby."

She pressed my shoulder back on the bed. "Right now, you need to rest."

She injected pain medication into my IV, closed the khaki curtain, and placed the call box near my hand. "This will help you relax. Let us know if you need anything." She tucked the sheet up under my chin and stroked my long blond hair.

I had as much strength as a mouse, and I succumbed. The dim yellow light from my night lamp cast soft shadows across the half-empty hospital room. I sunk into the mattress and listened to the two girls across the hall giggle about their stretch marks. No roommate for me. I caught the closing tune of *MASH* before they turned off their TV. My television stayed dark, the remote control strategically out of my reach. Doctor's orders. Any excitement could spike the toxemia.

And now—a premature baby—struggling for life in the nursery. For the moment, his fate was in someone else's hands. I closed my eyes and allowed myself to slide into a cocoon of sleep.

* * *

"You gave the nurses quite a run for their money last night, young lady."

I startled awake. Was it day? Night? The doctor stood at the foot of my bed, perusing my chart. Colonel Reeves, six foot one, towered over most of her OB staff. Her silver hair was cropped an inch longer than the standard military cut. No makeup. No jewelry. Her finely shaped eyebrows the only hint of femininity. The years had etched a permanent scowl on her face. Rumor had it she had been scorned in love during medical school and was now married to the Air Force.

"You were just upset because your husband's overseas," The Colonel said. "That's why the baby came early. I see it all the time with you young ones."

I wanted to scream. *No! I was upset because my contractions started six weeks too soon.* Instead I said, "I may look young, but I'll have you know, I am twenty-seven years old, a college graduate, and a department head." I wanted to add that if I ran my department like she ran hers, I'd be fired. But I held my tongue. Thankfully, a blood pressure of 190 over 140 got me admitted to the OB ward. Had the nurses ignored my pains because of an order from The Colonel? From my first appointment, something told me not to trust this woman.

She tapped on my chart with her pen, as if pondering a battle strategy. "Does the baby have a name?"

"Not yet. We were expecting a girl."

"Best to plan for all contingencies." Her tone hinted that she was miffed that Mother Nature had pulled rank in the middle

;ht. "The boy weighed in at three pounds, eight ounces. ₩ɛ re not equipped to keep infants less than four pounds here. But we've got a new pediatrician—Khan. Good man. They called him at 0400 hours. He's been with your son all morning. We'll transport the baby to the Travis neonatal unit sometime today, as soon as there's an opening."

Travis was somewhere in Northern California, a couple of hours away. "I won't need long to get ready—" I said.

"You'll stay here."

"Like hell I will."

"Mrs. Wahlberg, you will stay on my ward for a minimum of forty-eight hours."

"Do you know who my husband is?" The pilots of the SR-71 supersonic spy plane were an elite breed, the best of the best. If Mike were here, he'd get his commander to pull some strings.

"His rock-star status holds no sway with me."

"But—" I sunk in the bed, too drained to argue. I needed to regroup, find an ally, and form a plan.

The doctor palpitated my abdomen. "How are you feeling?"

My power to negotiate was hampered by the sharp jabs. "A little better." I was afraid to ask, but figured I'd better get it out. "Doctor, what are his chances? Will he … make it?"

"I'm going to order your IV removed. Then you can go see him. Under thirty-six weeks gestation, we monitor for breathing problems, but, so far, his respiration's good. Toxemia primes the lungs. He's in an incubator." She snapped the chart shut. "He seems to be a real fighter." Her tone softened ever so slightly.

Three pound, eight ounces. I'd never known anyone who'd had a baby that small. Jason, our three-year-old, had weighed over eight pounds. In college, I'd gone on a field trip to a hospital for handicapped kids. Children of five, even eight years, lay in cribs wearing diapers, drooling, with absent stares on their faces. I had never considered the possibility that my baby would be anything less than perfect.

"And his mental development? Can they tell?" I spoke just above a whisper, my voice trembling.

The Colonel slid the pen in her pocket. "Statistically, there's a good chance your baby will be 100 percent normal. But at this stage, we certainly can't determine these things."

After she left, I flopped back on my pillow. I felt totally confident with the younger OB doctors at the base hospital, but I couldn't get over this uneasy feeling about The Colonel. She always seemed too busy, too inflated with her rank and position. But in a military hospital, I didn't have the luxury of choosing my physician. I'd tried to talk Mike into letting me deliver at Ridner Hospital, just five minutes away from our house, but that would have cost a lot more money. He was way too frugal to spend the extra bucks. All the other military wives delivered at the base hospital, and so could I. If I hadn't been so obsessed with my work, with getting the new marinara sauce project completed, I would have gone behind his back and seen another doctor.

But playing the blame game wasn't going to earn me a do-over. From here on, I'd need to trust my instincts, not The Colonel and her team.

2.

Judy removed my IV and taped a cotton ball in the crook of my arm. "Can you stand, or do you want a wheelchair?"

"I prefer to walk."

I slid over the side of the bed and pushed up, carefully putting weight on my wobbly legs. She reached for my right elbow to steady me.

"I'm okay. Just give me a second."

"Let's get you covered."

She slipped a thin cotton robe over my arms. I followed her down the olive-drab hallway toward the nursery. We maneuvered past an airman who pushed a noisy vacuum and joked with the woman loading breakfast trays onto a tall metal cart.

The nursery was cheerier and quieter than the ward. On one wall someone had painted a huge Tigger, and on the other, Winnie-the-Pooh, his paw dripping with honey. Eight bassinettes held sleeping babies, some wrapped in pink blankets, some in blue, strategically placed near a viewing window so dads and visitors could catch a first peek. The other babies all seemed chubby and content, although one little boy started to squirm and whimper. I shuffled past them to the incubator in the far corner and peered in.

A monitor beeped softly. My baby lay naked, tubes and wires attached to every part of his body. My heart went out instantly to the little guy. He was all arms and legs—just like his daddy—but small and thin. His skin was almost transparent, his fingernails paper-thin. His delicate face was framed by soft blond hair—that he got from me. His tiny mouth moved in little sucking motions. I stood in awe, afraid to love him, fearing God might punish me for my obsession with having a daughter.

A short unshaven man came over and adjusted the leads coming out of the incubator. He looked barely old enough to be out of college. He extended a hand. "I am Dr. Khan. You are the mother?"

I felt strength in his warm grasp.

"Baby is still critical." The doctor's tired eyes offered little optimism. "We don't have a full neonatal unit here. Better if you'd been transported to Travis before the baby was born. You didn't realize you were in labor?"

I cast my eyes down in shame. I had asked the nurse for a watch to time my contractions, instinctively lapsed into Lamaze breathing, ignored my own body, and believed The Colonel. I should have listened to the gals at work and quit weeks ago. I'd been so selfish, so stupid.

"Sorry, little guy," I whispered under my breath. *I'll make it up to you.* I pointed at the little cotton shackles wrapped around each ankle and pinned to the sheets. "Bad behavior already?"

"This one's a fighter. Watch." He unpinned the left side, and immediately my little tyke lifted his leg and maneuvered his foot toward the IV that snaked out the top of his head.

"We don't want him to pull out the tube," added the doctor. "Don't worry. Fabric soft. Doesn't hurt him."

He gently pulled down my baby's leg and reattached it to the sheet with the safety pin. The leg was no bigger around than the doctor's thumb and shifted side to side, as if he were struggling to kick free.

"It's okay for you to touch him, but very gently. Wash hands first." The doctor nodded toward a sink along the wall near Tigger.

I complied, then returned, feeling like a surgeon with sterile hands. Dr. Khan opened one of the two ports on my side of the incubator and motioned for me to reach in.

The air inside the incubator was warm on my skin. "Hey, little guy. It's me, your mommy." His teeny fingers closed around my giant pinkie.

"See? Instinct. He knows his mama. Important for mother to bond with baby," Dr. Khan said.

I pulled my finger away slightly. But he held on. Definitely a fighter.

"You didn't pick name?" He pointed to the card that said, "Baby Boy Wahlberg."

"Angela." I paused. "I'm rethinking that choice."

"In my country, everyone wants boy. Grow up to be doctor, support parents."

"In this country, girls can be doctors—"

"Of course. The Colonel. My aunt is an internist. She studied in Boston. Go Red Sox," he added with a grin.

"I'm a Royals fan myself. George Brett?"

"Brett plays third base. He's a heavy hitter." Dr. Khan was clearly a fan of the sport. He jotted some notes on the chart, hung it next to the incubator, and wagged a finger at me. "Baby needs name before we transport to Travis. Pick a name today and let the nurses know."

My head swam. Pick a name? A boy's name? The odor of disinfectant was making me nauseous. My knees wobbled and I gripped the counter to keep from collapsing.

"Mother needs her rest," Dr. Khan said.

"Yes, I think I'll go back to my room."

"One more thing. Will you breast-feed?"

"I did with Jason, but now … can I?" How was I supposed to get past the wires, the tubes?

"It's very important for preemies. The nurses will give you bottles and help you." The young doctor stifled a yawn.

On the way back to my room, I stopped at the nurses' station and used the desk phone to call my parents. My dad answered. His usually cheery voice carried an unfamiliar tone of alarm. "Grandma Bernon had a stroke yesterday morning and fell in her kitchen. Your mother's still at the hospital with her."

I twisted the phone cord around my pinkie while Dad explained Grandma's condition. She had paralysis in her right leg, arm, and eye. She would need therapy. It would take weeks before they would know her full prognosis.

Last summer had been rough on Kansas farmers. My parents didn't have a lot of extra cash, and Mom had already bought a plane ticket to come out just before my due date, still six weeks away. I couldn't ask her to abandon her own mother now.

"Tell Mom to take care of Grandma," I said, "get rested up, and then come out to meet her new grandson."

"Grandson. Whoa. I thought you weren't due until the end of July. Are you okay? Your mother can be on the next plane."

Mom was a nurse. The best. I needed her desperately, but couldn't ask her to abandon her own mother now. I hesitated, running various scenarios through my mind, none of them working.

Finally I said, "Tell Mom to give my love and prayers to Grandma. Do you have a pencil? I'll give you the number and she can call me here at the base hospital when she gets home. I'll be fine. I will."

I wrapped my arms around my shoulders and hugged myself tight. A dark, dense feeling within me said nothing would ever be fine again.

3.

I got the preemie bottles from the nurses' station and returned to my room. A breakfast tray sat by my bed. I lifted the silver cover to Cream of Wheat, lukewarm now, but I was ravenous. My belly had been so bloated for the past week that I'd eat two bites, and my stomach was full.

I added milk, sprinkled on a little packet of sugar, and wolfed the paste down. Before starting into my task of the day, I tried to eke a little warmth from the cup of coffee on the tray. Maybe it would give me a boost of energy. What I needed more than anything was a day-long nap.

My breasts were starting to feel hard, like rocks, but I had no idea how to get the milk into the thin bottle. I worked at the task for ten minutes, and finally expressed about two teaspoons of my breasts' creamy yellow fluid. But it wasn't the same as with a baby at the breast. The first few days with Jason had been difficult. But, before long, we synched into a happy feeding team. Pumping my milk into a bottle felt so detached, so painful. Frustrated, I finally gave up and screwed on the lid. I tramped the bottle down to the nursery, and found Judy standing beside the incubator. A monitor alarm beeped. She reached to turn it off, then took the bottle and peered in. "That's all?"

"I tried. It just doesn't feel right."

"You need to relax, hon." She rubbed her hand across my shoulder. "It'll come."

Relaxing was not my strong suit. I was a food scientist with a "get 'er done" bent. With one child, I'd easily juggled deadlines and diapers. Now the simplest task left me stymied.

Judy added formula to make the requisite two ounces, and set the bottle on top of the incubator. She measured a piece of IV tubing by holding it from my baby's mouth, past his ear, and down to the middle of his stomach. She cut the tubing, attached it to a small syringe, and poured the milk into the syringe. Then ever so gently, she fed the tubing down my tiny baby's throat.

"We call this gavage feeding," Judy said. "A Frenchman invented it for babies who are too weak to suck." She held the syringe overhead while the milk slowly fed down by gravity.

I watched in awe. He looked like a fish on a line. Would he ever grow big enough to go fishing with Grandpa? He seemed to be sucking, his tiny lips opening and closing around the clear IV tubing. When the syringe was empty, Judy rubbed his bare belly until a tiny burp emerged.

"His skin looks bluer than yesterday," I said.

"That's a sign of neonatal respiratory distress syndrome. Dr. Khan has written orders to transport him to Travis, the minute there's an opening."

"Will they notify me before he goes?" I swallowed the bile that kept rising in my throat.

"We'll make sure you get to say goodbye. For now, you can stroke his forehead or hold his hand. Get to know him." She changed the diaper pad under his bare bottom and wiped his boy parts with a towelette.

I waited until Judy walked away, then leaned close and whispered, "You'd prefer mommy's milk, wouldn't you?" His legs kicked against the restraint, and I took that for a yes. "Don't worry. We'll get you healthy. You've got a big brother who wants to meet you. He's been so excited." I caressed the soft skin, then adjusted the cloth attached to his leg. "There, is that better?"

I glanced over my shoulder, half afraid that somebody would come and tell me I wasn't supposed to touch anything except my baby. I lingered, scanning the tags showing the names and weights of the other babies, paying special attention to the boys—Taylor, Zachary, and Morgan. One of the new moms stood outside the viewing window and pointed to a little girl. She was supported on one side by an older woman with an identical chin, clearly her mother, and on the other by an airman with a proud-daddy grin. I headed back down the hall, solo.

The nurses expected me to bring a little bottle of warm breast milk every three hours. But squeezing my hard breasts was agonizing. Only a few drops came out. I wanted to give up. But I couldn't let this little guy down.

Finally, the nurse on the afternoon shift brought me some pamphlets and suggested a hot shower. I raised the water temperature to steamy and stepped in. The trick worked. My breasts slowly relaxed. On my fourth try, I was able to fill the bottle. By the 9 p.m. feeding, I pretty much had the hang of it. My blood pressure was down, so I now acquired a roommate and television privileges.

I started to doze off for the evening. I felt a nudging on my arm. An orderly flipped on the hanging light over my bed. "Time to get your baby," she announced in a regulation voice.

"My baby's the preemie ... Are they transporting him now?" I turned to the clock on the wall behind me.

"Oh, sorry. You're on the three-hour schedule. Go back to sleep."

I was dead tired and pissed. Didn't one shift let the other know what was going on? The orderly walked over to my roommate, Natalie, who was on a four-hour schedule. "Wake up. It's time to get your baby."

Natalie yawned, flipped on the light, then trudged down the hall. She returned a few minutes later with her screaming baby, fed it, diapered it, and chatted at her newborn incessantly. I turned my back to them and pulled the sheet over my head, but it did little to block out the noise. Natalie would be going home with her baby in forty-eight hours. I longed for the comfort of my own house, my own bed. How long was I going to be stuck on this sterile corridor? Her baby cried for at least fifteen minutes while she sang an off-key rendition of "Hush, Sweet Baby." Finally, she took her baby back to the nursery.

I could not fall back to sleep. My mouth felt pasty. I hadn't planned to be admitted, hadn't even thought about packing a bag, so I didn't even have a toothbrush. I worried about Jason at the sitter's. He didn't have a toothbrush either, or his jammies.

And why hadn't Mike called? If all was calm, he usually phoned once a week from overseas, on the Air Force direct lines. If the world was in turmoil, he might be incommunicado for an indefinite time. Just when I needed him most.

4.

Mike soared twenty-five thousand feet over the South China Sea at near Mach speed toward the air refueling control point. The past three days had been crazy. There had been unusual troop movements in Cambodia. The Pentagon wanted reconnaissance photos. There'd barely been time to fly, sleep, then jump in the cockpit again. A KC-135 tanker loomed ahead. He flipped the switch to transfer fuel into the forward tanks and maneuvered the supersonic stealth jet fifty feet behind and ten feet below the tanker's boom nozzle. The boom operator, lying in the belly of the KC-135, moved the long metal fuel cylinder fore and aft to signal the SR-71 he was cleared for the "contact" position. Adding power, Mike eased the plane up toward the fuel boom, so that the operator could plug in, lock, and begin downloading JP-7.

The normal radios were silent, eliminating any chance of an enemy ship detecting his position. The boom operator's voice crackled through the interphone, "You're taking gas." Mike fingered the stick, keeping the spy plane straight and level during the fifteen minutes it took to fuel the thirsty machine.

His helmet was hot and itchy. He reached over to adjust the tiny valve that pumped cooling air between his body and six layers of high-tech fabric—the pressure suit that increased chances of survival, should the unthinkable happen at high altitude. He guided the "black serpent" in silence until the fuel gauge read full, then gave the signal to separate. He pulled up alongside the KC-135, gave a thumbs-up to the pilot, then accelerated, leaving the tanker behind.

At Mach 3, he climbed to 85,000 feet to begin the hour of aerial reconnaissance that would take him high over Cambodia and Vietnam, marveling at the varying hues of the heavens, almost baby blue reflecting off the beaches of Vietnam, nearly steel blue demarcating the horizon. From this layer of the stratosphere he could discern the curve of Mother Earth and gaze up at the stars in the middle of the day.

His thoughts returned to Kate. She'd had a ghastly look on her face when he kissed her goodbye before heading out on this trip. He should have put his foot down, insisted she quit work weeks ago. His cameras could capture troop and equipment movements in any hot spot on the globe. But he was woefully out of touch with what was happening with his three-year-old, his wife, and the precious bundle incubating inside her belly.

5.

Day 2

By the next day, I had pretty much synched into a routine of pumping breast milk, hovering over the baby in the nursery, and cat-napping—never sleeping—in my room. Dr. Khan had explained that the first forty-eight hours were critical.

At the 2100 hours feeding, I leaned on the wall next to my baby's incubator. His skin remained the same shade of blue. No better. No worse. His breaths were rapid and shallow. He was struggling. Still holding his own. An orderly tapped me on the shoulder.

"Mrs. Wahlberg, you've got an overseas call holding at the nurses' station."

I hobbled down the hall and grabbed the receiver off the desk phone.

"Kate. What's happening?"

I was breathless. "Mike, did they tell you?"

There was a crackle on the line and a slight delay in the voice transmission. "I called and called home. When I didn't get you, I dialed Brenda to see if she knew what was going on. She said you were in the hospital—"

"I had the baby. It all happened so fast."

"Are you okay? And the baby?"

"I'm alright. Our baby—they're still not sure. He's so tiny, only three and a half pounds. They're going to send him to Travis, to a special neonatal unit. So far he's holding his own, but he's still critical."

"He." Mike paused. "I know you wanted a girl—"

"You did too. Right now I can't even think about that. The nurses insist we pick a name, so they can complete the birth certificate before they transport him."

"Let me think—" There was long silence. "How about Robert? We could call him Robbie," Mike said.

Robert was Mike's Reconnaissance Systems Officer, or as Mike put it, "his RSO," the guy who sat behind him in the SR-71 and monitored the surveillance equipment. He and Mike had been a team for years. They were really close.

"Good solid name. I like Robbie," I said.

"Where's Jason?"

"With Lindsey. She's keeping him until we can figure something out."

"I can't talk much longer. They'll cut us off. Listen, I'm not supposed to come home for another five weeks, but—"

"Mike. I'm hanging in there, holding the fort together with blue duck tape and pink bubble gum." I tried to sound brave. "Please don't do anything stupid. After that flyover—" There was a click, then silence on the line.

Damn. I hung up, more apprehensive than assured after the call, longing for the comfort of Mike's touch. I could tell he was frustrated because he was half a world away. A lot of guys would be happy to have missed the whole birthing action, but Mike didn't fit the mold. He was hard as titanium in the cockpit, but soft as a tulip when it came to family stuff. He'd stayed up late many a night with Jason when my nerves were frazzled from a long day of mothering, snuggling our son under his shirt like a papoose, reading flight pubs to him until he drifted off to sleep, then tucking him into his crib.

I waddled back to bed. If only I'd listened to Molly, the secretary at work, back when my feet first started to swell. What if I'd delivered at home in my bed, or worse, in the hospital toilet? Scary images looped through my brain—Robbie lying in a pool of blood in our bed, or hitting the porcelain of the toilet with his fragile head.

Moonlight filtered through a crack between the linen curtains, casting a crooked line of light across my wall. I lay awake wondering if I'd ever get to take Robbie home to greet his big brother.

6.

The next morning I used the phone at the nurses' station to call our sitter, Lindsey. At twenty-five dollars a week, Lindsey was a godsend. She'd kept Jason for a week earlier in the year, when I was barely pregnant, so that Mike and I could take a much-needed vacation. I explained to Lindsey that the doctors wanted me to provide fresh breast milk for Robbie. It was a ninety-minute round trip from my house to the hospital. So driving back and forth was not an option.

"Jason must feel abandoned," I said.

"He misses you at nighttime. I keep telling him his mommy will come get him soon. I hope that's okay?"

I hung on the words, stung with guilt. "Put him on. I'll try to explain," I said.

"Mommy, guess what. Lindsey's cat had kittens." Compared to Robbie's thin cry, Jason sounded almost grown up. "Can I bring two home? One for me, and one for the baby? There's a striped one, Mommy. It's tiny. They're all tiny. And they go 'mew, mew.'" He brimmed with excitement. "They can sleep in my room. Pleeease, Mommy."

"Let's check with Daddy first. You know kittens have to stay with their mommy till they get bigger. They need their mommy's milk."

"Like our baby."

"Yes, honey."

For the past few months, Jason had been telling Stephanie, his four-year-old playmate down the street, that he was going to have a baby sister. They'd been playing "house" and

practicing diapering baby dolls. Stephanie had shown Jason
how to rock a baby doll and hold it to his breast.

"When are you coming to get me, Mommy?"

"Soon. Right now I have to stay with the baby at the hospital."

"Where's Daddy?"

"You know Daddy's flying. He can't come home for a long
time."

"Mommy—" Jason sniffed. "I wet the bed last night. Lindsey didn't get mad."

Jason had been potty-trained for over a year. He never wet
the bed. This holding-the-family-together via Ma Bell thing
was not working. "It's okay, Jason. We all have accidents.
Remember when I burned the pan on the stove?"

The nurse started giving me the *this is a community phone
and you've used it long enough* look. I glared back at her.

"Got to go, sweetie. Hang in there! I'll come and get you
soon."

"When, Mommy?"

The nurse pointed to the clock on the wall, and motioned
for me to hang up.

"Soon." I plopped the phone on the receiver and turned my
back so the nurse would not see my single-finger salute.

Later that morning, a couple from my church stopped in
to visit. They shared that everyone in the congregation was
praying for Robbie and left me a copy of the New Testament. I
adjusted my pillow and started reading the Book of Matthew.
It was boring, so I turned to the Book of Revelation and flipped
through the pages.

In Chapter 12, I found: "*She was pregnant and screamed in
the pain of her labor.*" Odd. I wasn't the screaming type. Unless
an unexpected snake slithered across my path. But just minutes before Robbie was born, I had gone to the toilet. There was
this huge gush of water. I knew something was terribly wrong.
I screamed. Probably scared every woman on the ward. Sure
got Judy's attention.

A coincidence. I knew from Catechism class that people could misinterpret Revelation. The whole Book was a mystery. I read on: "*Suddenly a red Dragon appeared .... He stood before the woman ... ready to eat the baby ....*" The Colonel had behaved monstrously. This stuff was creepy.

There was a knock at the door. I snapped the Bible shut and stuffed it in my nightstand.

Hillary, who ran QC in the lab at the small food plant where we both worked, stood in the doorway, her red hair flowing freely. In one hand, she held a bouquet of blue daisies, in the other, a teddy bear decked out in pilot-style goggles and scarf.

"Congratulations, new mama." Hillary set my gifts on the nightstand.

We hugged and I inhaled the familiar aromas of tomato, basil, and oregano on her shirt. "Come straight from work?"

"What gave me away?" She plopped her purse on the chair.

"Lingering aroma of marinara sauce."

We both chuckled.

"At least it's better than the stench of jet fuel. I make Bill shower as soon as he comes in the door."

"So you're managing to keep The Marinara Factory pumping out sauce without me?"

"We put the gourmet sauce project on hold until you get back. Any idea how long that will be?"

"Originally I planned to be back in six weeks. Now I don't know."

"Take it one day at a time. I know the baby will be here a while, but when do they release *you*?"

"The doctors want me to stay in the hospital, so my breast milk will be fresh for each feeding. I asked about refrigerating it, but they aren't sure about the sanitation, the distance. Fresh is safe."

"Makes sense from a micro standpoint. At least Chuck hasn't tried to move into your office."

I had been so preoccupied with the baby that I completely forgot about my rival at work. Everyone at the plant had assumed the job of supervising our team of seven food scientists, microbiologists, and technicians would have gone to Chuck, a chemical engineer with over thirty years of food-industry experience. Instead Fred, the plant manager, selected a lanky blonde with a passion for gourmet cooking, only five years out of college—me. Chuck, despite his ability to spout numbers and draw flow charts, was an abysmal failure at managing people. The man had defied my authority since the day Fred appointed me Director of Quality Assurance at Marinara.

"What's the weasel up to now?" I said.

"He's telling Fred you arranged this whole thing to get extra time off."

I let out a deep sigh. So typical of Chuck.

"He's working on replacing the real wine in your formulas with a wine flavor."

"No. He'll ruin them. He uses the cheapest ingredients. The stuff tastes like crap. Then he blames it on me."

"I keep telling Fred to wait until you get back. But if it's more than six weeks, Fred might give in. Chuck's pretty convincing." Hillary rolled her eyes.

"It's like I'm in limbo. No control. No idea how long I'll be here."

Hillary walked over and shut the door, then reached into her oversized purse. "I brought you a toothbrush, like you asked. And something else." She grinned, pulled out two cans of Coors, and handed one to me. Hillary was a woman after my own heart, comfy with bending a few rules and winking in the face of Uncle Sam.

The can was cold and inviting. I hesitated. "I don't know. I'm sort of drinking for two."

"After five days in this place, I figured you needed to loosen up." Hillary pulled the tab on her own beer and reached out to toast me.

When I nursed Jason, I learned that drinking beer is great for your milk production. Jason was a big baby. Robbie was tiny. Robbie needed my milk. Finally I gave in. "You're right. This is Mike's kid. He'll have to get used to beer eventually."

I pulled the tab, tapped my can to hers, and took a long cool gulp. Same great taste I'd been enjoying since college. I downed about half of the frothy brew and started to feel light-headed. "That's enough! We'd better wean Robbie onto happy milk slowly." I poured the rest down the sink, stifled a beer belch, and handed the evidence to Hillary for disposal.

"So when is Mike coming home?"

"I have no idea."

"Bill says they're talking about sending an extra SR-71 over to Guam. That thing in Laos and Cambodia. Have you been watching the news about the Khmer Rouge?"

"I'm out of touch." I collapsed on my bed. "Was banned from television for days."

"Nobody knows, but things may blow up. Speaking of blowing up, an F-4 exploded over the South China Sea. It's a mystery. Nobody can figure it out. All hush-hush. Mike might have to stay overseas even longer."

"Not with a new baby. They can't—"

"It's the military. Yes they can. Listen, I need to get home and make dinner." Hillary gave me a hearty goodbye hug, then reached in her purse and handed me a stick of gum. "For the beer breath."

* * *

The Travis neonatal unit remained full. Robbie improved every day. Dr. Khan finally announced that they would keep him here and not transport him. What a relief. I felt as if a boulder had been lifted off my back.

Standing over the incubator that night, I yearned to hold Robbie to my breast, just once. It might be weeks before I could take my baby home. I needed to be patient.

"Shouldn't I let him latch on to my breast, just for a few seconds. So he gets an idea where the milk comes from," I suggested to nurse Judy.

"Breastfeeding is a ways down the line," she told me. "But you can hold him for a few minutes."

After the tube feeding, she pulled a rocking chair next to the incubator for me.

I sat, crossing and uncrossing my legs, while she took Robbie out of the incubator and arranged all the tubes and cords. She placed him in my open arms.

My teeny tyke was light as a feather. He squirmed and curled a skinny leg up toward his head. I planted a kiss on his soft forehead and inhaled the mixed aroma of milk burp and baby wipes. This felt so unnatural. I yearned to slide him under my gown and feel the sweet communion of babe and breast. But Judy kept glancing at me while she changed the sheet in the incubator. Her manner convinced me to get both me and Robbie out of the hospital as soon as possible, to my own house. Where I could relax in my own comfy rocking chair, away from scrutinizing eyes, and feed my baby on demand.

A monitor beeped, and Judy held out her arms to take Robbie. Reluctantly, I handed my precious boy back.

"Go get some sleep, hon," Judy advised.

At the double doors that separated the nursery from the ward, I saw a parked gurney. On it, a body covered in a green sheet. Had somebody left a dead body in the hall?

Then the sheet moved.

Startled, I jumped. Then the medic rolled over and started snoring. I laughed at myself with nervous relief. This place was getting to me. Time to split.

7.

Day 8

Mike struck a deal with another pilot to switch TDY schedules. The Air Force had an acronym for everything. TDY was short for temporary duty, six-week stretches of overseas assignment. They kept coming and coming. Okinawa, Japan—then home to be the last person in the cul-de-sac to hear Jason's first "Dada." Mildenhall, England—then home to find Jason walking around the kitchen floor. Then back to Okinawa, the destination of this trip.

The other crew had arrived in Japan, and Mike and Robert were on their way home. After an eighteen-hour trip across the Pacific in a KC-135 tanker refueler, he would land sometime in the middle of the night.

One of the other SR-71 wives had brought me some makeup and a comb. I took a shower, fixed myself up the best I could, then peered into the narrow mirror in the bathroom. Not hot, but Mike had seen me looking worse. Natalie had gone home with her baby, and left me some Chanel cologne, which I dabbed on my neck. It covered the sterile hospital smell.

After what seemed an eternity, there was a loud tap at the open door. Mike stood in the doorway, tall and assured, wearing the signature SR-71 orange flight suit. His easy grin made my heart go flip-flop. I slid off the bed and rushed into his open arms. He smelled like he needed a shower, but I melted in his embrace.

"It's about time you got here, Flyboy."

"Would have hijacked an SR and been here faster, but you told me not to do anything stupid."

"And for once you listened."

I ran my fingers through his coarse auburn hair, grown over his ears since he'd left home, definitely longer than the limit for a military cut. But Mike relished pushing the boundaries of any Air Force rule.

He maneuvered the chair next to my bed, plopped down and pulled me into his lap. I sat gingerly, still smarting from the childbirth.

He nuzzled my neck with his whisker stubble. "Tell me everything I missed."

I poured out the whole saga, trips to the emergency room, the fast birth, my fears about Robbie's long-term prospects. "I can't touch my baby unless I wash my hands. They watch me every minute. It's like Robbie's their baby, and I'm an intruder." Finally, exhausted, I lay my head on his chest. The steady thump of his heart calmed me.

He gently pushed the corners of my lips into a smile. "You're getting yourself all worked up over nothing. It's a military hospital. You play by their rules. You don't have a choice. Trust me. Everything will be okay." He touched the hospital gown, and ran his fingers across my full breasts. "Nice outfit."

My breasts tingled. "Don't do that."

"Why not?"

Two wet spots formed on my chest.

He smiled. "You're breastfeeding."

I nodded. "I'm going to need that gown with the slits in the front, my nursing bra—"

"Make me a list. I'll bring it all tomorrow."

He scooted me off his lap. "I wanted to check on you first. Now, let's go meet our son."

The three o'clock bottle waited, empty on the nightstand. I grabbed it. "Give me five minutes. Don't watch."

"I've seen your breasts before, and I've kind of missed them."

"Stop. I can't let down if you're watching."

"Let down? Oh, yeah. The milk." He turned away. Out the corner of my eye, I watched him pull out his survival knife and tighten the loose screw on my overhead lamp.

I twisted the bottle cap closed. "Ready."

I led him down the hall to the nursery, and over to the corner where Robbie lay in the incubator, wearing only a preemie diaper. Mike was mesmerized. His mouth hung open as his eyes scanned the monitors and tubes, then settled on our tiny tyke.

"Hi, little guy. It's Daddy. Bet you were wondering when I'd show up."

I handed Judy the milk bottle and introduced her to Mike.

"I hear you fly the SR-71," Judy said.

"It's not nearly as impressive as this," Mike said, pointing to the monitors.

Judy prepared the gavage tube, and held it up to let the milk flow.

Mike leaned close. "Fuel from a tube. I can see the makings of an SR-71 pilot." He grinned, love in his eyes. "Hey Sport. I flew half-way across the world to meet you. You seem a little tied up at the moment."

"Robbie has fewer wires now than he did." Judy pointed to the bloody spot on Robbie's scalp. "He had an IV here."

They had removed the bandages from his legs. I leaned over and touched Robbie's soft cheek. "You're almost free, Robbie."

"Can I touch him?" Mike said.

"Sure." I demoed the hand-washing protocol.

Mike slipped his hand inside the incubator. Robbie's leg flailed up, greeting his dad with a swift kick on the wrist.

"Hey, guy. You pack a lot of punch for a four-pounder."

Having Mike here, solid, beside me, made me more eager to get out of this place, back to being a family. Mike fought back yawns, so we headed back to my room. I wrapped my arms around his waist and inhaled his familiar smells. "I don't want you to go."

"I'm here now. But I need some sleep. I'll be back first thing in the morning."

I stood by my bed. "I want to go home. We can transfer Robbie to Ridner Hospital. It's just five miles from the house."

"He's fine here. They're taking good care of him."

"No. You don't get it." I put my hands on his face and stared into his blue eyes. "This place is driving me insane," I whispered.

He massaged my shoulders. "You're the sanest woman I know. Just crawl back in bed. We'll talk about it later."

"Creepy things happen here. They watch me like a hawk. I don't sleep. My hands are raw from washing and disinfecting twenty times a day." I squeezed him close and clung to his waist. "I want to go home."

"Be patient a few more days. This is the best place for you. I can come and see you during the day and take care of Jason at night." He planted little kisses over my face. Soft warm promises of things that would come in due time.

Reluctantly, I released my arms from his waist and climbed into the bed.

"Get some sleep. I'll check on Jason. It'll all be okay. You'll see."

I nodded, my mind buzzing. I wanted to believe him. But my motherly instincts told me to keep a careful watch on my nest. Something wasn't right.

8.

Day 9

Every morning at 0700 hours, Colonel Reeves sauntered into my room and squeezed my breasts, like a farmer checking fruit. It hurt. It was all I could do not to scream at her.

After a breakfast of powdery eggs, I headed for the nursery, The Colonel and Dr. Khan stood talking in the hallway. She was beaming about how well *their* baby was doing. Robbie wasn't their baby. He was mine. Everybody seemed to forget that. I couldn't wait to get home and feed *my* baby on Mother Nature's clock instead of military time.

Robbie had graduated from tube feeding to preemie bottles. I again asked the nurse to let me introduce him to my breast. She refused. It was too soon. He would exert too much energy. They couldn't measure how much he was getting. A litany of excuses. I hadn't come this far for Robbie to end up as a bottle baby. But in a military hospital, rules are rules. There would be no exceptions.

I searched for Dr. Khan, to plead my case. He might be a bit more sympathetic. The nurse at the desk said he would be with patients all afternoon.

Mike stopped by that afternoon with my stuff. He presented me with a vase containing two red roses. They smelled heavenly. The accompanying card read: *Mommy, we love you, Jason and Robbie.*

He also brought a radio. "Some music might help you sleep." He tuned the radio to a soft jazz station. The rhythmic beats pumped up my tired body.

"I'm desperate to go home—but I don't want to leave Robbie."

"Relax, Kate. Don't ruffle too many feathers."

"I don't care if Dr. Reeves is a colonel. I wouldn't care if she were a general. She has the worst bedside manner—" I slammed my fist on the bed tray, sending the vase with the roses toppling.

Mike caught it in mid-air. Water splashed over his uniform and the floor. "Kate, calm down. You don't understand the politics. You just don't go around bad-mouthing a full colonel."

He refilled the vase with water from the bathroom faucet, and set it on my nightstand. "I promise. I'll talk to some people. See if we can get you a different doctor. Let me handle it. I've slept maybe four hours in the past two days myself. Give me a couple days, and I'll work it out." He hugged me and left in a tiff.

* * *

One of the SR-71 wives stopped by with fresh strawberries! I gleamed with joy, devoured three right on the spot, and offered the rest to my new roommate. Ophelia, a young black gal, talked incessantly about her difficult labor and her new son, Rodney. Something about Rh factor. This was her second, and the doctors were watching her baby closely. Ophelia kept the television on, day and night, and spouted a running commentary on the drama of every soap opera. The continuous noise was making my mind spin.

"Come see me when you get out of the hospital," Ophelia continued.

"Sure, give me your phone number," I said absently.

"In no time, our boys will be crawling. You'll see," she spoke between nasty coughs.

I nodded. "That would be nice."

I would force myself to be patient—a little longer. This hospital was boring. But I could survive a few more days. Once Mike was caught up on his sleep, he would take charge and get me out of this hell-hole.

Bored, I retrieved the New Testament that I had stashed in the nightstand and started to read. "*You have patiently suffered*

for me without quitting. You will be persecuted for 'ten days'."
Had I been in the hospital for ten days? That seemed about right.

I turned the page. *"I have opened a door to you that no one can shut."* I looked up. The door to my room was open.

I convinced Ophelia to turn off the television and listen to soft jazz for a few hours. The radio announcer came on with late breaking news: *A child disappeared from his home in suburban Los Angeles.* I tuned to another station. *A spectacular meteor shower was seen last night.*

Ophelia left for the nursery to get Rodney. I turned the radio off and the television on. *Another child has disappeared,* the reporter announced. *The authorities don't think it's a kidnapping.*

I tried to remember what the nuns told me in grade school about the second coming. There would be signs. It would happen when we least expected it.

Ophelia didn't come back after her 4 p.m. feeding. I headed to the nursery with Robbie's milk and didn't see her. The nurses were all in a tizzy. I asked them where Ophelia was.

In the hall, I heard whimpering, and a young girl was sobbing. A nurse said, "Oh, no, not another one."

Another one?

In Catechism class, they had said that when the Apocalypse came, no one would realize until it was too late. Except a chosen few.

Unnerved, bordering on panic, I charged into the hall. I bumped into an orderly, who was bringing my meal tray, spilling hot tea on both of us.

"What's the big rush, Ma'am? Your meal is ready."

"Later. Just leave it. I don't have time to eat now."

I rushed to the nursery to check on Robbie. He still lay sleeping in the incubator, his tiny chest moving up and down. Perhaps too sick to be chosen.

An orderly wheeled a large machine out of the nursery.

"What's going on?" I demanded. "What's this machine?"

"It's a special x-ray. Get back to your room, Mrs. Wahlberg."

I wrinkled my nose, but obeyed. Ophelia was not in the room. I paced back and forth, staring nervously at her empty space. I checked the bathroom. Where was she?

Amidst the quiet panic on the floor, and the hurried whispers of the nurses, I opened Revelation and pored over the pages. Study the signs. Understand the predictions. Before it's too late.

9.

Day 10

After a time, morning light streamed through the window. Ophelia still hadn't returned. I set out to investigate.

Two men were whispering in the corridor. One wore a doctor's coat, the other a staff sergeant's uniform. "Somebody's going to catch hell," the sergeant said. Both towered over me, looming taller, more menacing as I passed. They shrank back to normal as I slipped past them. Had I wandered down some black hole, into some other world, like Alice in Wonderland? I ducked into my room and closed the door. There was no lock. No way to keep them out.

Did they know about the chosen ones? Had they taken them somewhere? Why was I still here?

The Colonel stopped by for her morning check. I clamped my arms over my breasts. "Don't touch me," I said.

She snorted, then left. Didn't even ask me how I was feeling.

Judy came in to take my blood pressure.

"What happened to The Colonel?" I asked.

"What do you mean," Judy said.

"How did she get so tall?"

Her eyes widened. "How tall do you think she is?"

"Ten feet."

Judy wrote something in my chart and scurried out of the room.

I pulled out my Bible and turned to the pages I'd marked. *"She was pregnant and screamed in the pain of her labor ..."* I had not meant to scream. It was as if some force acted on me. Something out of my control.

"Suddenly a red Dragon appeared .... ready to eat the baby .... She gave birth to a boy who was to rule all the nations with a heavy hand .... The woman fled into the wilderness, where God had prepared a place for her ...."

I looked out the window, past Ophelia's empty bed. Dry grass surrounded the hospital. Brown fields gave way to craggy foothills. A wilderness. Beyond the foothills lay Donner Pass, where pioneers had resorted to cannibalism.

"... the Dragon ... persecuted the woman who had given birth to the child. But she was given two wings like those of a great eagle, to fly into the wilderness ...."

I grabbed a pencil and underlined the passage. *The woman was given wings. She could fly.* There was a message here. I closed the Bible. God had chosen me for something special. These words were written for me. Perhaps because I was a pilot's wife? My heart thumped loudly in my chest. Why me?

I turned on the radio. *They're disappearing right and left folks,* the announcer said. *You need to get here before it's too late.*

Was I too late? I rushed to the window.

Someone knocked at my doorjamb. He wore blues, the shade of his eyes, and held a clipboard. "I'm sorry to bother you," he apologized. "I'm Captain Quiry from social services. You're Mrs. Wahlberg?"

I smiled politely, while fretting and wary that Mike wasn't here yet. And where was Ophelia? What were they hiding? "I'm going home today," I said.

He pulled up a chair next to the bed. "May I ask you some questions?"

I sat on the bed, and nodded, twisting the coverlet as he talked.

"What's your name?" he asked.

"Kate Wahlberg." Didn't he just say my name?

He wrote my response on the form. "What day is it?"

I held out my hand, showing him the new watch Mike had given me.

"Can you *tell* me what day it is?" he repeated.

I looked at the watch. "June 30." I beamed.

"What year is it?"

I studied the face of the watch. Why hadn't Mike bought me a watch with the year on it? "Does it matter?" I said.

"I just have a few more questions. Who is the president of the United States?"

I could picture his face, his easy smile. But his name? Tears welled in my eyes.

The young man with blue eyes repeated the question.

"I can't remember."

"Who are you? What's your name?"

They mustn't know. Maybe they already know?

"Who do you think you are?" he repeated.

If I didn't answer, he would go away. I turned my head.

"How long have you been here?"

Don't answer—*Flee to the wilderness. Take Robbie.*

He left. Then a short, gray-haired woman wearing lieutenant colonel insignia, came into the room. She asked all the same questions.

They were trying to trick me. Just give them name, rank, and serial number. "Mike Wahlberg, Captain, 512-34-1926," I answered.

"That's your husband. What's your name?"

I studied my watch.

"Who do you think you are?"

"You will be persecuted for 'ten days'." The second hand was ticking away.

A few minutes after she left, Mike rushed into the room and took my hand. "What's going on, Kate? I got a call from the base commander telling me to get my butt out here ASAP."

"I want to leave this place, Mike. Now. And take Robbie. Something's wrong. People are disappearing."

"Calm down. The nurses say you haven't been sleeping. We're taking you home today, so you can get some rest." He reached into a duffle bag. "I brought you some sweats and shoes."

I stepped into the pants and tied the drawstring. Comfortable. Good choice for an escape. I slipped off the hospital gown and pulled the royal blue polo shirt over my head.

"We have to get Robbie."

"Robbie's going to stay here for a little while longer. He needs to gain more weight." Mike handed me white socks and tennis shoes.

"I've got to get Robbie … before the dragon … "

"The what?"

I didn't look up at him. I just said, "I'm not leaving without Robbie."

"Relax. Shoes—"

I grabbed the socks, then slipped on the shoes. I looked up after tying them.

The Colonel stood in the doorway, hands on her hips. "We're going to discharge you today, Mrs. Wahlberg. But the baby stays here until he's five pounds. I've ordered some pills. They'll help you sleep."

"It's all your fault." I started towards the door.

"Kate!" Mike grabbed my elbow.

I brushed past him, lifted my chin and glared at The Colonel. "I'm not leaving without my baby."

She blocked the door. "The baby stays here."

I rose up on my tippy-toes, all five-foot-nine of me. "Out of my way."

She didn't budge.

I slapped her. Hard. "You're the dragon."

The Colonel recoiled, stunned into silence. She reached to touch the red mark on her check.

My hand stung. I didn't realize my own power. I regretted the action. But it was too late. The forces were in motion.

Mike grabbed my shoulders from behind, twisted me around into his arms, and held me close.

I struggled, then gradually relaxed in his arms.

"Wait a minute," he said to someone behind me.

Two burly MPs came up to me. Two male nurses held out a white jacket.

I looked to Mike, pleading. *Don't let them do this.*

He stood there, his eyes flashing fire. But he didn't move. Where was my hero?

"No." I struggled. One of the men grabbed my arm, and stuffed it roughly into a sleeve.

They cinched me into the straightjacket. Sharp pain coursed through my tender breasts.

They led me down the hospital corridor, Mike one step behind. The MP said something about an ambulance outside.

We passed the nursery. Dr. Khan stood guarding Robbie's incubator. Judy, tears in her eyes, held her arms up, blocking the door to the nursery.

They were my last hope. "Judy, please," I pleaded. "Don't let the dragon get my baby."

10.

As the ambulance pulled away, I strained my neck to stare back at the hospital until rolling hills and trees blocked my view. *What would happen to Robbie?*

Mike sat close. I could feel his anger. He clenched his hands, tapped his thumbs together, and exhaled rhythmically. His personal trick to keep from going ballistic.

The straight jacket pinched if I moved, especially around my bottom, still tender from the stitches. I tried to sit still and take shallow breaths.

"Mike," I whispered so the guys in front wouldn't hear. "I told you. I begged you to get me out of that hospital."

He hesitated, then touched my face and spoke in a hushed tone. "Don't say anything, Kate. You'll only make it worse." He scooted closer and put his arm around me.

I stared out the window, couldn't speak the thoughts that were raging through my mind. I knew The Colonel was evil. "Where are they taking us?"

Mike put his finger across my lips. Then drew his hand back to his mouth, deposited a kiss to his finger, and transferred it to my lips.

A promise. He would protect me. He just needed to wait for the right moment.

We passed the base gates and headed toward town. I recognized the streets. Then we turned into an unfamiliar neighborhood. We pulled up to a sprawling brick structure I'd never seen before. The car stopped and the MPs helped me out. It felt good to stand. I stretched my legs and tried in vain to move my arms. A sign at the building entrance read *Yucca County Mental Health.*

The lady at the front desk seemed to be expecting us. She led us into a little room with lime-green chairs. The MPs stood me in front of a large maple desk. A tall doctor with dark hair and a pointed beard stood and peered at me with cold gray eyes.

"Mrs. Wahlberg. We'll take off the straightjacket, *if* you promise not to hit anybody."

I looked at Mike. He looked away, embarrassed.

When was he going to rescue me? Surely he wouldn't abandon me? Not here? Not alone? I stared down at my tennis shoes and whispered, "I won't hit anybody. I promise."

The MPs took off the straightjacket. I stretched in relief, the blood returning to my cramped fingers. The doctor nodded to the chair. I sat. Mike took the seat next to me. I stretched my fingers and ran them up and down the cold metal legs. Stay on your guard. This could be a demon.

The doctor sat at his desk with a clipboard.

"What year is it?"

"1980," I said tentatively.

"Can you speak a little louder, Mrs. Wahlberg. Who is the president?"

"Jimmy Carter." I spoke clearly. I can do this.

He peered close. "Who do you think you are?"

I remembered Mike's gesture to keep quiet. I twiddled my thumbs. Should I answer? No use getting into Revelation now. All would be revealed in due time.

"Who do you think you are?" The doctor asked, his voice more stern.

This seemed to be a sticking point. I glanced at Mike. He looked ready to catapult out of the chair any minute if I said the wrong thing.

"Kate Wahlberg." That's all they needed to know. Don't tell them about the dragon.

"Your address?"

I rattled it off.

"Who do you think you are?" We were back at the hard one.

"Kate Wahlberg," I answered, making sure I sounded confident. I smiled.

Mike smiled too, with apparent relief. The doctor nodded and relaxed.

It was that simple. All I had to do was to tell them what they wanted to hear.

I eased back in the chair. Mike and the doctor stepped out into the hallway. They spoke softly at first, then their voices grew louder. They were arguing. I couldn't make out all the words, but my mother's name came up, "Amanda," and "nurse" were said loudly several times. At last, Mike and the doctor came back into the room. Mike took my elbow. "Come on, Kate, I'm taking you home."

The doctor twisted his beard. "Don't forget what I said."

As we walked out, I leaned into Mike. "What did he say?"

"Never mind," Mike answered abruptly.

I saw the anger in his eyes and bent down to tie my shoes to escape its intensity.

The Air Force special transport was gone, so Mike used the phone at the front desk to call our neighbors, Wally and Brenda, to come pick us up.

Wally arrived in about fifteen minutes, and discreetly did not ask what we were doing at the cuckoo's nest.

When he turned into our neighborhood, the sun was just setting over the tall sycamores. I was elated to see our little green ranch house at the corner. Wally dropped us off at our juniper-lined driveway. Mike slipped the latch on our back fence, unlocked the garage side door, and led me through the garage into the family room.

Our neighbor Brenda, a petite brunette, was reading to Jason on the couch. He saw me, climbed off Brenda's lap, and dropped his teddy bear.

"Mommy!" He ran to me with outstretched arms.

I scooped him up and snuggled him tight, then stared at his face. What had happened to my son? I ran my fingers through the fine blond hair. It was so long. Somehow, Jason had turned into a girl! Was this God's way of answering my prayer for a girl? My punishment for obsessing over the sex of my baby.

"See, I told you Mommy would be coming home," Mike said. He reached over and brushed Jason's hair. "You need a haircut, boy. We'll work on that tomorrow."

Of course, how stupid. Just a haircut. I wasn't thinking straight. I needed sleep.

"Did you bring my new brother?"

"He's got to stay in the hospital until he gets bigger," Mike said.

Jason sucked his thumb and twirled my hair with his finger. He clung to me for a few minutes, then got down and tugged on Mike's jeans. "Dad, Lindsey said I could have the striped kitty."

"We'll talk about it tomorrow, kiddo." Mike stooped down and touched noses with Jason. "Want to spend the night at Brenda and Wally's house? Mommy needs her sleep."

Jason clung to me. "No. I want Mommy."

"We've got chocolate ice cream," Brenda said.

Jason looked from me to Brenda, undecided.

Mike scooped him up and gave him a belly kiss, sending Jason into a fit of giggles. "You can see Mommy in the morning. Okay, Sport?"

Jason finally nodded okay, and Brenda led him out the back door.

"Come on. Let's get some sleep, Kate."

I stopped at our bedroom door. "Mike, I can't sleep here." Our bedroom was decorated with red velvet curtains flanked by Mediterranean wall sconces, one a sword, the other a medieval ball and chain. Early married stuff we'd acquired at a garage sale years ago. Tonight the room screamed Spanish Inquisition.

"What do you mean?"

"In the hospital, I kept having these nightmares. All those times the doctors sent me home from the emergency room saying I wasn't in labor. What if I'd had him in the bed? We could have both bled to death." I reached in the closet for my gray nightshirt. "I *cannot* sleep here tonight."

I slipped off the sweats and polo shirt and pulled on my nightshirt.

"I want to sleep in Jason's room."

"Whatever." Mike held up his hands in surrender.

I walked down to Jason's room, a soothing oasis. Three walls were soft blue, the fourth, wallpapered with red, white, and blue ships sailing on blue waves. I switched on the aquarium light. All my fish friends were still there, two black angels, two white kissing gouramis, a school of neon tetras. Everybody alive and swimming. "Hi guys." I dropped in a few flakes of fish food, and my little buddies swam up to eat and greet.

Mike came into the room and pulled back the covers on Jason's captain bed, a twin. "I'll sleep with you."

"It's too small. You don't have to," I protested.

"No arguments."

"Can we leave the aquarium light on?"

"Sure."

Mike, wearing only his skivvies, snuggled in and wrapped his arms around me.

To the soft hum of the aquarium pump, I twined my legs into his for safety and blocked out the demons.

11.

In the middle of the night, I woke with a jolt. Mike nestled me and whispered, "It's okay. I'm here." I spooned into him. For the first time since he'd left, I felt safe.

In the morning, he made coffee and fixed me a bowl of Rice Krispies.

I knew I had disgraced Mike. Only the best of the best flew the SR-71. He had undergone a series of tough physical and psychological tests. And now, to have a crazy wife. Over the snaps and crackles, I said, "I've ruined your career. I'm so sorry."

"What's done is done," he interrupted. "I'll pick up the pieces at the base in a few days, apologize to your doctor, explain to the squadron commander, kiss a little butt."

I could tell he was still pissed. He punctuated that last phrase by tossing his spoon into his empty cereal bowl so that it clanged loudly.

"Can we go get Jason?"

"Let him play at Brenda's a little while. We'll get him later."

Mike didn't trust me. I wasn't sure I trusted myself. Two white dove statues graced the mantle above our fireplace. I stared. Their wings fluttered. Another sign. I looked to Mike. He had picked up the newspaper and was reading. He didn't see. Should I tell him? No. He might not be a chosen one. He wouldn't understand. He might even take me back to the crazy house.

I gazed out the patio door at our new green-and-yellow-flowered lawn furniture. Two large wooden planters of drooping petunias flanked the settee.

"I'll water the plants, see if I can resurrect them from the dead."

"Resurrect?" Mike turned and studied me.

Mental note to self: Watch your words. Only speak the truth to the other chosen ones, wherever they were.

I looked down at my pale arms. "A little sun will do me good."

Mike had always liked the way I looked in a bikini. I headed to the bathroom and stared at myself in the mirror, sucked in my gut and grabbed the huge rolls of loose skin in my hands. Ten thousand sit-ups in my future. Worry about that later. I found my yellow bikini top in the bottom dresser drawer and slipped it on. My breasts were painfully engorged with Robbie's precious milk. It hurt to touch them, but I chose to ignore the pain rather than try to express my milk.

My boobs overwhelmed the scanty top. I rummaged through the drawer again, but could not locate the matching yellow bottom. I settled for a pink polka dot one and slipped it on. Fortunately it fit low, below my bulging belly.

I grabbed a bottle of suntan lotion from the hallway closet and headed out to the patio, thankful that our back yard was surrounded by a six-foot privacy fence. First I turned on the garden hose, adjusted the water volume, and watered my parched petunias. Then I sprayed my legs and arms. Soon we'd be all perky again.

I adjusted the new chaise lounge chair to meet the sun, plopped down, and rubbed the coconut-scented lotion up and down my arms. The sun was warm and luxurious. I closed my eyes and savored the crimson glow though my eyelids. Wasn't there something in Revelation about the sky turning red? Or was that the moon? I blinked open.

The sky looked normal. Lack of sleep could make you pretty loopy. Why would God choose me? I was raised strict Catholic. Mass every Sunday, rosaries, patron saints. But saint I was not. Mike had corrupted me in the most delightful ways, teaching me to dance provocatively and drink whiskey straight.

My respite was disrupted by the phone ringing. After a few minutes, Mike came out, holding some shorts and a paisley blouse. "Some people from the mental health place are coming to see you. You need to change into these clothes."

"I don't want to see anyone. Especially not them." I ignored him.

"Kate, they'll be here in ten minutes."

"I said I don't want to see any fricking doctors. Make them go away."

"They have to see you."

"I won't see them."

"Just put on the clothes. And act normal."

I didn't budge.

"Do it. NOW." He laid the clothes next to me and went inside. The doorbell rang and I heard Mike welcome someone at the front door.

They came out to the patio. The doctor wore a white shirt and green-striped tie. His nose was cocked one notch higher than last night. Behind him, a curly-headed woman in a floral print dress and thick glasses gawked at me with a look that said, *My God woman, what are you doing in that bikini?*

I glared back at her, hoping she couldn't read my mind. *What the f--- are you doing in my backyard?* I tried to act normal.

The doctor introduced her as Delilah Johnson, a social worker.

Mike motioned them to the two lawn chairs. They sat rigidly. Mike held out my shirt. "Kate, honey, I told you we were having company."

I grabbed it and tossed it on the chaise.

The doctor leaned forward. "Ms. Johnson and I just want to talk with you." She pulled a yellow notepad from her leather purse.

"No more questions." I jumped up and grabbed the garden hose.

Mike was on his feet and stepped toward me. "Settle down."

"Don't come near me, any of you." I pointed the hose at them.

I discharged one blast, with glee. It splashed on Delilah's shoes and the doctor's trousers. They both bolted up. Mike walked over to the faucet and turned it off, then went over to the two visitors and spoke in a low voice. I overheard a few words, "still not stable" and "needs treatment."

Mike slid next to me on the chaise and put his arm around my shoulder. "We're going to take you back to the hospital where we were last night. They can take care of you for a few days while you rest. Please don't fight me." He dropped to his knee, and slipped my foot into the leg of the shorts. "Put these on, now." His tone was somewhere between pleading and ballistic.

I slipped my other leg into the shorts, stood, and pulled them up. Then I donned the blouse. "There, are you happy?"

Mike led me out the back gate and around the side of the house. The doctor held open the back door of their green sedan. I scooted in, and Mike slid in next to me. As we backed out of the driveway, he put his hand on my knee. I slapped it away and hugged the door handle.

12.

Before long, we were back at the cuckoo's nest. I sat, scowled, and clutched the arm of the chair, while Mike answered a bunch of questions. Then Delilah escorted us down a long corridor and into a room containing a twin bed, a three-drawer wooden dresser, and another green vinyl chair.

Delilah told me to sit on the bed. A hefty nurse with a scar across her cheek brought two pills and a little paper cup with water.

"No. No pills." I shook my head and held out my hand to block the two little white tablets. I'd had enough bad medicine at the base hospital.

"Take your medication." Scar Face barked at me like an army sergeant. She outweighed me by eighty pounds. She grabbed my wrist, pried open my hand, and laid the two pills on my palm.

"Kate Elizabeth," Mike said to me, like my dad used to when I was bad.

I glared at him. *Hey dude, you're my husband, not my father.*

Scar Face went out into the hall. "Assistance please," she yelled.

Suddenly five people had me surrounded—Mike, the nurse, the doctor, the social worker, plus a large gal in a blue uniform. The scar-faced nurse pushed my hand with the pills toward my mouth.

I tossed the pills on the floor, then threw the cup of water into the nurse's face. She gasped.

I waited for her to melt. Was surprised that she didn't shrivel.

The doctor motioned with his head to the large gal in blue. She exited the room, and was soon back with a long syringe.

This was the moment God had been preparing for me. I had to act. I scrambled to stand on the bed. Like Joan of Arc, I thrust out my arms in the crucifixion pose. "Our Father, who art in heaven—"

Like a well-trained SWAT team, they all knew what to do. Scar Face grabbed my right arm. The social worker gripped my left. The doctor and the gal in blue each grasped a leg, and they pulled me down onto the bed. The doctor told Mike to hold one leg. The gal in blue handed the syringe to the doctor.

They twisted me over, and the doctor pulled down my shorts. My flailing was futile. The needle stung as it bit my hip.

I didn't say a word, just buried my head in my chest. The nurse pulled the sheet out from under my legs, and slipped it over me. The others left.

Mike stayed and stroked my hair. "It's for your own good, sweetie."

I hissed at him. He had betrayed me. I twisted away, and curled into a tight ball.

13.

I woke to the chirping of a robin outside the lone window in my room. When I sat up to admire it, the bird flew away. My mouth felt like the Sahara desert, the rest of my body like it had been invaded by a virus. I pulled the sheet and frayed beige blanket up and surveyed the bleak room. Barren, ten by twelve. Stale.

The robin returned to the nest with a long worm in its beak. I went over to the window to watch the bird feed her babies, the way nature intended. She was a messenger. I knew. My heart ached for Robbie. My breasts felt hard as rocks and ached with abandonment.

Before long the same hefty nurse brought me two more pills and a glass of water.

"You can do this the easy way, or—" She didn't have to finish. I took the pills, put them in my mouth, maneuvered them under my tongue, and swallowed the water.

"Open your mouth," Scar Face said.

I opened my mouth.

"Let me see under your tongue."

Busted. I looked away. The robin had flown the coop.

"Like I said, you can do this the easy way—" Scar Face poured more water into the little cup and stood with her hands on her hips. This woman made The Colonel look like a wimp.

She waited.

With my tongue, I maneuvered one pill up behind my upper left gum, then swallowed the second pill and the water. I opened my mouth, lifting my tongue to show her that the pills were gone. Satisfied, she walked away. After she turned her back, I pulled the pill from behind my gum, and stuffed it under my mattress. Later I'd retrieve the pill and flush it down the toilet.

I had refused to eat lunch or dinner the previous day, despite my stomach growling in protest. So when Scar Face announced breakfast, I crawled out of bed, sluggish, every movement tedious. I followed three other women, grabbed a tray, and stood in line.

They weren't the kind of women I was used to hanging out with, so I sat alone and picked at my food. The toast was dry and smushed thin, the oatmeal lukewarm, the OJ watered-down. The Formica tabletop was chipped in several places. Someone had carved the initials "JC" in one corner.

I studied the carving. Signs would be in unusual places. HE was here, somewhere. I glanced around the room, studying the faces of the male patients. None looked the part. Perhaps HE was hiding, or had escaped. HE had been tortured too.

I forced down the nasty food and studied the grounds beyond the windows. There was a six-foot wooden fence along the rear of the property. Scaling it would be difficult, but not impossible.

Before lunch, Scar Face came back with more pills. I managed to slip them under the sheet, pretended to pop them into my mouth, and swallowed the water. My tormentor looked suspicious and repeated the oral cavity check. I tried not to look coy. Finally she left, but I could tell she had misgivings. After lunch I would reconnoiter and plan my escape.

I shuffled down the women's ward, past eight identical bleak rooms. Where the halls intersected, I noted to the left was the men's ward, to the right the dining room, and straight ahead— a short corridor with closed doors that led to front lobby and the outside world. Strategically placed at the intersection was the nurses' station, constantly staffed with at least one or two guards. I needed to figure out how to slip past that obstacle.

I decided to charge down the hall, like I was going to a meeting. A tall guy in whites stepped in front of me. We did the two-step, twice, before he said, "You need to go back to your room."

"Sure." I nodded nonchalantly, like I'd somehow gotten lost.

But late that night, when all was quiet, I slipped into my tennis shoes and tiptoed down the hall. A night-shift nurse emerged like a ghost from the shadows. "Are you looking for something?"

I didn't answer.

She spread her legs and crossed her arms, blocking any get-away.

I turned and trudged back to my room.

* * *

Mid-morning the pointy-bearded doctor stopped by my room. He stood at the side of the bed, an irritated expression on his face, and explained my medications. The Haldol would stop my racing thoughts. The Cogentin would counteract the side-effects of the Haldol, make me feel less like a zombie.

Then he leaned in, very serious, as if to warn me, as if he knew I'd been checking the pills. "If you want to get better, you must take your medication. If we don't see an effect, we'll have to increase the dosage."

I nodded like a good girl. No way was I going to drink his Kool-Aid. But I'd have to pretend to be a disciple. For a few days at least.

14.

After lunch, Scar Face handed me three pills, one at a time, then checked my mouth with a flashlight. The pills slowed mind and body, zapping all zest for life. My grandiose illusions of saving the world had evaporated. In their place, a desperate longing to escape this hell. I curled in my bed, closed my eyes, and shut out my prison.

"Kate, look who's here to see you." Mike's voice penetrated my cocoon.

I opened my bleary eyes. "Mom!"

She rushed to my bedside, horror on her face, her hand over her mouth, concealing shock. She smothered me with a mother's warmth.

I melted in her arms and sobbed.

"I should have come sooner. I knew it. I'm so sorry." She turned to Mike. "Jesus, Mary and Joseph. If I'd known—"

Mike held out his hands in a helpless gesture. Then he leaned over and kissed my forehead. "Your mom left work and got on the first plane out this morning. We came straight here."

Mom sat on the bed, then rummaged through her purse and brought out a hairbrush. She started brushing through my tangled hair, gently stroking my scalp as she worked out the knots. Her voice was calm and soothing. "We'll get you better. We'll get you out of here."

I calmed with her touch, then remembered. "Where's Jason?"

"Jason's taking his nap at Brenda's house." Mike reached in his shirt pocket, unfolded a piece of notebook paper, and handed it to me. "He made this for you." It was a crayon drawing of three stick figures, a mom, dad, and a child. The mom had a round red scribble with a smile across its belly. I assumed that was Robbie. I nodded my appreciation and curled up my lip. In Jason's innocent world, a red scribble could make our family complete.

Mom sat behind me and massaged my shoulders. Next she rubbed my back, her fingers soothing as a nightingale up and down my spine. Then she told Mike to sit by me while she went to find the doctor.

She came back about fifteen minutes later with a purple pitcher of ice water and made me drink some though a straw. The cool water refreshed my parched mouth.

"I talked to the doctor. You have to take your meds, so you can get better." I glanced from Jason's Crayola picture to Mom's face, then back at the picture. Maybe she was right. Maybe I was fighting this too hard.

Mom talked about Grammy, Dad, the crops. I mostly just nodded.

Mike glanced at his watch. "I want to take Amanda out to the base hospital to meet her new grandson."

Mom's eyes lit up when Mike mentioned the baby. She stuffed the brush back in her purse and stood.

At the mention of Robbie, I felt a surge of fullness in my breasts. I missed my precious baby, but my connection to him was drying up. I needed my mom, but knew she was anxious to see the baby. I kissed her goodbye and watched from my door as she and Mike walked past the invisible prison door at the nurse's station.

15.

The next morning, I was told to attend group therapy. Five other women sat in our session, our plastic chairs arranged in a circle around the bearded doctor.

I sat next to Lisa, a lanky brunette I met at breakfast. Over toast and scrambled eggs, Lisa babbled on for nearly an hour. Her husband had left her and taken their two daughters. I listened because Lisa would not stop talking. When I stood up to leave, Lisa gave me a shell necklace and declared me her "new best friend."

"Who wants to go first?" The doctor's eyes scanned the circle.

No one spoke. Lisa and I shot smirky glances at each other whenever the doctor looked our way.

"Rita, how about you tell us how you're feeling," he said.

Rita, a petite lady with a dried up mouth and stiff little hairs on her chin, started talking about her puppies, Rufus, Sparky, Sport, the list went on and on. Someone had taken away her dogs and sent her to "the big hospital." Nasty as this place seemed, evidently there was someplace worse. The rooms had locks on the doors. The whole place was surrounded by a large brick wall, topped with barbed wire.

Pointy Beard droned on about the importance of taking our meds and keeping a schedule. I ignored him and Rita, and stared at the calendar on the wall. There was a large numeral 3 under the word JULY. The page started floating off the calendar. It was a sign. I glanced around. Didn't anyone else see it? I had just enough wits about me to not broach the subject with the group. I envisioned racks and chains and row after row of locked doors at "the big hospital."

* * *

Mom and Mike stopped by every afternoon. Mom's face had acquired a few more wrinkles since I'd last seen her last winter, and her chestnut hair was starting to fringe with silver at the temples. Mike always brought a little gift—a magazine, a clean blouse, a flower. Mom and I chatted. I nodded, occasionally responding in mono-syllables. My tongue felt thick, and I had to wipe the drool from my mouth before speaking. It was less traumatic to just listen and nod.

Every day it was the same. Mike would kiss my forehead and ask how I was doing. He sat in the lone chair in my room. Mom sat on the bed and fussed over my hair or wiped the drool from my mouth with a warm washcloth. Before long, Mike started checking his watch. Then Mom would remember she needed to get back to Jason, or do the laundry.

After they left, I would sit on my bed and rock. Back and forth. Back and forth. I still had the watch Mike gave me at the base hospital, and a notepad and paper that I had requested. When no one was watching, I drew maps and arrows, noted times that the nurses came and went. I wrote messages for the chosen, in code. If I was taken away to the big hospital, they would understand. They would follow and rescue me.

After a week on the mental ward, I was deemed sufficiently subdued—make that drugged—to be allowed to go to adult "day care." They piled ten of us into a white van. I recognized the roads. The freeway. A wooded side street that led to my house. The turn-off to The Marinara Factory, where I had worked up until the week before Robbie was born. Sadness overwhelmed me. I might never find my way home again.

We stopped at a big white house with a blue porch swing and multiple doors. New escape routes. I got out of the van, moving in slow motion, as if I were walking on another planet.

A sidewalk encircled the house. Beyond it, a stretch of grass, then a three-foot wire mesh fence. Climbable. Beyond the fence, an orchard of peach trees beckoned me. I gauged the time it would take me to sprint across the grass, jump the fence, and escape into the orchard. I took a step, then remembered. Right now I couldn't outrun a snail.

"Where do you think you're going?" the man with a clipboard asked.

"For a walk." I smiled, exploring potential getaway routes out the corner of my eye.

"Walk back to the house." He escorted me into a yellow room with two large tables and told me to sit and paint.

I stared at the butcher-block paper and elementary-school watercolor paints. Great. I was now functioning at the same level as my three-year-old.

My friend Lisa, from the ward, fussed over her crude drawing. I dipped my brush in brown paint and drew a house. I didn't dare paint what I was feeling—a woman sneaking into a hospital, stealing a baby from the dragon.

For lunch, we could choose to help make either pizza or salad. I shied away from the pizza. The sauce reminded me that I once had a career. Now I had nothing. They'd never let a crazy woman work at The Marinara Factory. The attendant handed me a whole head of iceberg lettuce. Mike had told me to act normal. I ripped the lettuce apart with a vengeance.

Soon the aroma of baking pizza filled the kitchen. I closed my eyes and tried to identify the seasonings. All I could recognize was the overwhelming odor of garlic. Memorizing the aroma of various herbs had been part of my training. I used to be able to distinguish subtle difference in blends of basil, oregano, rosemary. Now it was all a jumble. My senses were dulled. What good would I be in the lab if I couldn't get past garlic? My career was over.

The medicine made me drool constantly. Lots of patients on the ward drooled. The meds also made it hard to control my bladder. I'd had several accidents. Was still wearing the bloody bikini under my shorts. I felt an urge to pee and searched for the ladies room. Luckily I found it in time.

After coming out of the stall, I pushed the soap dispenser, and counted to thirty as I washed my hands, like a good food scientist. I studied my reflection in the mirror over the sink. There were no mirrors in my bathroom on the ward. I gazed at myself in horror. The strange eyes. The woman staring back at me looked like someone come back from the grave.

And the wild hair—all knotted and straggly. Mom had not been by to fix it for me this morning. Even on a bad-hair day, my long blond locks and athletic frame were normally enough to make men turn and whistle. Now I was a mess. The other patients wore weird smiles, crazy hair. They belonged here. I didn't. I longed for a hairbrush, or even a scrunchie to pull my hair back. I searched the bathroom, found a rubber band with several long gray strands on it, but didn't want to touch anything that had been used by *those* people. I rushed out of the bathroom, paused at the door to the orchard, and mentally gauged the distance to freedom.

The male attendant walked up behind me. "No escape just now, but the pizza's ready."

How did he know what I was thinking?

I headed down the hall to the dining area. The group was just sitting down to a big round table to eat. I took the one remaining place and grabbed a piece of pizza. It was still hot and burnt the roof of my mouth. The guy to my right, a spastic teen, pointed at everybody as if he were shooting them with his finger, and laughed. He had a Pepsi. I stared at the cool drops of condensation on the can. I craved my own can. Pepsi was my one addiction, my afternoon treat at work. Why did he get one? Everybody else had iced tea. I didn't have a purse, or any money. Must remind Mike to bring me some cash.

A bearded man with missing teeth grabbed the Pepsi from the teen and took a gulp. He passed the can to a woman with shaky hands on his right. She spilled some down her chin and passed the can to the girl with a black eye. Next, the can went to Rita, then Lisa. The can passed to a quiet Asian girl.

I wanted my own Pepsi.

When the can came to me, it was almost empty. I raised it to my mouth, and took a long gulp—of warm drool. I wanted to gag.

I threw it to the floor and ran outside.

No baby.

No career.

No money.

No chance of escape.

The guy with the clipboard followed me. I cast my eyes down. I didn't dare let him see my soul, my death wish.

16.

One of the attendants at adult day care was a chubby girl with braided hair. Unlike the staff at the ward, Lucia liked people. She showed me pictures of her daughter, Carla, a miniature Lucia with golden braids. Lucia wore long skirts in colorful prints, kept notes in a spiral notebook, and helped me practice for my exit interview. If I passed, I could go home.

She huddled with me like a soccer coach. "You can't say, 'I don't belong in here with all these crazy people.'"

"But I *was* ... normal," the words flowed from my mouth like molasses, "before all *this* happened." I had been captain of the debate team in high school, excelled in forensics in college, once gave a speech to the whole university, always had a snappy comeback for Mike. Now I could barely speak. I just wanted to sleep in my own bed, tuck Jason in at night and make pasta sauce. If I could just close my eyes, tap my heels, and go home. I knew it wasn't going to be that simple.

"Just tell the doctor that you're ready to go home and take care of yourself and your son." Lucia cautioned that I not mention Robbie, or the dragon. Best to leave the lid on those subjects for now.

* * *

Finally the big day came. Lucia escorted me into the front room of Yucca County Mental Health, where the MPs had brought me the first day. I looked at my watch—July 18. In three days Robbie would be one month old. I had guarded the watch like a hawk, and only took it off to shower. It was my tenuous link to reality, a quartz and platinum reminder that days were ticking away. Life in the real world was moving forward—without me.

Pointy Beard smiled and leaned back in his chair. "Lucia thinks you've made a lot of improvement in the time you've spent with us."

I glanced toward Lucia for support, then nodded.

"How do you think you're doing?" he said.

"My name ... Kate Wahlberg ... I'm ready go home ... take care Jason," I managed to say my rehearsed speech. I wiped the drool from my lip and tried to sit tall.

"You do appear stable." He leaned forward. "Your husband is waiting in the lobby. Are you sure you're ready to go home?"

I wanted to leave this place. That was certain. Taking care of Jason, and eventually Robbie—things I'd considered a breeze less than a month ago—now seemed monumental. But anything would be better than staying here.

Mike came and sat beside me.

"I've written a prescription. You'll need to stay on medication for at least a month. And I want you to see a Dr. Falio, at our clinic down the road, for eight weeks. Understand young lady?"

I nodded.

"Make sure she takes all her meds on schedule, and keeps her follow-up appointments. We don't want to see her back here in a few weeks," the doctor cautioned.

"Yes sir," Mike said.

Mike had bought me a new outfit, a pair of beige shorts with elastic waistband, and a simple brown striped shirt with a white collar. He also purchased a small brown leather purse with a shoulder strap. Inside, per my instructions, was a comb, brown hair scrunchie, three dollar bills and eight quarters, the latter my soft drink allowance. I slipped into the new outfit, and he helped me pack my few things into a duffle bag.

"Robbie is gaining weight. I brought you a picture of him and Amanda." He handed me a snapshot of a proud Grandma holding a tiny bundle in front of the Tigger mural. "That was the day before she left to go back to Kansas."

"Thanks." The picture stirred up a lot of guilt. After staring at it for thirty seconds, I slipped it into the side pocket of the duffle bag. The base hospital existed on another planet. Our delicate mother-baby bond had been ruptured when they dragged me away in the straightjacket, and my motherly instincts had dried up along with my milk. A pouchy stomach was the sole physical reminder that I'd recently given birth. Mike took the duffle bag, and we walked out the front door of the county mental hospital. I didn't dare look back.

We arrived home. The house had an odd smell, like Mike had forgotten to take out the trash. I walked around the house, reconnecting with my old world. I touched my blue-flowered living-room couch—still velvety soft. I fingered the soapstone statue in my curio cabinet. A gift from Mike the first time he went TDY. These were all things I had once cherished. Signs of a solid middle-class life. They were all still there.

The walnut grandfather clock in the foyer was silent. I opened the door, set the time, and pulled the chains. It started ticking. I smiled. My world had stopped too. Hopefully in a few weeks my gears would be back in working order. It was going to take a while.

Mike had picked a bouquet of white daisies from our backyard, but forgot to add water. They were all droopy, like me. I knew there was no reviving them. I pitched them. Tomorrow I would pick fresh ones.

Then I went around the house and locked all the doors.

"Where's Jason?" I asked.

"He's at Brenda's house. Just until you get settled."

"I miss him."

"Tomorrow." He reached over and wiped my lip. "You'll be fine once you're off the meds."

He seemed to have read my mind. Maybe I wasn't fit to take care of Jason. Better check me out first. I bit my lip and blinked back the water in my eyes. I felt like such a moron. Drooling. Stuttering. Jerking.

"Don't watch me." I plopped on the couch and picked up a magazine. I was tired of being monitored. Told when to get up. When to go to bed.

His eyes followed my every motion.

"Leave me alone."

"I'll be in the garage." He stroked my hair and kissed my cheek. "Call me if you need anything."

I flipped the pages of *Better Homes and Gardens*. A cozy table set for two. A smartly arranged mantle. Things that used to excite me. None of this mattered any more. I tossed the magazine on the floor and curled into a little ball. It was a hot July day, but I wrapped myself in our afghan and stared at the blank television screen.

I eventually summoned the energy to unpack my bag. The clothes that I had worn for days on the mental ward, the burgundy shorts that I peed myself in so many times, were bitter reminders of a time I wanted to forget. I stuffed them in a brown paper bag and tossed them in the trash.

Over a simple dinner of canned soup, Mike chatted. "I'm going to be on 'light duty' for a while—flying paper airplanes," he said.

I was lucid enough to know he was unhappy. A pilot had to maintain absolute mental control to fly a supersonic jet over unfriendly territory. Being stressed out over a crazy wife wouldn't do.

"Jerome suggested I take a little time off flying, until things settled down on the home front," Mike said. Jerome was the new squadron commander, the person who controlled Mike's career. Mike was currently in the running for the recently-vacated assistant squadron commander slot. I'd certainly blown that for him. "I offered to teach anti-hijacking to the KC135 pilots. Something to pass the time," Mike added.

"How long ... light duty?" I asked.

He gave me one of his looks. I decided not to pursue the question. Flying was his life, and my actions had grounded him. I would give anything for a do-over, but that was not going to happen.

17.

The next morning, Brenda brought Jason back to me, just as Mike was leaving to run errands. At first Jason clung to Brenda's hand. Poor guy had been shuffled between neighbors, his sitter, Grandma, and Daddy for weeks. But he gradually relaxed and started playing with his LEGOs on the family room floor. He had come to visit me twice at the loony hospital, sporting a new crew cut and full of questions about when Mommy and the new baby would come home. I noticed the glance between them—*Is she normal?* Mike nodded and got into the car.

Brenda stayed for a cup of coffee. She had lived in the neighborhood for almost twenty years, and took me under her wing when Mike and I moved in. Wally was retired. Brenda had always been a stay-at-home mom. They enjoyed watching Jason on occasion.

"Did Mike tell you?" I searched her eyes.

"Just that you weren't sleeping. That they gave you some meds."

I rolled my eyes. "Who else?"

"What do you mean? Who else?"

"Who else … did he tell?"

"Honestly, other than me and your mom, I don't think he's told anybody. I came over a few times and chatted with your mom. Nice lady. She was real worried about you."

I looked down and sniffed. "I wish she lived closer." I stirred more sugar into my coffee and took a sip. It was lukewarm. I hoped Brenda was telling the truth. I didn't need the whole neighborhood knowing I'd gone loony.

Brenda stood to leave. "You stay here with your mommy. Okay, Jason?"

Jason stuck his finger in his mouth and nodded.

After she left, I went and sat with Jason on the floor.

"Are you still sick, Mommy?" He touched my forehand.

I adjusted the collar on his red polo shirt.

"Mommy's getting better."

"You look sick."

"Pills make me sloooow." I smiled, then tickled his belly. "How about ... I read you a story?"

He brightened, ran to his room and came back with *A Tall Book of Nursery Tales*.

I plopped in Mike's big leather easy chair. Jason crawled up in my lap and turned the pages to "Little Red Riding Hood."

"Once ... upon a time ... in a cottage ... at ... ," I read.

"Faster, Mommy. Read faster."

"... edge of ... deep woods ... lived ... little girl ... ."

The words were sticking in my head. I could see the words on the page. I knew the story by heart, but I could barely eke them out.

"Mommy, read."

"I'm sorry, Jason. Mommy's ... trying." I inhaled deeply.

"It's okay, Mommy. I'll read it to you." He positioned the book between us. "The neighbors called her Little Red Riding Hood." He turned the page. "Little Red Riding Hood's mother said, 'Take this basket to Grandma, who is sick.'" He looked up. "Sick like you, Mommy?"

I nodded and sniffed.

"Suddenly a big bad wolf appeared." He continued on, telling the whole story from memory, flipping through the pages.

I hugged him. "That was ... very good."

I closed the cover, stroked Jason's hair, and stared absently at the rabbits and roosters, the face of the gingerbread man. I had graduated top of my class in my high school, and breezed through college. *Valedictorian, Magna Cum Laude, Idiot.*

"I wanna go outside and play." He crawled down and opened the sliding door to the backyard.

I watched. He poured sand from a yellow plastic bucket into his trucks. He maneuvered the trucks around the sand, dumping each load until he had a tall pile. Normally I would be helping him build sand forts, planting flowers, trimming hedges.

The breakfast dishes were still on the table. I eventually summoned the energy to take one dish, rinse it, put it in the dishwasher. I walked over to check on Jason in the sandbox. Then I rinsed another dish.

Mike arrived home and started working on the sprinkler in the back yard. He came in, his hands covered with mud, and washed them in the kitchen sink.

"How's it going?" he asked.

"All these pills—" I sighed.

"Just take them. Please, Kate."

I bit my lip. He had read my mind, again.

He dried his hands, came over and planted a salty kiss on my lips.

"I should have asked your mom to come and be with you before I left on that last TDY." He brushed a lock of my hair behind my ear. "I noticed your ankles were swelling, and I knew something was wrong. I chose to ignore it, never heard of toxemia." His voice cracked. "But flying that damn black snake was more important than my family." He blinked and looked down to compose himself. He pulled me close. "I always thought of you as superwoman—capable of handling anything. But you'll be super again. We'll be fine. If you want, I can help make lunch."

I clung to him, then finally let go. "I think I can handle lunch." I needed to force myself to do things, to get my body back in motion.

I went to the fridge, pulled out a gallon of milk, lifted the lid and sniffed. *Blech!* Poured it down the drain. The lettuce was slimy, and white spots decorated the cheese. I would definitely have to go shopping for some fresh fruit and veggies.

Maybe tomorrow. I wasn't sure if I could even drive a car. I didn't dare chance anyone from work seeing the zombie.

18.

By the end of the first week back home, I was starting to speak in full sentences. Sometimes a word stuck in my brain and rattled around. An hour later I'd remember it. I prayed the short circuits in my brain were not permanent. I went for short walks, careful not to venture far from the house. My bladder was still unpredictable.

Mike took me and Jason out to the base to see Robbie a couple of times. Jason wasn't allowed in the nursery, but Mike lifted him up so he could peer through the window for a few minutes. Robbie was out of his incubator and sleeping in a bassinette, like the other babies. He'd grown so much. It broke my heart.

Mom came back from Kansas on July 25. She had a lot more wrinkles around her eyes, and I knew she'd been worrying over me. Robbie was five weeks old, and had reached the magical five pounds. Mom, Mike, and I headed out to the hospital to retrieve our baby. In the hospital, I clung to Mike's arm. The hospital smell still made my stomach knot up. To my relief, The Colonel was nowhere in sight, and the nurses acted as if they barely remembered me.

I slipped my pinkie into his hand and whispered, "Robbie. It's me, your mommy. Do you remember me?" His eyelids fluttered and he yawned. I took that as a maybe.

Dr. Khan was making rounds and stopped to chat. His face beamed and he shook my hand. "Take good care of our, no, *your* baby. He will grow big and strong, like his father."

I nodded. I hadn't planned for such a stormy start, like a mother ship without a rudder or sail. Mike had warned me that it took a strong woman to be a military wife. I had no idea. Now I was beginning to understand. For the moment, I was content to let Mike be the strong one.

Mom took the discharge instructions and chatted with Dr. Khan about Robbie's feeding schedule. Robbie had learned to suck on a preemie pacifier, and his mouth moved busily at odd moments.

"Do you want to carry Robbie to the car?" Mom asked.

I shook my head. Even though I was down to only two pills a day, my muscles twitched unexpectedly on occasion, and I was afraid I might drop him. Mike carried the baby and tucked him safely into his car seat in our Camaro.

Back home, Mom cradled Robbie and opened the receiving blanket to show Jason his baby brother. A size zero bootie slipped off a teeny foot.

"His feet are little."

"Yes, they are tiny."

"He'll never walk on those little feet. He'll fall over."

"He'll grow bigger and stronger. Just wait and see. Would you like to hold him?" Mom asked.

Jason's eyes grew wide. "Yeah!"

"You have to sit here by Grandma." She patted the spot on the sofa next to her.

I leaned on the kitchen counter and felt helpless, glad that Mom was taking charge. This was not the way I had imagined Jason meeting his little brother. But finally, we were all home, safe from monitoring, ready to take the first shaky steps as a new family.

Jason crawled up on the tweed couch and his eyes lit up. He grinned broadly as Grandma placed Robbie on his lap. She supported Robbie's head with her hand. Jason slipped his finger in the tiny hand. "Look, Mommy."

"He likes you," I said.

The pacifier fell out of Robbie's mouth, and he let out a "Waaa!" Jason retrieved it, sucked it clean, and plugged it back in, all the while making silly faces at his new brother.

When Jason lost interest in the new baby and starting plowing his toy tractor across the carpet, I sat on the couch next to Mom.

"My turn." I took Robbie, supported his head cautiously, and adjusted his giraffe-adorned receiving blanket. He immediately started fussing. "Don't cry. It's Mommy." I looked wide-eyed to Mom for support, feeling unsteady.

Mom glanced at her watch. "It's time for his bottle."

"I'd like to try to breastfeed him."

"It wouldn't hurt to try—" She wrinkled her nose.

I didn't care for the emphasis she placed on the word "try." Hopefully I hadn't pumped my breasts all those days in the hospital for nothing. "I'd prefer to be alone."

"Just be careful." She tucked the blanket around his feet.

I bundled him on my shoulder and headed down the hall to the bedroom. I propped a pillow against the headboard and settled onto the waterbed. My milk had almost dried up, but I pinched hard, and a few drops came out. I lay Robbie's cheek next to my nipple. He refused to latch on. He squirmed and arched his head away every time I tried to bring him close. Each squirm was like an arrow through my heart.

I tried several times over the next few days to get him to suckle. To no avail. I finally borrowed a mechanical breast pump from the county health nurse. The pump squeaked and grabbed, but nothing came out. My boobs had closed up shop. I'd grown up watching every pig, cow, and goat on our farm nurse their young. It wasn't that hard. Unless someone tromped on Mother Nature.

Maybe it was the medication. Maybe Robbie sensed that it was nasty stuff. I phoned the county health nurse for ideas. She asked which medication I was on. When she called me back, she suggested that perhaps it would be best if I didn't try to breast feed.

Finally, I gave up. Robbie was going to be a bottle baby after all. My baby had rejected me. I kept staring into his face, searching for splendor, but found only disenchantment. His face was bony, his eyes unfocused, his skin blotchy. A mother should love her baby unconditionally. I found it hard to care for him at all. My hatred for The Colonel grew darker each day. She had taken so much from me. So much that I could never get back.

I confided to Mom. "It's not the same as it was with Jason. It's so much harder to love him."

"Give it time. You've been through so much. Your brother Stevie only weighed four and a half pounds when I brought him home. Some days I thought he would never finish those two ounces of milk."

I had heard Mom's stories of her own preemie many times, but until now hadn't realized how difficult her struggle must have been. "How did you do it?"

"I prayed a lot."

I nodded. I was putting the last glass up in the cupboard when it slipped out of my hand and shattered noisily on the tile counter. I went to retrieve the broom and dust pan.

"Honey, go lie down. I'll clean up the mess."

"I'll do it, Mother." My voice was loud with anger. I brushed the little shards of glass into the dust pan and wiped the counter with a damp paper towel.

I turned to Mom, "I'm sorry I yelled at you. I'm really sorry." I paused and took a deep breath. "Maybe I *should* go lie down."

I shut the bedroom door and pulled the covers over my head, desperate for escape. But guilt seeped through the bedspread, despair laced the sheets, and shame shared my pillow.

19.

Mom stayed two weeks. On her last morning, we shared Danish and drained the coffee pot. I hugged her for a long time, wished she could stay longer, but knew she had to get back to her job. As Mike backed out of the driveway to drive her to the airport, I cuddled Robbie at the sidewalk and waved his little hand goodbye to her. Jason clutched at my trousers, waving too.

I was in a funk when Mike returned from the airport. "The house seems so empty without Mom."

He picked up Jason and zoomed him around the family room, one hand under Jason's chest in mock flight mode, an activity that always made Mom frown and Jason squeal with delight. "I'm glad it's just us. We're a family again. I can watch the boys for a while. Why don't you get out?"

"And do what?"

"Go to the mall. Anything. You've always loved bargain-hunting."

I looked at him, suddenly excited about the prospect of buying new baby clothes for Robbie. He was still so tiny. Most of Jason's clothes swam on him. "Are you sure?"

"Of course. You need some time to yourself."

So I went. This was my first time to drive a car since Robbie was born. I relished the freedom, but gripped the steering wheel and kept a safe distance from the car in front of me. My reactions were slow. On two pills a day, the fog was thinning. Still, I didn't trust myself to do so many things.

At the mall, I still moved in slow, robotic motion. I walked past the Baskin Robbins, resisting the tempting aroma of vanilla waffle cones. At Sears, I ignored the clearance sale on shoes and headed straight to the infant section. There I almost bumped into Pete, the night-shift manager at Marinara. He was often punching out on the time clock when I was punching in.

Before I could duck behind a display, he noticed me. "Kate, I was shopping for my new nephew, barely recognized you. You look awful."

No tact. Pete was forty and overweight by thirty pounds, with dark circles under his eyes. I suddenly realized why he was still a bachelor. The plaid shirt over striped shorts didn't help.

"Great to see you, too." I wiped my chin, hoping there was no drool.

"Sorry. You were always Miss Sunshine. How's the baby? What's his name?"

"Robbie. He's growing."

He shook his head. "I heard he came early—" I couldn't mistake the pity in his eyes.

"New baby, no sleep," I mumbled and turned away, empty-handed. Pete would probably report back to Fred. Everyone at work would know that I was a mess. Chuck would laugh in my sad face. I left the mall empty-handed and empty-hearted. I drove home, dejected.

Back in the shelter of my house, Mike was playing with Jason, the family room engulfed by an entire village of Lincoln Logs, Tinkertoys, and wooden blocks. Jason farmed the village with red and green toy tractors. A Roadrunner cartoon played on the tube. Jason sat cross-legged and shouted, "Beep, beep" along with the skinny bird. Through all the commotion, Robbie slept soundly in his infant seat on the floor.

"Mike, have you been watching television all afternoon?" I plopped my purse on the kitchen table.

"Great babysitter. See. Robbie's out like a log."

"You know the rules."

"Give it a break. I'm relaxing."

"Can't—"

Mike's icy glare stopped me short. After a stormy first year of marriage, Mike and I had settled into spheres of influence. I had strict rules about television. Jason was only allowed one hour per day. Now my authority in domestic matters had been swept under the rug. The longer "light duty" lasted, the shorter my flyboy's temper had become. There were more "fuck you" than "let's fuck" moments, and the strain was starting to pervade every facet of our lives.

I spied the cake pan sitting on the kitchen counter. Mom had baked her famous sour-cream chocolate cake. I'd already devoured a piece for my morning snack and another at lunch. I slid open the aluminum lid and grabbed a fork. Just one bite.

The icing tasted moist and fudgy. I shuffled to the left side of the kitchen, out of Mike's view. Soon only crumbs remained. I squished up every smidgen. Ran my finger around the pan to get the last lick. I hid the pan in the back of the bottom cupboard. Mike wouldn't look there. Maybe I'd tell him that I'd taken it to Brenda's house. But only if he asked.

I tromped back to the bedroom, curled up on the bed, and massaged the ugly roll of flab around my middle. Disgusting. I'd do better—tomorrow.

* * *

The next day, when Mike was at work, I curled up in a ball on the bed and rocked myself. Back and forth, back and forth— trying to get my body back to the old "tick-tock, tick-tock" after it had slowed to a "tick … tock … tick … "

I heard Robbie cry. *I'll get him in a minute.*

His cries grew louder.

I kept rocking, rocking.

Jason tapped lightly on the bedroom door. "Mommy, your baby is crying."

"I'll get to him." My toddler shamed me. I crawled out of the bed, plodded to the nursery, and grabbed Robbie. "Okay, bottle baby."

He wailed at my shrillness.

I held him tight and shushed his cries. The litany of drugs had transformed me into a monster mom, nothing like the cheery mother I had been with Jason. Where was the awe over my babe holding his head up for the first time, the joy at seeing my tyke first grasp a rattle, the wonder of his eyes meeting mine and recognizing his mama? All those feelings were buried beneath a blanket of medication. I fought the resentment.

Robbie squirmed unexpectedly and his head plunged toward the floor. I grabbed him up in a panic, my heart pounding. He wailed. Nerves clanging, I reached for his cloth Snugli. He needed protection from his own mother. "I'm sorry, Robbie. None of this is your fault."

Sweating, I strapped him into the body harness and jostled him quiet. I walked us to the kitchen, poured water in a pan, set it on the stove, and plopped in the baby bottle.

"Mommy will make your bottle just right. Be patient, little precious."

As we both calmed, I realized that carrying Robbie on my chest felt good. Each beat of my heart soothed his teeny frame. He needs you, I told myself. And I needed him.

I maneuvered him out of the Snugli, and we cuddled in the big round papasan chair that Mike had purchased on a trip to the Philippines. Robbie finished the bottle and I rubbed his boney back until a burp emerged. I touched his little button nose with my finger.

"We've been through a lot, little one? But we're survivors. We'll make it."

Then he smiled at me, a wide toothless grin. It wasn't a burp or gas. It was definitely a smile, his first.

I smiled back.

20.

Later that afternoon, I took the boys for a little walk around the neighborhood. Robbie was bundled in his red umbrella stroller. Jason ran ahead, his arms stretched out in airplane mode, making little jet engine noises. He almost ran into Brenda, who was coming out of her garage.

"This is my new brother, Robbie," Jason said proudly when Brenda leaned down. "He's the little brother. I'm the big brother." He pointed to the fat elephant on the big-brother shirt Grandma bought him before she left. Robbie's matching little-brother shirt was emblazoned with a curly-tailed mouse. He swam in a newborn size.

"He is teeny tiny, but cute as a button." Brenda bent down to admire the matching shirts. "I baked some cookies, chocolate chip. Would you like one?"

"Sure." Jason took Brenda's hand and tugged toward her house.

"I'll slip in the house. Should I bring one for you too, Kate?"

"No thanks. I've put on a few pounds." I sucked my gut in a notch. It was more than just not breastfeeding. It was the meds. My new shrink had explained that they caused weight gain, and I was too dopey to exercise, so I purposely avoided getting on the scale.

Brenda nodded. "I noticed, but that's a good thing. You've always been so thin, too thin if you ask me. You look more like a mom now." She and Jason went into the house.

I didn't want to look more like a mom. I wanted to look just like I did before I got pregnant—slim and sexy. It had taken a while, but I'd managed to eventually fit into my old clothes after Jason. Like that was ever going to happen. Like anything was ever going to be the same again. I clenched and unclenched my fists.

Brenda and Jason re-emerged a few minutes later, my boy with a full cookie in one hand, and a half-eaten one in the other. Brenda handed me two cookies wrapped in a napkin. "For Mike."

I politely thanked Brenda for the cookies and headed back into the house, cutting short our walk.

Somehow Mike never got his cookies.

* * *

The days dragged on. Mike was still on light duty, but was now spending time in the T-38 jet with another pilot to maintain currency. He was supposed to meet with the squadron commander soon to lay out a plan to return to duty on the SR-71.

Molly had asked if I could start work at Marinara part-time, just a day or two a week. The plant manager, Fred, was anxious for me to finish up the gourmet marinara project, which was due to launch in late October. I said I wasn't ready, that I was having trouble finding day care. That was at least half true. The other half was that I didn't have any clothes. I had outgrown everything except maternity pants and sweats. When I'd finally worked up the courage to step on the scale, I stepped off in horror. I weighed almost as much as I did when I was pregnant.

One morning I tried to squeeze into a pair of my larger work slacks, the ones I'd worn the first few months I was pregnant. I could barely get the zipper up two inches. I cast them in the corner of my closet in disgust. It was only ten o'clock, but I went to the fridge and took out a carton of rocky road ice cream that was about a third full.

Tomorrow would be a good day to start a diet.

Tomorrow I would begin with a clean slate.

Tomorrow I would eat only healthy food.

It would probably be best if there was no ice cream left in the house to tempt me. Ten minutes later, my stomach churned from an overdose of chocolate, marshmallow, and nuts. I tossed the empty carton in the trash.

I hated myself. I hated the Colonel. I hated Mike. I hated the whole world.

That night Mike snuggled up to me in bed. He massaged my tight shoulders. His strong hands soothed my stiff neck.

"That feels good," I murmured.

He planted tender kisses down the nape of my neck. "I know something else that would make you feel good."

"No. I'm not ready." I pulled away and wrapped the sheets tight around my body.

21.

After leaving the psych ward, I had been assigned to see Dr. Falio, a young psychiatrist at the Yucca County Mental Health facility. He had an athletic build and wore his wavy hair long. He always dressed in a sports coat over an oxford button-down-collar shirt. Never a tie.

The doctor's office was lit by a soft lamp. A philodendron sprawled out of a copper urn on the side table. I sat on a wing-back chair across from the doctor, bored.

He had switched me from Haldol to Prolixin, another antipsychotic drug. Today I was complaining about the weight gain.

"Can't I stop the medication? I feel groggy all the time."

"Not yet. We're gradually decreasing the dosage. There is some chance of a relapse, and we certainly don't want that to happen." He flashed a smile and waited for me to speak.

I stifled a yawn. I was here because Mike insisted. The doctor was weaning me off the drugs, and I was anxious to get back some semblance of my previous life. The prescription bottle said not to take the pills with alcohol. I wasn't a lush. But I used to join the Marinara crew for happy hour on Friday nights after work. Mike and I had enjoyed getting a sitter for Jason, and going to the Officer's Club. I missed the fun times— before I was pregnant, before the psychosis.

"Would it be okay if I have an occasional glass of wine?" I asked.

"That's not a good idea at this time."

I nodded like a polite child. One drink wouldn't hurt. He didn't need to know everything.

* * *

Two weeks later, Mike joined me during my appointment with Dr. Falio. I squirmed beside him on the couch.

Mike ran his hands up and down his thighs. He looked aside at me hesitantly, then spoke to the doctor in a low voice. "I think something happened to Kate ... either in the base hospital or on the mental health ward."

"What do you mean?" The doctor leaned forward.

"I feel really guilty about everything that happened. And I love holding Kate, snuggling, making her feel cherished. It's just that—" He let out a big sigh. "At some point ... well, a guy wants more than snuggling." Mike reached over to caress my hand. I pulled away and clutched both hands between my knees.

The doctor set down his notebook. "Have you talked to Kate about it?"

"She says she doesn't want to talk about it."

With Jason we'd violated the "wait six weeks" rule on about week three. But then he'd been c-section. No stitches. It wasn't about the stitches. It was about betrayal. About getting even. About my lousy self image.

Dr. Falio turned to me. "Did something happen to you in the hospital?" he asked gently. "Something bad?"

I curled my lip. Did something bad happen to me? The whole incident had been one hellacious nightmare. I nodded, yes.

"Did someone hurt you?"

I nodded, yes, again.

"Did someone rape you?" Dr. Falio spoke very softly.

I shook my head, no.

"Can you talk about it?"

Again, I shook my head, no.

"Can you show us what happened?"

I nodded, yes.

"Go ahead, show us." Dr. Falio waited.

I stood up and motioned for them to follow. Mike rolled his eyes, but I motioned again. They both traipsed down the hall after me. I stopped at the vending machine and pointed to a Pepsi.

My folks rarely bought soft drinks back on the farm. But the city kids—the cool kids—all had Pepsi in their fridge. At college I'd treat myself at the vending machine after passing a rough exam. Always Pepsi, never Coke. It was my favorite pick-me-up when I was down.

I reached in my pocket, as if looking for change. I pulled out my empty hands, and pointed at the Pepsi in the machine again.

"What Kate? What are you trying to say?" Mike asked.

I kept pointing at the machine, then started pounding on it with my clenched fist, then reached in my pockets, coming out with empty hands. *Haven't these idiots ever played charades? Don't they get it? In the hospital, I wanted a Pepsi. I had no freedom, no money, no baby. The one thing I valued above all else, my mind, was gone. And they want to know if something bad happened.* The rage built inside me. All the injustice. I pounded harder, harder, my fist throbbing, the machine swaying from the force of my blows. *All I wanted was a fricking Pepsi.*

Mike looked wide-eyed at Dr. Falio. "I don't get it."

"I'll be right back." The doctor went down the hall.

I was expecting him to come back with three quarters. Instead he brought a syringe. *No use fighting it.* The needle stung. My ego shattered. I turned to Mike. "Can I have a Pepsi?" I yelled.

"Why didn't you just ask?" Mike reached in his pocket, pulled out three quarters and jammed them in the machine. The can of Pepsi rolled out with a welcome thunk. He popped the top and handed it to me. "I don't understand any of this, Kate."

I'd tried once to tell Mike. Tried to explain how humiliating it had all been. How betrayed I felt. He listened, but I could tell he didn't understand. "You said show you," my voice cracked.

Mike threw up his arms.

"Let's go back into my office and talk," Dr. Falio said.

We followed him down the hall. Mike sat. I plopped in the wingback, but he pulled me onto the couch, close to him.

"Kate, you're keeping a lot inside. You need to tell us what you're feeling. Talking about it will help you get past this," Dr. Falio said. "You also might need a different medication. You obviously responded quickly to what I just gave you."

I glared at him. Medication had transformed me from a winner to a weenie. The last thing I needed was more medication.

"Come here, sweetie." Mike took the Pepsi from me and set it on the table. "Listen, I can't help you when you shut me out. You've got to talk to me."

Tears came to my eyes. "You can't begin to comprehend what I went through."

"I'll try harder." Mike reached up and brushed a tear from the corner of my eye.

I pushed his hand away, grabbed the Pepsi, and took a gulp. It was cold, and I liked the way the bubbles tingled in my mouth.

22.

By the end of August, I was off all medication. Minus the "Prolixin stare," I almost recognized the woman who looked back at me in the mirror. Robbie now fit in newborn clothes, although his arms and legs were rail thin and his face delicate. He was smiling regularly. I sat in the rocking chair in the boys' room with the aquarium light on, and poured out my heart to him. "So what do you think? Are we gonna make it? We're tough, you and me."

I picked up his favorite rattle, the one with the kitty face, and shook it. He grasped it with his tiny fingers.

"Mommy's sorry she couldn't be with you in the hospital. What did you think of that Colonel? Did you know her mother was born wearing army boots?"

Robbie let out a long burp. I put the little tyke on my shoulder, patted his back gently, and closed my eyes. "She was a scary dragon." The episode was now more like a fairy tale gone wrong, less fire and brimstone. The everyday reality was settling in. Calendar pages no longer floated in mid-air. The days passed slowly, monotonously.

I was beginning to realize that doctors were not perfect. They made mistakes. But I still despised the woman. "At least Dr. Khan was there to protect you." Robbie let out a loud belch of confirmation.

"Such a big burp for such a little guy. Do you feel better now? Mommy's starting to feel better." I continued rocking and rubbing his back. Five neon tetras played tag in the aquarium. I started humming "Lullaby and Good Night." There was laundry to wash, dust to wipe, and dirty dishes on the table. But for now, I just sat and rocked Robbie, trying to make up for all those lost days and weeks.

* * *

In my world gone crazy, food was my one joy, my secret comfort. Unfortunately those extra pounds that I gained on the meds settled on my waist and hips. No matter how hard I tried, they declined to budge. I kept telling myself that I would stick to that diet—tomorrow—but my willpower was shot.

At the clinic, I found a brochure for Overeaters Anonymous, so I decided to give the group a try. OA met in the basement of the First Presbyterian Church every Saturday morning at 10 a.m., in a little room with two long tables and no windows. I arrived a few minutes early and timidly entered the room. Multi-colored stars on the bulletin board featured snapshots of children. In one corner, a dozen or so metal folding chairs were set in a circle.

Before long the room began to fill. One woman appeared to be pushing three hundred pounds. She slowly waddled in, paused to catch her breath, and sat on a chair. The chair creaked, and I worried that it might collapse. Eventually six women, including me, were seated in the circle. The others appeared to be hard-core overeaters, most fifty to a hundred pounds overweight. Carrying only an extra twenty-five or so pounds, I felt out of place. Apparently these women had been hurting for a long time. This is how I could end up, if I didn't stop binge eating.

A woman started the meeting. "Hello, I'm Marie, and I'm a compulsive overeater."

We prayed, and then went around the room introducing ourselves. When it was my turn, I followed the lead of the others. "I'm Kate—a compulsive overeater."

A woman read from the Twelve Traditions of Overeaters Anonymous. Then came time for each woman to share. One of the older ladies started, "Sometimes I open a can of Crisco, and eat spoonfuls of it."

I cringed at the thought.

"When my husband drinks, I eat," Marie confessed. "He drinks a lot."

Finally it was my turn. The room grew silent and everyone's eyes fixed on me. I clenched my hands tightly on both sides of the folding chair, and stared down at my navy and white tennis shoes. I raised my head to meet everyone's eyes, my voice barely above a whisper. "I'm punishing myself for having a postpartum psychosis."

There were blank stares around the room, but it felt good to get it out.

Marie reached over and patted me on the arm, "You poor thing." Her paisley smock-like top barely concealed two bulging layers of fat around her stomach, but her dark brown eyes brimmed with compassion.

I tried to imagine what it would be like to carry around all that misery. I was on a downward spiral. My eating had been out of control for a few weeks. But these people had been out of control for years. What could I learn from them? I left the meeting determined never to go back.

That night, after putting Jason and Robbie to bed, I pulled a bag of Oreos out of the pantry. I didn't want them to be around to tempt me in the morning. Tomorrow I would start my diet. I tossed them in the garage trash can and turned to go back in the house.

I stopped with one hand on the door knob, went back, and pulled the bag out of the trash. Just one Oreo wouldn't hurt.

Five minutes later, I lifted the bag over my head and poured the last chocolate crumbs into my mouth. I tossed the crumpled bag in the trash and slammed the lid with a clang. My stomach grimaced in protest. I disgusted myself.

Mike was snoozing in front of the television. He didn't see me. Thin, healthy, athletic, sexy Kate was slipping away. Would Mike love pudgy Kate? Today, maybe. Forever, I wasn't sure. Could I love pudgy Kate? If I couldn't respect myself, how could I expect Mike to love me?

I stared at myself in the master bathroom mirror. The extra pounds showed in my cheeks. I opened the medicine cabinet behind the mirror. I kept a bottle of ipecac syrup, on the chance that Jason might somehow eat or drink something poisonous. I studied the bottle, held it in my hand, read the instructions to induce vomiting.

I put it back in the medicine cabinet, praying for will power.

I locked the bathroom door and turned on the shower, so Mike wouldn't hear. I opened the cabinet, took the lid off the bottle and downed the syrup in one long gulp. Nasty.

In a few minutes, my stomach wrenched. I hung my head over the toilet and spewed little black chunks mixed with the spaghetti. I flushed. Then again. If I could only pull a lever and make all the bad memories go away.

My gut ached. I downed a glass of water, brushed my teeth, and rinsed with mouthwash to get the pukey taste out of my mouth.

I couldn't resist looking in the mirror. Disconsolate eyes stared back at me. Stop punishing yourself. Pull yourself together. Stop flushing your life down the toilet.

The next day, I went to the drug store and picked up another bottle of ipecac. The following day I was back again.

23.

As my culinary creativity gradually returned, I started to get antsy to go back to work. I missed the lab and my work friends. Mike had pooh-poohed the idea, so I decided to make him his favorite breakfast—bacon, eggs, and hash browns—to get him in a good mood so we could talk about my going back to work. I slid six strips of bacon in the frying pan. Within minutes the tantalizing aroma of bacon filled the kitchen. Robbie started to cry. I turned the burner down and went to comfort him.

"Okay little guy. Let's get that diaper changed." After the diaper, I wound Robbie's mobile. He kicked and reached his arms as colorful plastic puppies twirled to the music of "Here We Go Round the Mulberry Bush."

A shrill alarm sounded. *Shit.*

I rushed to the kitchen and wafted my way through the smoke. The bacon was burnt to a crisp.

Mike charged into the kitchen, a towel wrapped around his waist, his hair dripping wet. "And you think you're ready to go back to work."

I slammed the skillet into the sink. "Yes ... and then you can start making your own damn breakfast."

Ten minutes later, wearing his flight suit, he slammed the garage door on his way out.

* * *

My conversations with my shrink were typically sedate and boring. Today I let loose. "They say 'till death do us part.' What they really mean is 'till you get fat and some skinny chick comes along.'"

Dr. Falio set down his pencil. His eyes were steel-blue. I had never noticed their color before, or felt the warmth behind the steel. "What happened?"

I ranted on. "Nobody really loves anybody anymore. As long as you're skinny and hot in bed, everything's hunky-dory. It doesn't matter that you were up half the night with your baby. Sooner or later, he betrays you."

He leaned in. "Mike has betrayed you?" His cologne was musty, like a walk in the woods on a misty morning.

"Yes ... no. It's just ... nothing's been right since ... ." I blinked hard. "I'm losing him."

Last week he had taken down the red velvet drapes and replaced them with beige curtain panels. He repainted the bedroom a soft blue because somebody told him that blue soothed the soul. Brought home color samples with fifteen different shades of blue, asked me which one I thought was most calming. Finished the job in one week-end. He was being so nice. So damn capable. But my anger and resentment bubbled out at odd moments, over ridiculous little things like burnt bacon. It cast an icy chill over our bedroom. Each day the river between us grew wider.

"What would you do if you lost Mike? If you guys divorced?" He said it in a big-brother way, like he cared, like he understood.

"I don't know. I'd—" I wanted to crawl in his strong arms and have a good cry. Then I remembered the needle. I drew back. I felt so lame. Would I ever be normal again? I glanced down at my hands. Long overdue for a manicure. I'd let myself go these past months, in so many ways.

I stared into his steel eyes for the longest time, then stood and left without a word. I hurried to my car in the parking lot, and sat, gulping to catch my breath.

I stopped by Macy's on the way home and browsed through the lingerie department. I used to dress sexy when Mike came back from a TDY. The luscious homecoming romance would last for days. This time he'd returned to a premature baby and a crazy wife. I shopped a long time, searching for something seductive—that could cover my flabby stomach. I finally selected an outfit, complete with four-inch stilettos. The saleslady swore they'd knock my man off his feet—assuming I didn't trip and fall first.

That afternoon I did sit-ups until I petered out. Then I whipped together the perfect dinner: baked chicken, herbed rice, green beans topped with almonds and olive oil. I carefully portioned out small servings for myself. Resisted seconds. Afterward I bathed and shaved my legs—all the way.

I emerged in the new black teddy, silk stockings, and high heels. Mike was absorbed in a rerun of *MASH*. I stepped in front of the television. "Haven't you seen this episode before?"

"Wow." He picked up the remote and turned the television off.

I strutted over and put a high-heeled foot on the coffee table.

"What's gotten into you?" He ran his finger along the top of my black garter.

I leaned down and opened the top button of his shirt. "I just wanted to surprise you."

"This surprise I like."

"I thought you might."

My first orgasm came on the couch. I had forgotten how good it felt. Then Mike picked me up and carried me back to the bedroom. I closed my eyes and imagined Dr. Falio carrying me away. Dr. Falio? That was insane.

But what the ... I was a certified crazy woman. And somewhere there was a little piece of paper to prove it.

24.

Gradually, my libido escalated. At odd moments I pondered accidental meetings with Dr. Falio—in the park, in a restaurant. I had noticed on a brochure at the clinic that the doctor's first name was Rex. I hoped that I didn't slip and scream "Rex" in a moment of passion with Mike.

Mike was strutting with a cocky air, partly because of what was happening in our bedroom, and partly because he had been approved to go back on flying status.

I felt uncomfortable with Dr. Falio during my next appointment. I avoided looking in his eyes.

"Has something changed?" he said.

"This is the real Kate. Not that pathetic woman who's been coming to see you the past month." I relaxed in the chair and smiled. My hot pink nails exactly matched my new silk blouse and high-heeled sandals. I'd been skipping breakfast and eating salads. I could squeeze into my looser blue jeans. My new push-up bra and my silk blouse revealed just the right amount of cleavage. Two thin gold bracelets jangled on my wrist. I sucked in my gut.

His gaze was … questioning? Mocking? Pitying?

Suddenly I wondered if my perfume was too strong.

"I'm wondering if it would be good for you to work with another doctor," he said. "In addition to the work I do here at the clinic, I also have a private practice. We have a female psychiatrist in our group."

He knew. He could read my mind. Was he just being professional, or did he not trust himself?

"The last thing I want is to see another doctor. I'm more like my old self. I have lots of energy now."

"Too much energy is not necessarily a good thing. We want your mood stable. I'd like you to see this other doctor. I suspect you might have a mood disorder. We might want to consider a different drug, lithium, to even out your highs and lows."

"I hate drugs."

"Kate, you've got to understand what you're up against."

"But I was so normal before."

"Once you have a mood disorder, you're much more likely get out of control again. We don't want anything to happen to you ... or your children."

"But I'm fine. I'm a good mother. I would *never* hurt my children." I was furious that he would even suggest such a thing.

"Postpartum psychosis is pretty rare. We don't understand all the contributing factors, but we do know that both heredity and hormonal changes are involved. You'll definitely be at risk if you have another pregnancy. It's important that you understand, if you're not careful, you could end up spending more time in a mental institution."

I studied his shoes for the longest while, cordovan penny loafers, neatly buffed to a soft glow. I remembered one of the crazies talking about "the big hospital," definitely not a place I cared to visit. Up until that moment I had considered this whole psychotic thing to have been a big mistake. One of those things that happened and you recovered completely. Now I wasn't so sure. I looked up, bit and then released my lip. "I understand."

I missed my next appointment with Rex. The clinic called several times to reschedule. I ignored the calls and erased them off the answering machine, so Mike wouldn't know. I couldn't trust Mike, and I definitely couldn't trust the sexy doctor. I was basically on my own—to recover over time.

25.

My six weeks of maternity leave stretched to thirteen weeks. Molly called twice and warned that if I didn't come back to work soon, there wouldn't be a job to come back to. So I started back to work at Marinara on September 22. The new gourmet line was set to launch in the next month, and my expertise was welcome. I wasn't quite sure how I'd hold up, but decided to take it one day at a time. I had no sick leave, but Fred had agreed that I could take a day or two off without pay here and there if I needed a break. Lindsey preferred just pre-schoolers, so that she could take them for walks to the park, but she reluctantly agreed to watch Robbie until I could find someone who cared for infants.

The first week was hell ... and nirvana. I came home dead tired every evening, but it was exhilarating to be back in the groove, to get dressed up and put on make-up every day, to have a break from diapers and bottles. Everyone in the lab was glad to have me back—except Chuck, who was cool and aloof.

People stopped by to catch up and see pictures of my new baby. I had a framed five-by-seven of Robbie perched on Jason's lap. Most of my co-workers thought Robbie looked more like Mike than me.

A huge pile of correspondence overflowed my in-box. By Wednesday, I had whittled down the pile to a short stack of follow-up and to-do items, methodically organized in folders. It felt good to toss the unneeded—and compartmentalize the unknown, which is exactly how I filed my ongoing nightmares.

Fred's secretary, Molly, took me out to lunch and quizzed me about what had happened the last three months. Molly, short and stout with silver streaks in her hair, had once worked as a lumberjack. I stayed mum about my episode, but I could tell she knew more than she was letting on. Maybe she had wormed it out of Hillary, who had visited me at the hospital. Still, she didn't bring it up, and I sure wasn't going to go there. *Yeah, I spent a couple of weeks on the loony ward. You should try it!*

Thursday, my team conducted sensory panel tests on the new marinara sauces, including two of my formulas, Basil Cabernet and Red Pepper Chianti. I had left the formulas nearly complete before Robbie was born, but had made a few tweaks on my return. Chuck had concocted "improvements" to each flavor. All four samples were coded by one of the lab techs, so no one knew which were mine and which were Chuck's. Three groups of five people tasted all four. I recognized my sauces immediately. They tasted rich, with the perfect hint of a full-bodied Cabernet. Chuck's tasted like someone had doused them with cheap wine, that strawberry stuff I drank in college. Everyone ranked my formulas above Chuck's. I couldn't wait to report the results to Fred.

Friday, the crew insisted I join them for happy hour after work, a "Welcome back Kate" event. Chuck begged off, professing he had a prior commitment.

Twelve of us gathered at *Tres Margaritas*, a local bar with greasy nachos and the tastiest guacamole north of the border. The smoky dive was decorated with red and green piñatas and Mexican flags. Mariachi music blared over the stereo.

Hillary sat to my right. Wooden bowls of chips, pitchers of margaritas, and empty shot glasses littered our large round table. She set down her second shot glass. "It's great having you back." Wisps of her coppery hair trailed loose from her ponytail, accenting her green eyes.

"It's great to be back. But this is my first time drinking since I found out I was pregnant."

Before long, my mind started spinning. I should have gone home after the first round of drinks, but I was having too much fun being Kate again, not just Mom.

"I'll drive you home," Hillary slurred. "Just one more round."

"You're barely in shape to drive yourself. It's only a few miles." I fished for my keys.

Fred offered, "I can drive you home, Kate. One of the guys can bring me back to my car."

"Thanks. I'll be fine."

Five minutes later, I was lost. I drove aimlessly. In the rearview mirror, I spotted a police car following me. At the next stop sign, I counted to five under my breath, then pulled out. He turned on his flasher.

I pulled over and grabbed a mint from my console. When he came to my door, I rolled down the window a couple of inches, so he couldn't smell my breath.

"License and registration, please."

The officer flashed perfect white teeth.

"You were driving a bit erratically back there."

I debated: lies or tears? "I'm so sorry." Tears. "I just had a baby. This is my first night out. Please don't give me a ticket."

"Give me a few minutes." He went back to his cruiser.

After what seemed like an eternity, he came back. "You live on Butte View."

I nodded.

"Know Ted Lindstrum?"

"Sure. Ted and Rose. They live just down the street." I smiled. Ted worked for the highway patrol.

The cop handed me back my driver's license. Then he leaned down. "Have you been drinking?"

Busted. "Only one. Actually, more like half. You know, baby ... milk."

He looked embarrassed. Hesitated. "Look, I'm going to give you a break. But just this time. And I'm going to follow you home, make sure you get there safe."

Mike was waiting up. He took one look at me and laughed. "I see you had a good time."

I hung my head low and moaned. I needed to show Mike that I was getting back together. That I could handle responsibility. What if the cop hadn't bought my mommy-milk story? What if I'd been arrested? I couldn't afford any crazy screw-ups.

Mike took my hand and steered me to the bathroom, obviously amused at my misery. Usually worshipping the porcelain goddess was Mike's trick, but tonight I paid my homage. Between the margarita and the terror of the traffic stop, no ipecac was necessary. He helped me out of my clothes and into the shower. "Don't worry, Kate. This I understand. You'll be fine in forty-eight hours." He swatted me on the rear, turned on the water, and closed the glass shower door.

Mike handled Robbie's 3 a.m. bottle and Jason's demands for pancakes at the crack of dawn. By Sunday the throbbing in my head had abated, and I was back to being Mom. It would be a long time before anyone talked me into doing shooters again.

26.

Mike got the nod to take the Air Force's multi-million dollar baby out for a spin and start prepping for his next overseas trip, two weeks in Mildenhall, England. This would be a quick trip, a trade he'd made with another pilot so he could come home early from Okinawa after Robbie was born.

I sat on the edge of our waterbed while he packed a small metal footlocker. We'd built the frame together during our first year as newlyweds. Mike had fashioned a wooden base out of two-by-fours, and covered the edges with foam and black Naugahyde. I had pitched in by staining the wood and pounding hundreds of little decorative nails, spaced evenly at one inch intervals, along the side. Mike whistled as he pulled socks out of his armoire and tossed them in. "No going crazy on me this time."

"I'll do my best." I rolled my eyes and bobbled my head.

Mike threw a pair of socks at me. I caught the socks and tossed them into his footlocker.

He grinned. "I'm glad to see you're getting your sense of humor back. I missed that."

"Me too." Mornings were good. I had a lot of energy and optimism, but by evening—after work and putting the kids to bed—I was whipped. Mike had been a trooper. Giving both the boys their baths and reading Jason bedtime stories. "It's going to be a challenge keeping up with the boys while you're gone. Two weeks is a long time."

"You'll manage," he said. He tossed a pair of Fruit of the Looms into the air. They landed in the footlocker. "Promise me. No more fruit basket upset."

"Do you think I had any control? That I chose to go off the deep end?" I stuck out my tongue.

He pulled me close. "I know it wasn't your fault. But, you're getting better now. You're almost back to the old Kate."

"Sure." I tried to sound confident. But Dr. Falio's warning about spending time in a serious mental institution kept looping through my brain. I couldn't let that happen. Would die before I'd let that happen. I plopped down on the side of the bed. I had once told Mike that I was having nightmares about having Robbie in this bed. Mike just didn't get it. He thought changing the curtains and re-painting the walls would wipe the slate clean. But the gaping holes in my psyche remained.

"I'd still like to get a new bed." I tilted backward. "This one has too many bad memories. I would sleep better. And I wouldn't break my fingernails every time I try to tuck in the sheets."

He tickled my bare foot. "I love this waterbed. We've had a lot of good times on this bed."

"We could have good times on a new bed." I ran my big toe down his tummy.

"Absolutely not. I like this bed." He slid his hand up my inner thigh.

Even through my blue jeans, his caress sent a bolt of energy coursing through my tired body. I brushed his hand away playfully. "Give me fifteen minutes to take a shower and slip into something sexy." I had bought a new pair of black nylons and a lacy black camisole, just for the occasion. *Service a pilot properly before and after each trip, and he won't be as likely to stray.* I knew that there were women who hung around military bases, ready to provide comfort and "whatever else" to a lonely crew member in exchange for a few drinks and a few bucks. TDYs grew long, even for the best family guys.

"Leaving at oh-dark-thirty?" I said.

He nodded. "I'll try not to wake you."

"I won't mind." I started singing "The Stripper" tune and slithered out of my blue jeans.

He slapped me on the ass. "Shower, woman. Let me finish packing, and then I'll say good-bye." After two glasses of wine and delightful, farewell love-making, I slept like a baby. I heard Mike's alarm go off in the middle of the night, and felt his warm goodbye kiss on my lips.

* * *

I juggled work and getting the boys to day care without any major hiccups. Mike had taught Jason to fold the laundry. The task took three times as long with Jason's help, but he was so proud of himself, matching up socks by color and putting them in piles. I lauded his efforts and figured I'd pair up the socks properly during Jason's nap time.

Saturday, I had an unexpected visitor. There stood Betty Lou, or Snooty Lou, as Mike called her behind her back, holding a package wrapped in blue paper adorned with miniature airplanes and clouds. The gift was topped with an enormous blue-and-white bow. Betty Lou wore a silk floral jacket over a soft peach shell that exactly matched the color of her fingernails and toenails. I was decked out in frayed jean shorts and one of Mike's old fraternity T-shirts.

"I thought I'd take a chance and drop by." She handed me the baby gift. "This is for the new arrival."

"You'll have to excuse the mess." My eyes scanned the piles of laundry strewn across the living-room floor, lunch dishes on the table, breakfast dishes in the sink. I picked up a plastic truck so that she wouldn't trip, and pointed her to the family room.

Betty Lou scouted the room, as if the chaos required caution. "Sorry I haven't been by sooner. Jerome and I were on vacation." At one time her husband Jerome had flown the SR-71, but since his recent promotion to squadron commander, he currently flew a desk.

I cleared away the stuffed animals off the couch, felt her eyes on me.

"We don't have any children, but I'm constantly picking up after Jerome."

"Would you like tea or a soft drink? I have diet."

"Tea is fine."

I was just ready to set our glasses on the coffee table, when Jason came around the corner, carrying Robbie, like a running back would carry a football. Jason wore the proudest smile. Robbie squirmed and whimpered. "Here's my new brother!"

Betty Lou jumped up and grabbed Robbie. I spilled one of the glasses of tea, and grabbed a towel from the kitchen to wipe up the mess.

Jason picked up a rubber squeaky bear. "Robbie likes this. See, it makes a noise." He squeezed the bear over and over.

"Jason. Enough!" I shouted. "Go out and play."

He unstuck a half-eaten Tootsie Roll Pop from the coffee table and stuffed it in his mouth. "Can I take Robbie?"

"No. Shoo."

Betty Lou cradled Robbie's head to her shoulder. She stared at the coffee table, out the door after Jason, back at me in my chaos. She smiled lamely.

We chatted for a few minutes. "I've got to run some other errands. It was good to see you. I'll go now." She placed Robbie in my arms, then adjusted my hand under his head, as if I needed a class in how to hold my own baby.

As squadron commander, Jerome had the power to make or break Mike's career. There were a couple of bachelors in the squadron, but most of the SR-71 pilots were stable family men. Guys with solid personalities and proper wives. We had just made a lovely impression.

27

I picked up the boys from their sitter after work and arrived home reeking of garlic and basil. Jason ran into the backyard to play in the sand pile and I cradled Robbie on my hip.

"Did you miss Mommy?" I cooed to him.

He flashed me his cute cross-eyed smile. Dr. Khan had said that preemies take longer with certain motor skills. *Same for crazies*, I thought to myself.

The red message light flashed on the answering machine in the hallway. I grabbed a pencil and punched *play*.

"This is Sally Sterm from Yucca County Social Services. This message is for Mike Wahlberg. Please call me as soon as possible." I knew in an instant. Betty Lou had reported me. *That bitch!*

Mike wouldn't be home for another ten days. I bit my lip and considered my options, then pushed the erase button.

Who could I ask for help? Who could I trust? Not Dr. Falio. Brenda? No, I had been leaning on her too much. Besides, she was more of an I'm-here-for-you type than a skilled-in-crisis-negotiation personality. I was running out of people to turn to. I'd deal with it later.

Jason was busy driving his tractor in the sand pile. I went out and took his chin in my hand. "Listen, young man. You are never to carry Robbie again. Do you hear me? You can sit and hold him on your lap. But an adult has to be present."

"But he's not heavy."

"I said *never*." I plopped on the edge of the sand pile and let the warm sand trickle through my hands. I took off Robbie's booties, and stood him in the sand. He pushed up with his legs. He was getting strong.

Jason handed Robbie a plastic shovel. "I love my brother," he said.

"I know you do, honey. You just can't carry him." Right now it was my job to carry the family. I wasn't doing such a hot job.

* * *

After a restless night, I lacked motivation. I managed to empty the dishwasher, load the breakfast dishes, and get dressed for work. I had to meet with the night shift crew, so I wasn't due in to work until ten o'clock. I took extra time to comb Jason's hair. He needed a haircut again. I was falling behind in all my motherly duties.

The phone rang. I let it go to the answering machine. The caller did not leave a message.

Twenty minutes later, the doorbell rang. Through the peephole, I saw Delilah from the mental health ward, and an unfamiliar lady in a navy suit, carrying a briefcase.

She rang a second time. "Mom." Jason said in his outside voice.

"Shhh." I knelt down and whispered in his ear. "Let's play hide-and-seek, okay?" It was Jason's favorite game. He would often hear Mike's Camaro pull into the garage and go hide behind the couch in the family room, or under the kitchen table.

He nodded and flashed a grin. We went to the boys' room and hid in the closet, leaving Robbie asleep in his crib.

The doorbell rang again.

"Should we jump out and go, 'Surprise'?"

I snuggled him tight. "No. Let's just stay here. Be quiet." I held my finger to my lips.

Delilah knocked loudly, this time on the back door. "Mrs. Wahlberg? Are you home?"

Robbie started to whimper. His tummy was tiny, and the formula didn't always sit well. We might have three minutes more before he started wailing. I squeezed Jason a little tighter and prayed that Delilah would leave before Robbie erupted.

Robbie's whimper turned into cry. I slid the closet door open and brought him in with us. His hungry cry grew louder.

"Hush, Robbie."

The front doorbell rang again, three long rings. "Kate," Delilah yelled.

Robbie opened his mouth to scream. I put my hand over his mouth to smother his cries. I held my breath. Another knock.

"Mommy," Jason pulled on my sleeve and pointed to Robbie's face.

I looked down. Robbie was blue.

I jerked my hand away. My heart raced like a freight train.

Robbie gasped, then started wailing.

I shushed Robbie with kisses and listened. Jason stuck his thumb in his mouth and scooted to the back of the closet. I cradled Robbie to my chest until I heard the car drive away.

Oh, my god! What did I almost do?

28.

Two hours later, I sat in the office of Paul, an attorney who attended my church. Paul had silver hair and a golden heart. His thin frame was lost behind a massive oak desk.

"Thanks for seeing me."

"What happened, Kate?"

I hadn't told anyone about the psychosis. Other than Mom and Mike, only Brenda knew. I'd refused to talk about it with anyone else. "This is all lawyer-client privilege, right?"

"Of course. Everything you say is confidential." He pulled out a legal pad.

I took a deep breath, inhaled the faint odor of lemon furniture polish, leaned back in the deep leather chair, and tried to imagine being on trial. There was no turning back now.

"Ten days after Robbie was born, I had a postpartum psychosis. I spent two weeks in a mental hospital, and I've been trying to get my life together ever since." I paused, waiting for Paul's mouth to drop open.

"Go on." He did not judge.

"This woman, Betty Lou, she came to see me Saturday. She reported me to social services. I know it was her, because Jason carried Robbie into the family room, almost dropped him. Jason has never carried Robbie before. It all happened so quickly. I guess she thought I allowed this every day."

"Just relax, Kate. We know you're a good mother and you've been through a lot. What did you say to the social worker when she called?"

"She left a message on the answering machine for Mike—but he's out of the country and I didn't call her back. Then she came to my house this morning, with the woman from the mental health center. I didn't answer the door, but Robbie was crying. I suspect they heard him and knew I was there."

He wrote a bit more, then put down his pen and spoke in a soft voice, as if hoping not to startle me. "Where are your sons now?"

My knees started to knock. Thank God I had pulled my hand away from Robbie's nose in time. It was close, too close. I quelled my fear. "They're with Lindsey, their sitter. They're safe there."

Paul leaned back in his leather chair. "Social workers get hundreds of reports. They're overworked. They have to respond, just to make sure there's no risk to your children. If you'd like, I can give her a call."

"Please." I exhaled, trying not to sound frantic. Mike had left me in charge, and I'd promised I'd be fine while he was away. "Mike's such a hothead. He's been upset over this whole psychosis thing. He was off flying status, which made him even more volatile. Now he's in England. I was afraid I'd say the wrong thing and end up back in the mental ward."

Paul smiled confidently and took off his cheaters. "I don't think that will happen. If you need some help with the kids, especially while Mike's overseas, it can be arranged. Maybe somebody from the church would be willing to pitch in."

"Thanks. I'm okay. If everybody would just leave us alone. But—"

"Is there something else you'd like to discuss?" He glanced at his watch. He had been nice enough to work a thirty-minute consultation with me into his schedule.

Could I trust Paul with the rest? Occasionally I'd helped his wife, Lydia, with Sunday school classes. Still, I didn't know Paul that well. I studied his eyes, the injustice of my whole situation seething in me.

"It was all *her* fault," I blurted. "*She* kept sending me home without catching my toxemia. *She* told the nurses I wasn't in labor. *She* said I could stay in the hospital as long as I pumped my breasts every three hours. I never got any sleep—for over a week. I told Mike we should sue her for malpractice."

"Slow down a minute. Who is this 'she'?"

"The Colonel."

"This was someone at the hospital? A doctor?"

I nodded. "Head of the OB ward. It was all her fault. It should never have happened." Hysteria took over. "Sleep deprivation is a form of torture. The Japanese used it to break prisoners in the war."

Paul scratched his head, then leaned forward and looked me square in the eye. "Life isn't always fair, Kate. Bad things happen. First, it would be hard to prove a direct causal relationship. Second, we're talking about a military hospital, which makes it next to impossible to win. Third, the trial would drag on for years. It would be emotionally devastating for you."

I blinked to fight back tears. I opened my mouth to protest, but no words came out.

"Kate, I'm going to give you some free advice." He leaned forward. "You need to get on with your life. Stop talking about it. Stop dwelling on it. Pretend it never happened."

Easy enough for him to say.

I hurried out of his office, avoiding his secretary's eyes. My heart scorching with black hate for The Colonel. I'd get my justice—one way or another.

29.

Mike had always made me feel safe, spooning me in the night, his body warm and close should a scary thought dance across my dreams. Sleeping alone was creepy. All the "what-ifs" came rushing back. What if I'd had Robbie in the bed, with no doctors or nurses? Who would have cut the umbilical cord? What about all the blood? Would his tiny brain have been damaged? Would he have survived?

I told myself, *Get over it.* But I couldn't. Sometime in the wee hours of the morning I came to a resolution. The water-bed had to go.

I put an ad in the paper the next afternoon. On Saturday morning, a couple called and came to inspect the bed. After a few minutes of haggling, they handed me $100 in cash and helped me disassemble the bed, then loaded it into the back of their yellow Ford pickup. I vacuumed the carpet and stared at the bed's crush marks criss-crossing the carpet, wondering if the damage was permanent.

After Robbie's nap, I headed downtown with both boys to Yucca City's three furniture stores, which were all in a two-block section. Robbie sat in his stroller while Jason helped me test endless mattresses. After two hours of plopping, gig-gling, and fake snoring, we gave our nods of approval to a Serta mattress, which would be delivered on Monday. That left two nights of sleeping on the couch.

In the middle of the night, I woke with a start. I had been dreaming about having wings, soaring high above the earth. The dream was so vivid. My back ached, and there was a crick in my neck.

I couldn't get back to sleep, so I retrieved my Bible to do some reading. I turned to Revelation, to the pages I had underlined in the hospital. *The woman was given wings.* Wow. I'd just had the flying dream. I still had this nagging feeling that God had been trying to tell me something in the hospital. But I had somehow misread His message. I stashed the Bible, and tried to focus on getting ready for tomorrow. A visit from social services had been scheduled for Monday at four thirty.

* * *

Monday after work, the two men from WoodKing furniture arrived with the new bed, apologizing for being an hour late. They carried the new mattress and frame back to the bedroom. As I was about to close the front door, the social worker arrived.

Sally Sterm introduced herself. She looked to be in her upper fifties, blond hair with gray roots. She wore an old-fashioned perfume, something my mother might wear. "How are you doing today, Mrs. Wahlberg?"

Jason was all wound up. Lindsey had gotten a new puppy. "Mommy, please. Daddy wouldn't let me have the kitty. I want a puppy!"

"Jason, not today." I gave him my sternest Mom look and turned apologetically to Sally. "Jason's babysitter loves animals, but right now—" I stopped myself midsentence. She could see I had my hands full.

She smiled, then wrinkled her nose. I nervously surveyed my clean and organized house, fresh with the scent of Pine-Sol, then excused myself to show the furniture guys where to set up the new bed.

"Sorry about that," I said, flustered. "The furniture guys should have been out of here by now. But they're running late." I felt her judgment bearing down on me as her eyes scanned the house, every detail scrutinized. The afternoon light revealed sticky fingerprints across the coffee table that I had somehow missed. What did she expect? I was a working mom.

"Maybe you can show me around the house."

"Sure." I grabbed my purse and Robbie's diaper bag, which I had plopped on the kitchen counter, and stashed them in the hall closet.

I had deposited Robbie on the living room floor, and he was busy playing with his red and yellow shape toy. A rank odor greeted us. "Hey little guy. Whew!" I scooped him up to change his diaper, just as Jason tugged on my slacks. "Mom, I'm hungry."

I glanced at the clock. "Can't you wait?"

"I'm hungry now."

I feigned patience and forced a calm smile. "What sounds good?"

"Peanut butter and jelly."

"Sure. They're in the fridge. Bread's on the counter. I'll come help you as soon as I finish up your brother's diaper." I blew him a kiss, then remembered I'd just emptied the peanut butter jar. My kitchen was woefully small, and there might be an extra jar on the overflow shelves in the garage. I ran a hand through my hair.

Jason bolted for the kitchen.

"Don't run. Don't climb," I yelled after him. "If you can't reach something, wait for me."

Sally hovered. As if I couldn't change a diaper without supervision. I grabbed the Lysol spray from under the bathroom sink, gave the living room a quick shot, and fastened the child-proof latch, like a good mother. I set Robbie back down with his toy.

I nervously wiped my brow. "Miss Sterm, can I offer you a glass of—"

At the crash in the garage, and Jason's shrill scream, I dashed to the garage door. Sally was two steps behind me.

Jason stood next to a broken jar of peanut butter, blood dripping from his lip. "Mommy," he blubbered, his mouth dripping with brown goo.

I scooped him up and deposited him on the kitchen counter next to the sink. "Spit it out."

He spit out peanut butter, glass, and blood.

Miss Sterm had visibly paled and looked like she was about to pass out. I had been trained in emergency protocols at the plant, and seen plenty of blood growing up hunting on the farm. "Open wide. Let Mommy look."

I gently ran my finger through Jason's mouth. There was a small cut on his inner lip. "Did you swallow any glass? Does your throat hurt?" He shook his head bravely. I grabbed a flashlight and inspected his throat. No signs of bleeding there. I ran warm water over his hand to melt the peanut butter, and found a small cut on his finger.

From the living room floor, Robbie wailed. En route to get bandages for Jason's finger, I shoved a pacifier in his mouth. "Sorry, guy. You've got to wait your turn."

I poured peroxide over Jason's cut. He screamed again.

"It's just bubbles. Don't cry."

Sally diligently jotted down notes, her face tight.

Then the shorter of the two guys from WoodKing came into the kitchen. "You want to check the placement on the frame before we place the mattress?"

"Yes. Give me a minute. Can't you see—" I stopped myself, took a deep breath, and set Jason on the kitchen floor. Then in a calmer voice said, "Minor emergency. We're under control now." Who was I kidding?

I gave my approval to the bed placement. When the furniture guys finished I signed the receipt and let them out. At last, Jason was bandaged and rescued, and Robbie was entertaining himself. All that remained was to sit down and answer Sally's questions.

I plopped next to Sally, whose color had returned. I responded to all her queries, then said, "Well … ?" *Now go away and leave me alone.*

She looked at me with an inscrutable stare. "This is all highly unusual, Mrs. Wahlberg. I've had enough for today. But, I think we should schedule another visit. I'd like to stop by when things are a bit calmer. Just to make sure things are going okay. I'd also like you to rearrange the food in the garage, to make sure something like this doesn't happen again."

When I made the trip to the base commissary, I liked to stock up. Mike had built the shelves in the garage for overflow. It had seemed like the perfect solution, until today. "Sure. I'll figure out something."

I let Sally out the door, using all my self-control to keep from slamming it in her rear. *Damn that Betty Lou.*

30.

Basil Cabernet, the first flavor of our new gourmet marinara line, was set to launch in late November, just four weeks away. Fred paced back and forth from his office to the plant. Marinara sauce didn't cook exactly the same in the ten-quart kettle in the lab as it did in a five thousand-gallon kettle in the plant. A lot of things could go awry in the scale-up, so new products always ran on the plant's second shift, 3 to 11 p.m.

I was scheduled to be in the plant for the first few runs. Working late when Mike was TDY presented new challenges. I would need a second babysitter. Luckily, I persuaded Guntha, wife of one of the Punjabi guys who worked at the plant, to babysit the nights I had to work late. She liked to read nursery tales to the boys in her broken English.

I nervously oversaw the initial stages of the first plant run. Tomatoes were received, conveyed, and deposited into one of our five-thousand-gallon tanks. A variety of metal stairs and walks allowed the workers to stand at the top of the kettles and add pre-measured ingredients as the sauce reached the prescribed cooking stage. The place reeked with the odors of cooking tomato and basil. I was getting my exercise shuffling back and forth between Pete in the plant and Hillary in the Q.C. lab.

Solids and pH were just right. It was time for the critical addition. We'd never tried to put wine in a sauce before. Fred had constructed a special locked room, modified to hold the red wines at an optimal 58 degrees Fahrenheit and 60 percent humidity. Cecilia's orders. She had personally selected the wine, a full-bodied Cabernet with good tannins. I unlocked the room and poured the wine into a plastic container. Wine was expensive, and we were starting with the lowest possible level, one that should give just a hint of authentic wine flavor.

I met Pete, the night supervisor, near kettle five. He wore white pants and shirt, his name embroidered above his left shirt pocket. "If it isn't the wine queen," he said as I approached. "The batch is at 145 degrees. Let's add the wine, let it cook for another five minutes, and you can take a sample up to the lab for the final taste test." He winked at me.

I carefully carried the sample up to the lab. Hillary and I dipped our plastic tasting spoons into the quart sampling container, closed our eyes and tasted, then looked at each other.

Hillary shook her head. "Sorry, Kate. I can't taste any Cabernet Sauvignon."

Dejectedly, I agreed. "Not enough wine, and what's in there totally cooked off."

"I know you worked your butt off. But you'll get it. This is only the first plant trial."

I had staked my reputation on this project. Now it was back to the drawing board—and more late-night shifts.

* * *

I tossed and turned on the couch, trying to figure out where I went wrong. When the phone rang, I reached for it, knowing Mike was due back from his TDY.

"I'll be home in forty-five minutes, and I expect you to be wearing something sexy."

I responded in a low, husky voice. "Think red lace."

"And what else?"

"You'll be surprised." I hung up the phone. Left him in suspense. I showered off the smells of marinara, and tried to erase the images of Mike exploding when he found his waterbed missing.

As I slipped into the new Victoria's Secret red bra and garter belt, I mentally rehearsed my plan. Sex on the patio. By the time he hit the bedroom, he'd be so wasted he wouldn't notice the switcheroo on the bed.

Who was I kidding?

As the garage door hummed open, my heart raced. I plopped two fresh ice cubes into a second whiskey glass and poured Mike a double. I'd already downed one shot of Jack Daniels for courage.

He walked in looking beat—stubbly beard, flat hair, weary eyes, flight suit zipped open down his chest. He plopped down his flight bag, then stopped and stared at me in my sexy best. A smile crept across his tired face. "Now this is more like it." He took the Jack with his right hand. "Red heels, nice touch." He took a sip, then pulled me into his arms and ran his hand over my bare ass.

He pulled me close. "It's good to come home to sexy Kate," he said. He kissed me, his mouth tasting of Jack.

Instead of crazy Kate, he meant. I pushed the thought aside and leaned into him.

"I'm wearing five-thousand miles of sweat and grime. Let me take a shower first."

"I want you just the way you are." I grabbed the whiskey bottle, and led him out the sliding door to the patio.

Jim Croce's "Time in a Bottle" wafted over the patio speakers. Votive candles cast soft light beneath the full moon. We slid onto the two barstools at our six-foot teakwood bar. The fragrance of jasmine filled the air.

He fingered the lace of my front-hook bra. "You smell good," he murmured.

I slid a small plate of olives and cheese in front on him. "Hungry?"

"Hungry for you." He popped an olive into his mouth, then nibbled on my ear, sending tingles down my spine.

I trailed my finger slowly down his chest. He took another drink of Jack, which he shared with me, kissing my mouth and depositing the fiery liquor and a sliver of ice in my mouth. He pulled me off the barstool.

I let him have his way with me, hoping he'd remember this when the darker side of his passion would want its say.

Mike was smashed by the time we headed to the bedroom, he in his briefs, me fully bare. He stopped at the bedroom door. "Where the hell is my bed?"

"Shhh. You'll wake the boys." I pulled him into the bedroom and shut the door. "I sold the bed. I was fine while you were here to snuggle with me. But once you were gone—" I sat down and patted the bed, trying to look seductive, hiding my quiver. "Wait till you try this one. It's a pillow top."

He glared. "I don't like surprises. I want my wife, my kids, my bed, just like I left them."

"I couldn't sleep. I kept having nightmares." My heart pounded. My head, too.

He pulled me close. "I'm sorry. Let's not fight tonight. I'm beat."

"Thank you. I've got to go to work tomorrow." I glanced at the wall clock. "Actually, in a couple of hours."

On no sleep, I barely trusted myself to show up at work. But I had no choice. Fred would be pissed because the trial failed. Chuck would be gloating. "I don't suppose you could take care of the boys tomorrow?"

"Kate, I haven't slept in forty-eight hours." He collapsed on the bed. "And you expect me to get any rest on this hard monstrosity." He punched the mattress and turned his back to me.

"Never mind. I'll get them to daycare." I curled up and stared at the bedside clock, desperate for sleep, sensing that I was freefalling into the danger zone.

31.

I managed to consume sufficient caffeine to make it through work on Friday, guarded my every word, and postponed the meeting with Fred until Monday.

On Saturday morning Mike got in his Camaro and headed to the WoodKing furniture store. He reported back a few hours later, claiming that he had tried every bed in the store, and not one was comfortable. He had spoken to the store manager and agreed to sleep on the bed for one more week. If he hadn't gotten used to it by then, they would take it back. I knew there was no point to the week trial. Mike had already made up his mind.

Mike and I took turns resting and watching the boys over the week-end. At night our sex was quick, hard, and loveless. My body responded, but afterward felt empty. I rolled over and curled up into a little ball, listening to his snores, a million problems charging through my brain.

On Friday, Mike went in to WoodKing and demanded that they come back and pick up the bed. The same two guys who delivered it arrived late the next afternoon and took it away. Mike camped out in the family room, with Johnny Carson and a Jack Daniels. I snuggled up to him on the couch. "I'd say come to bed, but there isn't one."

"I'm going to Sacramento tomorrow. They have a waterbed store." He downed his drink.

"Maybe there's a new and improved waterbed."

"Maybe I can find a new and improved wife."

"Give it a break." I punched his thigh.

"Kate, I'm just teasing." He pulled me close and massaged my spine with his thumbs. "I want you. I want our marriage. Like it was before. We'll get through this. As soon as we have a new bed, you'll start sleeping. You'll be back to your old self."

Back to my old self. Was that possible? Parts of the old Kate had been annihilated on the mental ward—my spunk, my self-confidence, my witty come-backs. Mike still believed that the old Kate would make a comeback. With each passing day, my doubts grew stronger.

I finally retreated to the living room couch, a piece of furniture we had purchased for its decorative value, rather than for comfort. I heard David Letterman start his monologue, and drowned the noise with a pillow.

* * *

"Mommy," a soft voice whispered.

I opened my eyes.

"Why are you sleeping here?" Jason asked.

I yawned. My back had a kink from the stupid couch. "Because Daddy doesn't like the new bed."

Mike stood in the doorway, sipping coffee. "Because Mommy doesn't think before she does things."

I wanted to say, *Because Daddy is stubborn as a mule.* But I held my tongue. I sat up and stretched my arms. Mikes eyes had that glazed over look I'd seen when he arrived home after a long overseas flight. "Did you get any sleep?"

He snorted into his coffee cup. "What do you think?"

"I'm sorry." I flexed my back again, trying to work out the kink.

"You know I've got a check ride next week. I can't climb into that cockpit feeling like death warmed over."

He was right. His career, his very life, would be on the line. At Mach 3, the slightest mistake could be fatal. I knew that. A pilot's wife was supposed to be supportive, not sabotaging. I exhaled deeply "Do you want breakfast? Pancakes?"

"Yes." Jason did a little jig on the carpet.

"None for me. I'll stop at Denny's on the way to Sacramento."

"I could make you —"

"Don't bother." Mike headed for the garage.

I rushed after him. "When are you coming home? I could use some help with the boys."

He opened the door to his car. "Maybe never."

"Asshole."

He put the Camaro in reverse.

"Wait. Talk —"

My words were drowned by the roar of the car engine as he sped away.

32.

He didn't come home for lunch. Or for dinner. I gave the boys a bath, read them Mother Goose, and tucked them in.

I took a shower and made myself as comfy as I could on the couch. Maybe if I read, I'd get sleepy. Something boring. I picked up my Bible. I tried to focus, but scary scenarios ran though my mind. What if Mike had a car accident. Maybe he was in the hospital. More likely he was out carousing with the bachelor pilots. A list of suspects ran through my mind. I thought about calling a few, but didn't want to appear that desperate. I read through a few chapters of Matthew before my eyes grew heavy.

I woke with a start. Remembered a dream. Mike and Jesus arguing.

Mike saying, "Don't give her wings. She can't fly. She'll just kill herself."

Jesus saying, "No. I promised her wings. I always keep my promise."

Finally, caught between realms, I pulled on my sweats and headed into the kitchen, hoping that Mike had come home in the middle of the night. The first blush of dawn filtered through the window. Mike was not on the couch. I stopped with my hand on the doorknob, took a deep breath, opened the door to the garage. The Camaro's spot was still empty.

A cold chill descended over me. Waiting around for Mike was only making me angrier. I needed to get out. I had been negligent about going to church the past few months. Friends would be there. I packed a diaper bag with raisins for Jason and a pacifier for Robbie.

I was raised a Catholic, Mike a Presbyterian. After checking out both churches, we'd settled on a small Presbyterian congregation. We sat in the glassed-in room at the back, the cry room, though my boys rarely made a peep. The sermon was on the temptations of Jesus. "He will command his angels concerning you, and they will lift you up in their hands, so that you will not strike your foot against a stone." I remembered my dream of Mike and Jesus arguing over whether I should have wings.

"I enjoyed your sermon," I shook Reverend Charles's large moist hand.

"Mike flying?" the reverend asked while adjusting his wire-rimmed glasses.

I stood there open-mouthed, not wanting to admit that I had no idea where Mike was.

"Something wrong, Kate?"

"Nothing. I'm fine."

He beckoned to his wife, who was chatting with another parishioner. "Ellen, would you mind getting Kate something to drink. I want to chat with her."

She took one look at me and put her arm around me. "Kate, what's wrong?"

"I'm fine. I just haven't been sleeping." I knew I wasn't fine. Coming to church was a mistake. I was slipping, sliding off the edge of reality. I should have kept my crazy self at home.

"Here, let me see how big this boy's grown." Ellen took Robbie from my arms, lifted him in the air, then balanced him on her hip. She reached a free hand to Jason. "Would you like a cookie?"

"Sure." He skipped along as she led us back toward the church office.

She motioned towards the couch, handed me a glass of water, reached into an apple-shaped cookie jar, and produced an Oreo for Jason. She sat next to me. "Where's Mike?"

"He left me. He might never come back."

She wrapped her arm around my shoulder. "When did he leave?"

"Yesterday morning."

"Give it some time. He's probably just blowing off steam."

"We fought. It was so stupid. I sold his bed, and he was really mad. And then he was fighting with Jesus about my wings."

"Your wings?" She leaned closer. "What wings?"

"Jesus promised me wings, but Mike said I'd just kill myself. He thinks he's the only one in this family who knows how to fly."

"Oh, Kate —" She patted my hand. "Just sit here until Charles is finished saying goodbye to all the parishioners."

She lifted up Robbie. "This little guy is so strong. He wants to stand already."

She balanced Robbie on her hip and led Jason to the toy box in the corner. "Jason, you can play with this." She handed him a wooden train engine with carved wheels that turned. "It belonged to Charles when he was your age."

I nodded approval.

The reverend came to the door. Ellen whispered to him then sat next to me on the couch, juggling Robbie on her knee. She wrapped a free arm around me. Charles closed the door and sat beside me on the couch.

"Kate." He reached for my hand. "Is there a doctor you've been seeing, somebody who looks after you when Mike's gone?"

They knew about the psychosis. Mike must have told them. Who else did he blab to? "I don't see those doctors anymore. They don't understand." I bit my lip. Sanity was a magic carpet. You tread on it effortlessly, until it was pulled from under you. I felt as if the rug had just been jerked away.

"What about your mother?" Ellen said. "Can she come spend time with you?"

I sunk my face in my hands. "I'm not sure if she can get off work."

"It's hard when Mom's so far away." Ellen spoke softly. "I bet you miss her."

I nodded.

"What about your neighbors? Friends? Is there somebody you trust?" Charles said.

My mind wasn't working. I shook my head and inhaled deeply, forcing back the dam that was about to break.

Charles scratched his head, then suggested, "Do you know Betsy Borden? She leads the local La Leche League, teaches first grade Sunday school. She has a little girl Jason's age. How about if she came over, just for a few hours? Would that be alright?"

"I don't want to bother her."

"You've met Betsy. She's very warm," Ellen said, "and funny."

"Is there a number where we can reach Mike? His squadron?" the reverend asked.

"He left in his blue jeans, not his flight suit. He's not at work." How embarrassing. Coming here was a mistake. I stood up. "I'm going home now."

"How about if Ellen rides over with you?" Charles asked. "She'd like to catch up on how the boys are doing. I'll call Betsy. Maybe she can come by later. Okay?"

"Fine. Come on, Jason."

On the ride home, Ellen chatted about the plans for Sunday school and their vegetable garden. When I rounded the corner on my block I punched the garage door opener, held my breath as the door rolled up, then exhaled into the emptiness.

33.

Betsy stood at my door, wearing one of those crinkly skirts that looks like you slept in it. Her three-year-old daughter clutched at her skirt and peeked from behind. I smiled and vowed not to do anything weird. Ellen phoned Charles, who arrived to pick her up a little later. I promised to call if I needed anything else.

Tall, with long braided hair, Betsy was one quarter Cherokee. I had first seen her breastfeeding her daughter Abrianne in the cry room at church. Betsy and I had chatted often at church, but she had never been to my house. I'd attended a couple of Betsy's La Leche League meetings with Jason, but soon dropped out. Like most of my friends, I figured if I breastfed Jason for six months, I'd done my duty. No one I knew breastfed past a year, except Betsy.

She plopped on the floor beside the family room sofa and deposited a large cloth purse, quilted in multi-tones of emerald and forest green. "Abrianne, this is Jason," she introduced.

"Why don't you go show Abrianne your LEGOs," I suggested to Jason.

Abrianne looked at him shyly. He took her hand and led her to his room.

Betsy slipped off her sandals and made herself comfortable on the couch, "Is it all right if I put my feet on your coffee table?" she asked.

"Sure." I tried to be polite, but honestly I was wrung out. The fewer people who witnessed me in my wacked out state, the better. If I didn't get some sleep soon, I'd lose control.

She stretched her legs out, leaned back, and adjusted a throw pillow under her arm. "So you're having trouble sleeping."

Right to the point. Charles and Ellen must have told Betsy about the psychosis. Might as well put a sign on the front lawn: *Caution. Crazy mom. Enter at your own risk.* Maybe I was paranoid. I decided to play it casual with Betsy. "I was just panicky this morning when Mike didn't come home. I'm fine."

"So tell me about Mike."

I was about to break. I slowly exhaled, then relayed the saga of selling the bed.

Betsy scooted over and put her arm around me. "There must be more to the story—"

I reached for a tissue and dabbed a tear.

What to say? "After Robbie was born ... I was in a couple of hospitals."

"So you had some postpartum issues. It happens. You're home now. How's it going with Robbie? Are you breastfeeding?"

That brought me to the brink of tears. "No. Are you sure you don't want a glass of water."

She took my hand. "Talk to me. Let it out."

"They gave me a lot of drugs. My milk dried up. Then Robbie refused to nurse." I choked on my sobs. "It's hard to love—"

Betsy rubbed my hand. "It's hard to love who?"

"Robbie. Mike. Myself. Some days I wish—" My voice trailed off.

"Everybody has rough times. But things get better. Some days I do stupid things, and I want to kick myself. But I just keep telling myself, 'This is all I can handle at this moment. I'm a good enough mom for today.'"

"That's an interesting thought. Maybe I'm just expecting too much. Trying too hard. Robbie does seem to be doing fine on the bottle."

"I assume you're off the medications now? I have a breast pump you can borrow."

"I am off the meds, but I tried a breast pump once. It didn't work. I think it's too late."

"Don't stress over it. Tell me what's been going on with you and Mike."

My head was throbbing. "He was really mad because I sold our waterbed. I not sure if he'll ever come back."

"I know Mike. Beneath all that macho is a solid family man. He's probably kicking himself and missing you like crazy. Jose and I split up once, when we were first married. He was gone for a month."

"But you worked it out?"

She nodded. "We've both matured a lot since then, learned to accept each other. He gets his baseball on Sunday afternoons. I get La Leche League. It works out."

Abrianne appeared, proudly holding a LEGO house. "Mom, I'm hungry."

"Would you like lunch," I offered. "I'm starving."

"Do you have any organic veggies?"

"I've got fresh spinach."

"A blender?"

Five minutes later, after scrounging through the fridge and pantry, we produced a smooth blend of milk, bananas, almonds, spinach, honey, and apples. I poured us each a glass, and sippy cups for Jason and Abrianne.

Betsy retired back to the couch. I warmed a bottle for Robbie, who was due for his nap.

"Why does your mommy feed her baby that way?" Abrianne asked Jason.

Jason shrugged his shoulders.

"Are you still hungry?" Betsy asked Abrianne. She nodded, and Abrianne climbed onto Betsy's lap. Betsy lifted her blouse, and Abrianne started suckling. Jason gave Abrianne a weird look and ran back to his bedroom.

"I'll finish feeding Robbie in the nursery." I headed down the hall. Watching Betsy and Abrianne was painful. I sat and rocked as Robbie slowly finished his bottle, then thumped his back until a loud burp emerged. "Sorry, little guy. Mommy's having a rough day."

Before long Abrianne came looking for Jason, who was quietly building a LEGO wall. I returned to the family room to find Betsy thumbing through a magazine. "I've taken up half your Sunday," I said.

"Jose's watching baseball. Sports bore me to tears. How about a walk?"

"I don't want to be a bother."

"Just once around the neighborhood?"

I reluctantly agreed and put Robbie in his red umbrella stroller.

Jason and Abrianne skipped ahead of us singing "Mary Had a Little Lamb." As we walked, Betsey chatted about her La Leche League group.

"We meet in a different house every month. Somebody always volunteers."

"Maybe you should meet at my house." I regretted the offer as soon as the words left my mouth.

She looked at me weird. "Wouldn't you feel awkward, not breastfeeding?"

"We could try it once," I said lamely. Too late to back out.

We returned from our walk and there was a message on the answering machine from Mike. "Hey, it's me. I'm staying with Spencer."

I seethed with rage. Mike sounded like he'd been drinking. Spencer was bad news—a senior pilot notorious for his flavor-of-the-month affairs. His claim to fame was that he had flown "Rapid Rabbit," the SR-71 with a playboy bunny painted on its tail.

"Mike will be coming home soon," I said. "I just got all upset over nothing."

Betsy gave me her phone number. "Until he gets his head on straight, you can call me—any time of the day or night. I mean it."

After Betsy left and the boys were down for the night, I called Mike. "Please come home."

"There's no place to sleep. Spencer's got a spare bedroom with a king-size bed."

"Who else is there?"

"Actually, Mandy and Candy."

I closed my eyes, trying to block the scenes I could only imagine. "That man is going to end up with a disease. He'll be dead by the time he's forty-five."

"Yeah, but he'll die with a smile on his face."

"Why don't you just come home and sleep on the couch." I tried to hide the whine in my voice.

"Don't you trust me?"

"Can't you stay someplace else?"

"I'll stop by and see the boys at the sitter's in the afternoon. Love you, Kate."

"But—"

Mike hung up before I could argue.

34.

For some reason, I had lots of energy. I decided to clean out my bedroom closet. My tightest jeans, the ones that would never fit again, had to go. I tried on one after the other, holding my breath. Buzzing with energy that even I couldn't explain, I packed three pairs plus a dozen shirts into a large brown paper bag, and parked it in the garage for Goodwill.

With all that extra oomph, I then tackled my technical journals. The guilty pile. I glanced at the covers, skimmed the table of contents, then pitched them, one after another.

At midnight, I was still wondering when the buzz would wear off. I headed to my bed on the living-room couch and put my faith in warm milk. My mom swore by it, and it had helped me through many a tense evening. But tonight it failed to work its magic. I tossed and turned on the narrow couch.

Somewhere between three and four o'clock, I drifted off. At 6 a.m., I gulped a cup of coffee, got the boys ready for day care, and scooted us out the door. It was time to get serious about my job.

Molly was coming out of Fred's office, and stopped to greet me. "You've got to get more sleep, girl. You look like something the cat drug in."

"Robbie's getting a tooth. He was fussy." My standard lie. How many teeth did babies get? I hoped nobody was counting.

"Fred's worried about the sauce project. He didn't like the results of the first trial. Said if he was going to spend money on good wine, he'd darn well better be able to taste it in the sauce."

"I spent half the weekend thinking about how to fix it."

"Just a warning, Fred's thinking about giving the project to Chuck. I told him to give you another week."

"I owe you." I couldn't afford any more mistakes. I headed to the lab to stash my purse and jot down some notes before staff meeting.

Fifteen minutes later, I was in the board room, ready for Monday morning staff meeting. I grabbed the chair to Molly's right. She and I always sat on the east side of the table so we could look out of the wall of windows at the stately almond trees that flanked the parking lot. Normally I was a one-cup-of-java girl, but today I was already on my third cup, and it wasn't even nine o'clock.

When my turn came, I cleared my throat. "I've evaluated what went wrong in last week's plant trial. We need to lower the cook temperature, and add the wine in the cool-down stage. I've already ordered a micro test, to be sure it'll be safe." I tried to sound confident.

Fred nodded in approval. "Go on."

I drew a blank and panicked, searching for my next point. I shuffled through my notes, and retrieved the paper with my team assignment. We were all supposed to present ideas for the plant expansion. Fred had told us to be creative. I took a deep breath to calm myself.

"As for the company's long-term growth potential, there are only a limited number of customers who are willing to purchase high-end marinara sauce." I paused for that much to sink in, knowing Chuck had been campaigning for a cheaper brand. I had to bring all my wits to bear. This was my chance to show them I was back in control, even though my brain was reeling from the lack of sleep and the caffeine buzz. All eyes were on me.

"I think we should expand to an international line. We could include both Northern and Southern Italian sauce, quite different. The next target would be Mexico. Not the typical thin and runny salsa, but a true gourmet product."

"Mexico is crazy!" Chuck blurted. "We make Italian. Aunt Cecilia would have a fit if we started making salsa."

Crazy. I scanned the faces of the management team. Everyone knew. I fought the impulse to bolt from the room. I shrank down and stared at my hands.

"Kate, I think your idea has some merit," Fred said. "We could utilize the new equipment. Maybe add a third shift."

I recovered my composure enough to nod.

Pete scratched his head. "Salsas can be chunkier. There'd be some capital investment. But if the market was there, it could pay for itself in months."

Bill from sales piped in. "With the way that population is pouring over the Mexican border, I think there's good growth potential."

"I agree." Fred jotted some notes. "Your idea is a stretch for our company, but I'll mull it over."

I hid my hands under the table, so no one could see them shaking, and nodded. Thankfully my turn was over. For now, I was off the hot seat.

After the meeting I called Chuck into my office, a ten by ten cubicle adjacent to the lab, adorned with a single poster of wildflowers in Aspen.

"Sit," I demanded.

"I didn't mean to use the word crazy." Chuck sounded as sincere as a snake-oil salesman.

"My idea is not crazy. It's innovative. I'm still department head. You filled in while I was on leave. Well, I'm back now. And you need to remember your place."

"Is that all?" His voice dripped with contempt.

"Let's just make sure you got it. You need to report any issues or suggestions directly to me."

"Are you saying I shouldn't talk to Fred?" Chuck bristled.

"Think about it."

"Sure." He rolled his eyes. "Anything else?" He stood to leave.

"That's it for now."

Chuck paused at the door. "Maybe I'm out of line, but I want to say one more thing."

"Make it quick."

"When we first started working together, I thought of you as the daughter I never had. Enjoyed showing you the ropes. I was a happily married guy, way back. But when my wife went back to work, after the youngest boy started kindergarten, things changed. I knew she was under a lot of stress, trying to work and keep up with the boys. Eventually the marriage crumbled."

I glared at him. "Your point—"

"You've been looking haggard, Kate. I'd hate to see anything happen to you." Chuck turned and left.

He knew. Who told him? It didn't matter. I needed more time—to get myself back on solid ground. How much time, I wasn't sure. But the hourglass was emptying.

35.

With no bed and limited sleep, I was so edgy, I didn't trust myself. Feeling almost out of body, I reluctantly scheduled an appointment with my shrink on Wednesday afternoon. Maybe he could give me something to sleep.

Being back in Dr. Falio's office was intimidating. I couldn't afford to say anything crazy. I came from work wearing blue jeans and a simple knit top—hoping I looked sane.

Dr. Falio was as hunky as I remembered, but now tanned.

"Have you been somewhere sunny?" I asked.

"My family just returned from a vacation in Hawaii."

"Family?" I had somehow assumed he was a bachelor.

"My wife, son, and I."

"Oooh." Thoughts of him as a family man shattered my fantasy of meeting him in some secluded spot and doing the nasty.

"You look tired," he said. "Tell me what's been going on."

"I sold our waterbed. Ever since the bed's been gone, I've had trouble sleeping. I need you to prescribe something mild, not like the drugs before."

He leaned forward. "I don't think what you are experiencing is simple insomnia. I suspect you have a mood disorder. It requires a different type of medication. I can't just prescribe a sleeping pill."

"I refuse to take drugs that make me a zombie. I was doing fine up until this past month—sleeping, working, taking care of the boys. Ninety-eight percent normal."

I smiled to hide my uncertainty. My psyche had been permanently altered. My innocence destroyed. I knew I'd never be a hundred percent like I was before. Life was different, now that

I had experienced life outside of the winner's circle. I had no desire to go back to the world of the droolers and crazy hairs. I smoothed my hair and waited.

My sexy doctor stared at me, waiting for me to speak. I hated when he did that. I came for answers, not more questions. I had to figure out all the answers on my own. Even scarier, I was unsure of the behind-the-lines communication between him and social services. Did my shrink know about Jason carrying the baby and the broken peanut butter jar? I decided to test the water.

"Jason's so grown up. He likes his new brother, hugs him a lot. He's really proud of him. Sometimes too proud." There was no visible change in the doctor's expression. Maybe he didn't know. "We've been practicing how to hold the baby. Jason has to sit on the couch. An adult has to be present."

"Sounds sensible."

So far so good. Do I ask if he knows Delilah? Best keep that to myself. There was a long awkward silence.

Dr. Falio shifted in his chair. "Maybe it would be helpful if I asked you a few questions."

"The president is Jimmy Carter," I offered.

"No." He smiled. "You seem coherent enough. I'm just trying to assess where you might be in an upward cycle."

"Ask away."

He looked at me purposefully. "How long have you had issues with your sleep?"

I mentally ran through the calendar. "I think it's been three weeks since I sold the bed. I haven't had a decent night's sleep since then. Mike couldn't sleep either. He's been staying with a friend for the past four or five nights. I'm usually exhausted at the end of the day and fall asleep as soon as I hit the pillow. Then, almost like clockwork, around midnight, I have a panic attack and I'm jerked out of my sleep. Did I forget to lock the doors? Did I turn off the steam kettle in the lab? Is Mike having an affair?"

He raised his eyebrows at that one. "Mike. Having an affair?"

"No. I trust him. But he's so distant, so angry."

"He's angry?" Dr. Falio leaned forward. I caught another whiff of that cologne.

I sat back, afraid to be any closer. "He didn't like the new bed."

We went on for fifteen minutes. He reviewed his notes, then set down his pad. "I suspect you have a condition we call bipolar disorder. I'm going to recommend that you start lithium. It's a drug that helps to control mood swings. You'll probably need to be on it the rest of your life." He went on to explain that I would need regular monitoring, blood tests, to ensure that the drug was at the proper level. I listened in horror as he described the potential side effects—confusion, poor memory, frequent urination, weight gain—all the things I'd worked so hard to overcome. This was not what I expected to hear. I squirmed nervously in my seat.

"But you don't get it. If somebody took your bed away, you'd have trouble sleeping too. I don't want heavy drugs, just something to help me sleep, like a sleeping pill."

"Kate." He shook his head. "After one episode, you're more vulnerable. Your body gets speeded up, and before you know it, you're out of touch with reality. We can't let that happen."

This was all a mistake. I rose to leave.

"Wait." He stood and maneuvered between me and the door. "Remember the female doctor in our group. I think you might like her. I'll get her card." He fished in his top desk drawer, then handed me a business card. "If you're not comfortable with me, please make sure you see somebody." He raised his eyebrows. "Don't let this go on too long."

This was like quicksand. The harder I fought, the faster I sank. I slipped the card into my purse. "Sure," I said, knowing I was not going to see his colleague.

As I drove home, I realized I was unraveling. Occasional bits of craziness might slip by. But I didn't dare let my doctor talk to my pastor. I prayed my boss wouldn't run into my neighbor. For sure I couldn't let Sally talk to Dr. Falio.

36.

The next day I got a call from the woman shrink, Dr. Tomay. I reluctantly agreed to an appointment on Friday at eleven.

Thursday evening was the next scheduled plant trial on the new gourmet marinara sauce. The trial would last from 7 p.m. until 3 a.m. I had convinced Cecilia to use a less expensive Cabernet, but at a higher level in the formula. The temperature of the batch when the wine was added was critical, and I had to get it right this time. If I failed, Fred would give Chuck's cheap formulas a try.

I perched on a steel walkway, forty feet above the plant floor, supervising the process. After five hours on my feet, my eyes grew heavy. I closed my eyes and tried to focus on the herbal aromas emanating from the kettles.

I felt a tug at my lab coat. "Kate."

I startled awake. Pete handed me a sample cup of the sauce. I grabbed it awkwardly, spilling sauce on my sleeve.

"Sorry, I was concentrating." Another lie. I carried the sample to the lab. Hillary took one look at me and laughed. "You're definitely into this project. I've heard of wearing your heart on your sleeve. You wear your marinara."

"Let's run these tests and get out of here." I forced back a yawn.

Together we performed the analytical tests. All were within the specifications we had set. Then I headed back to the plant to watch Pete add the wine, then back to the lab with another sample for the critical flavor assessment.

Hillary and I rinsed our mouths with tap water. We closed our eyes and held the spoon just under our noses, evaluating the subtle aromas. Finally we tasted one spoonful, rolling it around in our mouths before swallowing.

I waited, anxious for Hillary to confirm my verdict. My heart pounded.

She looked me square on. "I get them both—hints of basil and Cabernet. This is the best pasta sauce we ever put in a jar," she said.

We hugged each other. My idea of adding the wine on the cool-down stage had worked. I glanced at the wall clock. It was 2:30 a.m. I headed back to the plant and told Pete to start up the filling line. Within hours, Aunt Cecilia's Basil Marinara would be in quart bottles. If it passed the final micro tests, it would be on store shelves in two weeks.

"Great job," he said. "Maybe we should put you on permanent second shift, that way you could play with the boys during the day and work at night."

"And when would I sleep?" Now that the excitement was over, exhaustion rapidly overtook my body. By the time I got to the parking lot, I couldn't stop yawning.

I slid into my Buick, and relaxed with the sounds of Kenny G. Thank goodness it was only four miles home.

Suddenly a loud honk. I jolted awake and stared at the grill of a huge semi-truck barreling toward me. The driver honked a second long, piercing beeeep. I heard the thunderous exhaust of air brakes.

I was in the wrong lane. I jerked the steering wheel hard right, narrowly missing having my rear bumper clipped by the monster truck.

My car skidded. A black and yellow caution sign loomed ahead. I braked. Slammed into the sign. Heard a loud snap. Felt the jarring impact. Slid into a ditch. My car teetered. Slithered down. I heard metal rip.

I sat, dazed, gripping the steering wheel.

A man yanked open my door. "Lady! Get out."

He reached over and turned off the ignition switch. "Are you hurt? We've got to get you out. Now! I smell gas."

I felt the stubble of his whiskers on my cheek. He lifted me out of the car and carried me up to the road.

"Just sit here. I've got a two-way radio." He rushed to his truck.

The odor of gasoline wafted up to me, nauseating. As I peered down the embankment, my car exploded and was engulfed in flames. I stared in disbelief. That could have been me.

I heard sirens. Within minutes, police cruisers and an ambulance arrived. A fire truck pulled up, its siren screeching. Two firemen jumped out and started spraying my car.

"Just relax." A paramedic made me sit, then slapped a blood pressure cuff and an oxygen mask on me. "We're going to take you to Ridner Hospital. Is that okay?"

Still in shock, I pulled the oxygen mask off and struggled to get to my feet. "I don't need to go to the hospital. I'm fine."

The paramedic pushed the mask back on my face. "We'll decide that."

37.

It was nearly dawn when I got home, bruised and achy, but thankfully all in one piece. I called in sick to work, and was nursing a cup of coffee when Dr. Tomay's office called. "Mrs. Wahlberg. We were expecting you for an eleven o'clock appointment."

"Something came up. Sorry. I forgot to cancel."

The receptionist asked if I wanted to reschedule. I said I'd call her when I figured out my work schedule.

I hung up. Desperate for help. Knowing that I wasn't going to make that call. How could I explain this to Mike? He was already lobbying for me to be a stay-at-home mom. I needed to be at work on Monday. Car dealers were closed on Sunday. I had one day to find transportation. The Buick dealer offered to send a guy out to pick me up, and I coerced Brenda into watching the boys.

Bobby Blithe showed up promptly at 9 a.m., wearing a red polka-dot tie and an overdose of cheap cologne. When I explained that Mike was an SR-71 pilot, his eyes gleamed.

First he took me to see the '81 models. Five new cars glistened on the showroom floor. "We've got—"

"I can't afford a new car. I just need reliable transportation."

"Let me just show you one feature on this new LeSabre." He held open the door of a navy blue model. I slid into the driver's seat, inhaled the aroma of new vinyl, and ran my finger over the soft leatherette.

"Twenty miles to the gallon. And watch this, Mrs. Wahlberg." He demonstrated the child safety latches. "Just press this button, and the kids can't get out until you let them out. Not a single car in the used lot has these."

I was intrigued. Mike would be furious over the old Buick. And he was still pissed about the bed. I didn't care to experience more of his wrath.

"You've got a toddler. He's safe and secure in the back seat. Think how sporty you and the mister would look driving to church, taking a little weekend outing to the Bay Area." He leaned in, ruining the new car aroma. "How about you just drive it around the block?"

I nodded skeptically.

"Comes with a four-year, forty-thousand mile warranty. Any problems, you just bring it in. We'll take good care of you."

Taking care of me was supposed to be Mike's job, at least between TDYs. He was always quick to fix any rattles with the old car. At this point, I wasn't sure if he was ever coming back. For the first time in six years of marriage, divorce seemed like a distinct possibility.

I agreed to take a test drive. At first I was white knuckled. Past the city limits, I stepped on the accelerator. Snappy. I did feel sporty behind the wheel.

By the time we got back to the showroom I had bonded with the LeSabre. Then I looked at the sticker. *Ouch.* My dad had taught me to always pay cash for a car. A car was not something you bought on time—a house or a farm—those were investments. When it came to cars, you only bought what you could afford. That was one area where Mike and I agreed. His old man had instilled the same philosophy. Up until that point, our only debt was the home mortgage.

"Show me what you've got in the used lot," I said.

"What's your budget?"

We had roughly six thousand dollars in our savings account. "Do you have something under five thousand?" I asked.

He led me to a white Century, with scratches on the door. It reeked of tobacco. There was a cigarette burn on the cloth seat. I would not look hot in a scratched up Century.

Bobby leaned on the door. "Mrs. Wahlberg. If you don't mind my saying so, I've never seen a woman look as good as you did in that LeSabre."

I wavered. "The beige interior color did complement my hair."

"You shine in that car. You literally glow." Bobby led me back to the showroom and handed me the keys. "Just sit in this one a few more minutes."

I sat in the car, pulled down the visor, and admired myself in the vanity mirror. Child safety latches. Mike would want the boys to be safe.

"So what would I need to buy it on my own?"

"We'd need proof of employment, your pay stubs," he said.

Two hours later, I drove out of the dealership in my new Buick, proud as a peacock.

I stopped at the first stoplight.

Then it hit me. I hadn't even bargained. I'd paid full sticker price. Nobody in their right mind paid full sticker price. No wonder Bobby looked like his rich aunt just died.

Temporary insanity—again.

38.

I called Mike when I got home, being careful not to mention the accident or the new car. We chatted for a few minutes, then I asked the million-dollar question, "When are you coming home?"

"Not until I have a bed to sleep in. I miss you. I know I've been a total jerk. But you do realize I couldn't climb into the cockpit feeling all foggy-brained because I hadn't slept in days."

We agreed to meet that evening at *Chez Richard*, a French restaurant in the Eastern suburbs of Sacramento. I donned my little black skirt, and an emerald silk top with a low v neckline. My hair in an up do, I slipped into the new LeSabre. I did look hot. Let's see Mike try to stay away.

I was fashionably late. Let him want me. I strutted into the restaurant, wearing my new black stiletto heels, proud that I had whittled off another five pounds of baby fat.

Mike looked surprised. "Wow." He kissed me behind the ear. I caught his familiar fragrance of Drakkar Noir, reminding me of the many good nights we'd spent in each other's arms. Even when our whole world was falling apart, the sex was still earth-shattering.

That's why I was there. Dinner was just foreplay. I hoped Mike wouldn't be pissed when he saw my new car and leave. I desperately needed him back home.

The restaurant walls and ceiling were painted in a faux finish to resemble stonework. Intimate dining areas had been partitioned off with wooden lattice intertwined with artificial grape vines. Soft saxophone music drifted through the room.

Mike slipped the waiter a bill, and we were seated at a private corner table. He ordered a bottle of merlot.

He slid his hand to my knee. "You look tired, Kate."

I pushed his hand away. "The couch isn't all that comfy." Don't let this be easy. Make him want it.

"I've ordered us a new bed. It's like a waterbed inside a conventional mattress. They call it a soft side," Mike said.

"Never heard of such a thing."

"It will be delivered on Thursday. You'll sleep better."

I wasn't sure it was that simple. "And then you'll move back home."

"I'll move back home. I miss you and the boys."

"Jason's been asking about you."

The waiter came back to take our order.

"I just want a salad."

"You're losing weight too fast. You need to eat," Mike said.

"I like being thin."

"Bring us two of your top sirloins. Medium rare," Mike said.

I picked at my salad, then set down my fork. "I don't want to fight. That morning you left, I was so mad I almost hit you. But it was like somebody grabbed my hand and pulled it back. I remembered what happened after I hit The Colonel."

"The doctor realized you weren't in your right mind. Everybody did."

Once or twice in the first year of our marriage I'd gotten so mad that I slapped Mike. "If I hadn't slapped her. If I could have slept for a few nights. If this whole thing hadn't snowballed."

"It's over, Kate. Just put it in the past and move on."

"I never want to hit anybody again. Not Jason. Not Robbie. Not you. When we were growing up on the farm, my mom and dad spanked me. It was what people did. But there's a better way."

Mike put down his fork, then put his hand over mine. "There's something I've wanted to tell you, Kate. Something I've never told anyone." His eyes were wet.

"I grew up hearing my parents fighting downstairs. Dad calling Mom names. Her shouting Bible verses back at him. It was usually about money, some piddling amount that Mom had spent. Then I'd hear this smack. Just one. My mom never said another word. I'd hear her steps on the staircase, then she'd crawl in bed with me. She'd hold me in her arms, shaking."

"I'm so sorry. That must have been hard." I laid my hand on Mike's.

"One morning, the bedroom was cold and there was frost on the windows. I went over and scraped off the ice. A foot of snow blanketed the farm. 'No school today,' she said. I turned to her with a smile. And then I saw her face in the morning light. A bruise had formed on her cheek. She made me sit on her lap. 'Promise me one thing, son. When you grow up and have a wife of your own. Promise me you'll never hit her. No matter what.'" Mike paused.

I bit my lip. I had never met Barbara. She died in a car accident just before we met. Mike had grown up in a family where the father ruled. At my house, both parents shared decision-making. After all these years of marriage, I had no idea what Mike's poor mom had been through. Mike's dad Gustav was a good man, but a hard man. I squeezed Mike's hand. "I'm sorry for your mom. But I'm glad you kept your promise."

"I was mad at you for selling the bed. Furious that you had defied me. I left because I was afraid I might hit you." He took my chin in his hand. "When I said I might never come back, it was a verbal slap. I knew it stung. I kicked myself all the way to Sacramento. Can you ever forgive me?"

I sighed. "These last few months have been hard on both of us. It's going to take time—"

"I want us to be a happy family, like we used to be." He took my hand and his lips grazed my knuckles. "Okay?"

I still deeply doubted whether I'd ever be happy again. I pulled my hand away. "Mike. It's not that simple. You just can't up and leave, and expect to waltz home whenever it's convenient. I know you had to get some sleep before your check ride.

But you don't understand what I've been through this past week, these past months. I need to lean on you for a while, until I get my head on straight again. You need to come home. Tonight."

"Just one more day. Please. Brenda agreed to watch the boys tonight. You and I are shacking up at the Marriott down the street."

"No." I had been mulling this over all week. I had to force it out, before my will power buckled. "I am not sleeping with you unless you agree to see a marriage counselor."

Mike's head jerked back. "But … Kate. I love you."

"Love is more than sex." I struggled to keep my voice from breaking. I leaned in to Mike. "It's changing the diapers. It's being there for the 2 a.m. feeding. It's sleeping on the god damn floor if that's what it takes."

Mike hung his head. Gradually his eyes rose to meet mine. He took both my hands in his. "I know I've been an absolute jerk. But my check ride is over. Give me one day to finish up something at Spencer's. I'll be home tomorrow night. I'll see a fricking counselor. Whatever you want."

"Promise?"

He pulled my hand to his mouth and kissed my wedding ring. "I promise."

I chewed on my inner lip. I wanted to believe him. Had he ever lied to me? Not once in the six years of our marriage. At least not that I knew about.

I hesitated. "Okay. We'll go to the Marriott. You can drive my new car."

"New car?" Mike's eyes flashed. "What new car?"

39.

I woke with Mike's body wrapped warmly about me. Faint morning light filtered through a slit in the hotel curtain. After the incredibly hot sex, I slept well and felt more rested than in weeks. I scooted closer, slipping into the spoon position. He pulled me into him. Even his morning breath was sweet.

I arrived home around nine. I'd never seen Brenda in such a foul mood. "Wally's complaining that he wants his short-order cook on duty at 8 a.m."

I could tell by her tone that the overnight babysitting thing was getting old.

"I owe you big time."

"Wally's given me a one-week ultimatum. No more over-nights."

"I understand." *Shit*. Who would I trust to come to the house? Guntha had agreed to work occasional weeknights. No week-ends.

"Mommy." Jason came running from his room. "Where's Daddy?"

I had hinted to Jason that his dad would be coming home with me. "He's coming home tonight." Spencer was overhauling the engine on his Corvette. Mike had promised to give him a hand. Like Spencer needed Mike more than I did. I was miffed, but I told myself I could hold it together one more day.

Jason hung on my arm. After Brenda left, I knelt down to give him a bear hug. For good measure, I lifted his red polo shirt and gave him a belly blubber, trying to interject a little laughter into our world.

After lunch I said, "What would you like to do today little man? Play outside in the sand pile or go to the park?"

"Park." Jason's eyes lit up.

"Park it is. Is your brother awake?" I headed down the hall. Robbie was in his crib, busily playing with his feet. He greeted me with a happy lunge and put his arms out to me.

"Come here, precious." I picked him up and he promptly grabbed and scratched my cheek. "Ouch. Mommy needs to trim your nails." The little details of mothering were slipping past me. I trimmed the nails with a baby nail clippers, then deposited him in his stroller.

The neighborhood park was two blocks away. We paused to chat with Wally, who was trimming the boxwood hedge that ran between our two properties.

"You want me to trim your side too while I'm at it?" he asked.

"Mike will get it when he gets home." I was embarrassed to let Wally help with the yard work. I had been leaning too hard on their neighborliness. Add trimming the hedge to the growing list of things that needed to be completed before Sally's next visit.

At the park, there were two sets of swings, one for the toddlers on the north side, and a larger set for bigger kids on the south. A grove of tall oaks ran through the middle. As soon as Jason's feet hit the sidewalk, he jerked free of my handhold and bolted for the toddler swings.

I spread the blanket for Robbie under the shade of the oaks, took him out of his stroller, and laid him down. Mike should be here, so I could push Jason while he entertained Robbie. I kept telling myself, *One more day. You can do this.*

I positioned a blanket behind Robbie's back, propping him up so that he could watch Jason. The sky reflected off my baby's eyes. They had been a soft steel gray since birth. For all these months, I hadn't been sure if they would end up hazel, like Jason's and mine, or blue like Mike's. Today I had my answer. They were definitely blue. Not just any blue, but the same exact shade as Mike's, a blue that challenged the splendor of the sky.

Not a day passed that I didn't feel guilty over the whole postpartum thing. Guilty and angry. The peanut butter thing had been so stupid. A hundred other moms could have had a similar incident. For them it would have been just a call to the pediatrician, and an anxious forty-eight hours of checking stools. Not another mandatory visit from Gestapo Sally. Not fair. I had no idea if or when the monitoring would ever stop. There might as well be a red "P" stitched on my chest. Psycho Mom.

I glanced up to check on Jason. A little boy and his parents had entered the park from the opposite street. The new boy was riding a shiny red tricycle. Jason ran to check out the trike.

"Jason, come back," I yelled after him.

The couple waved at me and headed the two boys in my direction. I stood and shook hands. "Thanks for bringing Jason back."

"Today is our son's birthday. He wanted to try out his new tricycle," the athletic-looking dad said.

"Mom." Jason tugged on my shirt. "I want one of these. Can we ask Daddy?"

I wanted to scream, *Daddy should be here.* I scooped up Robbie and buckled him into the stroller. "Nice meeting you. We have to go."

"Mooom," Jason whined.

Jason pouted on the way home. It was all I could do to keep from smacking him. I kept telling myself, no violence. I kicked a rock and sent it rumbling across the street.

As I was taking Robbie out of the stroller, the doorbell rang. "Betsy?"

She entered with wave-skirt flowing. Abrianne skipped behind, clutching mom's skirt in one hand and asked, "Where's Jason?"

"I'm sorry. Was I expecting you?"

"We're here for the La Leche meeting. You said you'd host. Did you forget?"

"I'm so sorry. I've had so much on my mind ... come in. Make yourself at home."

I looked about my disorderly house. Toys everywhere. Half-eaten hot dogs and spilled catsup on the kitchen table.

"Jason, take Abrianne to your room," I said, piling lunch dishes in the sink, already overflowing with remains from breakfast and the previous day's lunch. Brenda had tired of cleaning up after me. I couldn't blame her.

Ten minutes later, two other women showed up. A tall red-head with a two-month-old introduced herself as Shannon. The other mom, Dorothy, was an extremely buxom brunette with a teeny newborn. I ushered everyone into the back yard, where it was slightly less chaotic, and pointed everyone to seats on the patio furniture. I offered tea or lemonade that I could fabricate from powder and water at a moment's notice.

Betsy started off the meeting by asking everyone to tell a little bit about themselves. Shannon was in a bit of a tizzy because she had to go back to work in two weeks, and she was going to have to pump her breasts. From a large bag, she produced an Ameda breast pump, which Betsy helped her place on her breast. It was noisy.

"How does it feel?" Dorothy asked.

"The trick is to close your eyes and think happy baby thoughts." Betsy smoothed her skirt.

"So how do you store the milk?" I said.

"If you're going to use it the same day, then the fridge at work is fine, or a cooler with ice packs," Betsy explained. "If you're pumping extra, then you can freeze it."

Freeze it. I slammed down my glass, spilling lemonade on my leg. I could have frozen the milk and gone home and slept in my own bed. Not gone through hell. That damn Colonel Reeves. I exhaled slowly to calm myself.

"Betsy. Where were you when I needed you? No one at the base hospital told me I could freeze my breast milk." I was incensed.

"Oh, Kate. I'm sorry." She hugged me comfortingly. "Robbie was a preemie. They're stricter about milk for preemies. But I'm pretty sure you could have pumped and frozen. I'll check for you."

"Too late now," I murmured.

"So what happened?" Dorothy asked. "Did you stop breast-feeding?"

I searched for the right word. "I was *separated* from Robbie. They weren't exactly into breastfeeding in my second hospital." I stared at the oak tree in the corner of my backyard. The leaves were starting to don their fall color. So much misery. All because The Colonel was behind the times.

As they left, Betsy asked, "Same place and time next month?"

I looked at her blankly.

After Dorothy and Shannon scooted, Betsy lingered. "Bitterness is a poison. You need to talk about it, get it out."

"It may be poison, but currently it's my drug of choice. What am I supposed to do? Scream? Pout? You can't even begin to understand."

"Maybe not everything. But I know you're not alone. Other moms have problems. I read an article just the other week. There was a number to call for help. Let me see if I can find it."

After she left, I collapsed on the couch, intrigued by the idea that I was not alone. I was drained. In my previous life, before Robbie was born, every event was faithfully logged into my daily planner. My life had structure. Now I couldn't keep the simplest things straight.

The phone rang. "Sweetheart," Mike stammered.

"Don't tell me—"

"The Corvette overhaul is taking longer than expected. It's Spencer's only way to get to work. I'll be home before midnight."

"You'd better be. If you're not—" I slammed the receiver down. Maybe I should ask Paul if he handled divorce cases.

40.

I woke on the family room couch to find Mike asleep on the floor, snoring. I tip-toed toward the kitchen. His hand reached out and grabbed my ankle. He pulled me down to the floor, rolled on top of me, and tickled my tummy.

"Stop. What are you doing?" I laughed.

"Sleeping on the god damn floor. If that's what it takes."

"Welcome home."

"That living room couch is a torture chamber. No wonder you haven't been sleeping. I'll figure out something until the new bed arrives on Thursday."

"Good. Cause I've got to get to work." I headed for the shower.

I was stir-frying some celery and water chestnuts for dinner when Mike arrived home from the base with a bouquet of roses and a "Sorry for being such a jerk" card. He had purchased a used sleeper sofa that was advertised on a bulletin board at the base. Two airmen delivered it that evening, and we rearranged furniture so it would fit in the spare bedroom. It would make do for a few nights. It would also come in handy if Mom came out again. She hadn't complained about sleeping on the family room couch all those nights. What a trooper.

After the boys were asleep, Mike and I plopped on the couch.

"You said you ran the old car in the ditch," Mike said. "But where is it? Can't it be fixed?"

"It sort of—" I looked down. Shit. Might as well get it all out. "It crashed and burned."

"Burned?"

"Not so loud. You'll wake the boys."

"How'd you get out?"

"This guy helped me. I was just dazed for a minute."

"Kate, what if the boys would have been in the car? Could you have gotten all three of you out in time?"

I hadn't thought of that. Scary. I rubbed my forehead, then shook my head. "But the boys *weren't* in the car. I'm fine. It was only a car."

"Kate. I know your job is important to you. But you need to take a few weeks off. Until things settle down here. Until you're sleeping."

"I can't. Not now. Not in the middle of the wine project."

Mike clenched and unclenched his fist. He got up and paced. Opened his mouth to speak, then shut it. "Do you mind if I have a drink?" He headed for the kitchen.

"Go ahead." As if he needed my permission. I exhaled slowly.

He poured a shot, then came back and sat next to me. He took both my hands in his. "I know I should never have left. That was a mistake. And I do want to see that marriage counselor like we agreed. But we need to talk to him about your work. You need to get your priorities straight, woman."

"I am *not* quitting my job. End of discussion."

"I'm not asking you to quit. Just to take time off. Until you're more stable. Maybe until Robbie's a year old."

"A year?" I coughed. "You think I'd have a job to come back to? Chuck would have my stuff in a box in the parking lot."

"The Boticellis won't let him do that. Aunt Cecilia loves you. Everybody in the company knows you're good at concocting tasty food. You're the best cook in the whole state."

"Just give me a few weeks. Once we get through these plant trials, it'll be Thanksgiving. I'll have four days to get caught up on my sleep."

"Two weeks. I'll give you that much. I'll make dinner. Do the dishes. Give the boys their bath. Whatever you want me to do. We can take turns on Robbie's night feeding. But promise me." He took my chin in his hand and ran his finger across my check. "Promise me, if you're not sleeping after two weeks with the new bed, you'll reconsider this work thing."

I sighed. Two weeks. Was that enough time? I doubted it. "Can we see what the marriage counselor says first?"

41.

As I was punching out on the time clock Tuesday evening, Pete from the night shift came up to me. "We heard about the car accident. Are you okay?"

I paused. I hadn't told a soul. "How did you hear?"

"The pallet driver. He told Bill about some crazy lady who pulled in front on him."

"Crazy?"

"Hey—his words. Not mine." Pete held up his hand. "Then Chuck noticed your new car in the parking lot, and he put two and two together."

My secret was out. Too bad Chuck wasn't better at detecting herbs in pasta sauce.

"You did look pretty tired that night," Pete said. "Maybe you should try Xanax. Good stuff. I can snooze right through all the neighborhood noise during the day. Now I can't sleep without it. I'm hooked."

"Thanks. I'm not a big pill person."

"Just remember to never mix it with alcohol. Deadly combination."

I turned to leave, then paused and pulled out my pen. "What did you say that pill was called?"

* * *

Dr. Khan was all smiles when I brought Robbie to his office for the four-month checkup.

"Let's see how our future pilot is doing." Dr. Khan shook a little rattle. Robbie's eyes followed to the right, then to the left. Dr. Khan took off Robbie's diaper and rolled him over. "Good reflexes and muscle tone. Your son is growing up fast. His dad must be proud."

"Sure …" I answered foggily.

"Everything okay?"

"It will be. This back to work stuff … the nighttime feedings."

"Normally by four months, babies are starting to sleep through the night. But preemies take longer, maybe a few more months. Does your husband help out at night?"

"When he's not MIA."

"MIA?" Dr. Khan's eyes widened.

"Just joking. I'm a military wife. We spend half our lives being single moms. The next TDY is just around the corner."

"I'm relieved. MIA isn't a joking term around here. You know about The Colonel?"

"No?" I leaned in, curious.

"Her boyfriend, an F-86 Sabre pilot, went missing in Korea. Story has it he parachuted out of a burning plane, but they never recovered his body. She still has his picture hanging on the wall above her fireplace."

If I didn't hate the woman so much, I would feel sorry for her. Now I could understand why she was so cold, so bitter.

Other than a bit of diaper rash, Robbie was doing great. We chatted about preemies while Dr. Khan finished the check-up. "Throw out the book," Dr. Khan said. "He'll develop at his own pace."

I thanked him as I left, relieved that at least one person was non-judgmental. I had been thinking about the sleep aid that Bill had mentioned. The base hospital had a walk-in clinic. Sometimes the wait was minutes, sometimes hours. I checked after leaving Dr. Khan's office. There were two patients ahead of me. I fished in my purse for the piece of paper with the name of the pill that Pete recommended.

Twenty minutes later I was explaining to a doctor that I was occasionally required to work the night shift, and that I wanted a prescription for Xanax. He pulled out his pen and started writing. "How long do you expect to be on shift work?"

"A couple of weeks." I lied.

"I'll let you have fourteen pills. But I want you to listen, Mrs. Wahlberg. These pills can be addictive, so I'm not authorizing any refills. Never, ever take these with alcohol. The combination can be deadly."

I nodded. Of course.

I left the base hospital with Xanax safely tucked in my purse. A simple sleeping pill. That's all I needed. Forget that lithium. I wasn't crazy, or bipolar, or whatever Dr. Falio had said. I just needed sleep. Only fourteen pills. I'd better save them for an emergency. I hoped that wouldn't be any time soon.

42.

Okinawa, Japan

Katsurou, Kat as the GIs called him, trimmed the quince bushes lining the walkway to the Kadena Air Force Base Officer's Club. Out the corner of his eye, Kat watched the KC-135 tanker land, taxi, and park on the flight line. The crew of four deplaned, then headed to the crew quarters. The three SR-71s that were stationed at this base were always parked in a guarded hanger. There was no way Kat could get near the Habus, the black snakes. But the tankers were vulnerable.

He put away his pruning shears and passed quickly through the gate in the concrete wall that surrounded the base. He found his younger brother, Akira, waiting in the backyard of their small red-tiled home, on the bench under the gajumaru tree.

"Is it ready?" Kat's voice trembled.

"Patience, brother." Akira smiled at his brother's anticipation, nodded and held out a yellow glob of plastic. Two thin wires ran from the plastic to a small timer.

The two had plotted for many years. Kat had been only five, Akira three, the day the earth shook. They were playing inside on that dreadful day. Their mother had run to them, screaming "*Nante Koto!*" and blocked the door so they couldn't go outside. They had stayed in the back room for weeks, while their mother went searching for food and checking on relatives. "Stay here, Katsurou. Keep your little brother safe," she said to her older son each time she left.

Their father, an American citizen, was working in Hawaii at the time. He had assumed Hiroshima would be safer for his wife and two young sons when the talk of war started. Fatal assumption. Their mother's eyes had turned yellow and glazed over after staring at the mushroom cloud. She slowly and painfully succumbed to the effects of radiation poisoning.

Their cousins had lived closer to the city and were playing outside the day the sky turned gray. They had come to the brothers' house for refuge. Kat remembered their burnt and bubbled skin. He still shivered with despair. The brothers had watched their entire extended family—grandparents, aunts, uncles, cousins—wither away, some taking as long as twenty or thirty years to die from the cancers. The two brothers were the only survivors of a large and proud family.

Before Akira started college, they made a pact. Kat followed in their father's footsteps, staying in Okinawa and working on the base. But Akira went to America, attended M.I.T., and earned a degree in chemical engineering.

The first plane sabotage had been easy. A simple explosive, packed into a parachute. The second would be more difficult. But Akira had promised that the special plastic would go unnoticed in the fighter's wheel well until the plane was well over the ocean. By the time the Air Force recovered enough pieces of the fighter from the ocean floor to piece together the puzzle, their third and final act—bringing down the pride of the United States Air Force—would be complete.

43.

When I got home, the delivery man had arrived with the soft-side waterbed. Mike proudly explained that it had dual bladders, we could each choose our own level of firmness. Even dual heaters, so I could sleep cool and Mike could sleep hot. Life was going to be good. Included in the waterbed package was a set of royal blue fitted sheets.

While I entertained Robbie, Mike filled the bladder on my side of the bed, using a green garden hose which snaked from the bathroom faucet to the bed. As the water level rose, so did my spirits.

Jason jumped back and forth over the garden hose. "Can I get a trike Dad? Pleeease." It was amazing how a three-year-old could sense a moment of opportunity.

"Yes. Jason. Tomorrow. We'll go to Sears and check out the tricycles."

"Are you home to stay, Daddy?" Jason asked.

I smiled and put my arms around Mike. "Daddy's home for a while—until he has to fly the spy plane and take pictures of the bad guys."

"Can I go with you when you fly?" Jason stretched out his arms in airplane fashion.

"Someday buddy. You can't even sit in Daddy's plane unless you have top security clearance. But I'll take you to the next air show. You can sit in a T-37, and I'll show you the ropes."

That night, Mike and I gave the new bed a proper initiation, after which I slept like a log.

* * *

When I got home from Marinara on Friday, Jason danced up to me. "Guess what Daddy bought me."

I dropped my purse and hugged my boy. "What?"

"A new tricycle. A red one! With a bell!"

"Some assembly required," Mike added. "I'll have it together before dinner. Teach my buddy to ride over the weekend."

"And I'm helping Daddy. I hand him the screwdrivers."

Mike winked at me and tussled Jason's hair. "You're a big help, Sport."

On Saturday morning I got up early and tidied the house. I was pretty much of a free spirit when it came to the boy's toys, allowing them to be strewn about the house, but the next Gestapo visit was on Wednesday. The house needed to shine, and I couldn't afford any last-minute surprises. I piled their favorites into the toy box in the family room, and put the rest on shelves in their bedroom.

I was scheduled for a nine o'clock haircut. I needed a little sprucing up too. As I was putting on my make-up, the doorbell rang. It was Sheree, one of the wives from the squadron.

"Sheree. I'd love to chat, but—"

"No protests allowed," Sheree said. "We have instructions from Mike to kidnap you for the day."

Mike appeared behind me and handed her a wad of cash. "Don't bring her back before five."

"Got it. She'll be a new woman."

We climbed into Sheree's Mazda Bumblebee. On the way to the salon, she confided that Mike had been worried about me. "He thinks you're working too hard. He asked a couple of us wives to lunch earlier this week."

"Let me guess. All wives who don't work."

"Kate. We're in awe of you. Working with two kids. None of the other SR-71 pilots' wives work. But if it's your thing, more power to you. We told him so. A lot of military wives work. But it's a lot easier for the gals whose hubbies don't have to pull so many TDYs."

"At least Mike has six weeks off before he has to leave again. I was hoping Robbie would be sleeping through the night before the next overseas trip. That may or may not happen." I let out a deep sigh.

"In the meantime, you've got to find a way to unwind. Mike said that he only had a brother, and he needed help to understand female psychology. We put our heads together and decided you needed a day of relaxation. So after your hair, you're getting a manicure, pedicure, and facial. Then lunch, and to top it all off, a massage. Just go with the flow and enjoy it."

I had a long list of mommy chores scheduled for the afternoon, but I decided they could wait. The pampering was exquisite. French manicure, lunch at a new soup shop, massage, and a final surprise, wine with Karen and Charlotte, two other wives from the squadron, at a little bar on the edge of town.

It was nearly six when I opened the door from the garage to the kitchen, a little light-headed from the second bottle of wine, and announced, "I'm home." What I saw on the couch stopped me dead in my tracks.

Mike cradled a whimpering Jason, an ice pack on his head.

I ran to them. "What happened?"

"Crashed and burned on initial test flight," Mike stared at the ceiling.

Jason sported a big shiner on his left eye and scratches down the left side of his face.

"Michael, you have the boys for one day. How could you—" I scooped up Jason and examined the scratches. None appeared very deep.

"We were sort of pre-occupied with a project. I thought he was fine riding his trike on the patio."

"What project now?" I slowly counted to three and exhaled.

"Look for yourself." He pointed to the patio.

I walked over to the sliding glass door. There was Jason's new trike—tipped over on its side, its wheel stuck in the planter that ran along the side of the patio. I had been so happy with that planter when Mike poured the concrete. Beyond the planter, the corner of our back yard had been transformed.

It now contained a little water garden and a stone bench surrounded by flagstones.

"Come check it out." Mike pulled the sliding door open.

I shook my head, then walked over to explore my new oasis. I plopped on the bench, still cradling Jason in my arms. The pond was kidney-shaped, maybe six by eight feet. A half dozen goldfish darted beneath the heart-shaped leaves of a pink water lily. A merry stream of water trickled out of a big lava stone, creating a soothing melody as it splashed into the pond. "You did all this. In one day. It's incredible."

"Wally, Spencer, and Joe all pitched in. We planted you some roses, all hand selected, just for you." He cupped a delicate blossom, pink on the outside and fading to a yellow center. "This one's called Peace," he said proudly. "And the pink one is called Chuckles. We were almost finished when Jason took the spill." He threw up his arms. "I'm sorry, honey. I'll explain to Sally. He's not the first or the last kid on earth to overturn a tricycle." Mike touched the puffy area below Jason's eye. "It does look pretty nasty."

"It's not the end of the world. It's just the timing."

Jason squirmed in my arms. "I'm better now, Mommy. Can I go ride my trike?"

"I'll take him out on the driveway," Mike said.

"Watch him like a hawk," I snapped.

Mike picked up the trike, and off they went. I sat there and watched the water trickle into the pond. How was I supposed to relax? Just when I thought my world was coming together, this.

That evening after the boys were in bed, Mike and I sat on the little stone bench. "So how'd you decide to do all this—the spa, the fountain, the roses?"

"Sheree suggested the spa. Roses were all mine. The fountain was Spencer's idea. After his divorce he used to go out to a stream behind his house and watch the water for hours on end. Said it saved his sanity. I could see how stressed you were every night after work. I knew if I didn't do something you'd end up back in that mental hospital. Part of the reason I stayed in Sacramento so long was to figure this out. We spent days researching and ordering the pump and liner, then built a little prototype in his back yard."

"It's sweet. But now I'm dreading Sally's visit."

"Maybe you could put a little make-up on Jason's eye."

"That would make it look like we were hiding something."

"Just tell Sally what happened. I'll arrange to be home, and explain that you weren't even on the property when this happened. I'm good at schmoozing women."

Mike did have a way of charming women. Let's hope it worked on Sally. I vowed to be extra vigilant until her next visit.

44.

Cecilia Boticelli, the company founder, was short, dark-haired, and amazingly spry for a woman who had just celebrated her seventieth birthday. There had been a big party at the plant in April to celebrate the occasion. I learned from Molly that Cecilia's husband and three teen-age sons had died in a boating accident at Lake Tahoe in 1960. She had opened a restaurant in downtown Sacramento the following year, drowning her sorrow in marinara sauce. She inspired me—what can we do with the problems life hands us, other than try to find our way back?

Before long she was bottling the extra pasta sauce in the back of her small establishment. After three additions to the restaurant, The Marinara Factory had outgrown its original location, and her two nephews, Fred and Francis, built a state-of-the-art plant near my home.

When the plant first opened, Cecilia made the sixty-minute drive up to Yucca City faithfully once a week. Over time she had turned most of the plant operations over to the nephews. But the old woman still insisted on sampling all new products before they launched.

Both passionate about food, Fred and Francis occasionally lapsed into Italian, especially when they were talking to Cecilia. I had picked up a few phrases over the years. As Fred reminded us, "Nothing goes in a Marinara Factory jar, *finché la vecchia signora dà la sua benedizione*," which meant something like, "Until the old lady gives her blessing."

Cecilia was a hoot. In the early days she and I would stand together over the ten-quart steam-jacketed kettle in the lab with our little plastic tasting spoons, me in a white lab coat, Cecilia in a large white apron. She added herbs by the sprinkle. I measured by the gram. I learned the art from her. She picked up a bit of the science from me. We respected each other. She would smile, her dark eyes lit up like candles, pat me on the shoulder, and declare "*i gusti grandi*" when the sauce had simmered to perfection.

On Tuesday morning, Cecilia was scheduled to taste my new gourmet salsa and Chuck's everyday marinara. I wasn't sure how the old lady would react. Chuck's everyday pasta sauce was bland. I had loaded my salsa with chunky tomatoes, jalapenos, and cilantro. There would be mild, regular, and hot varieties. The Hispanics in the plant raved about the hot version.

Tastings were held in our sensory room, with private tasting booths along one wall and a large round table that seated eight in the middle. Cecilia liked to do tastings at the round table, family style. I brought out the trays of samples, six different varieties in little plastic cups, and set a tray in front of each panel member. Cecilia took the seat to my left. First we sampled Chucks's everyday marinara sauce. I put a little in my mouth and swirled it around. It reminded me of that stuff Mom used to buy in a can. I held my breath, trying to predict Cecilia's reaction.

Her face spelled disappointment. Chuck's sauce got a few "okays" and a "needs something."

"The costs look good. But I think it's too thin," I said.

Cecilia was not so diplomatic. "I don't want Aunt Cecilia's name associated with this garbage." The old lady paused for effect. "Maybe you could call it Up-Chuck."

Next came the three salsas. My stomach churned nervously.

I studied Cecilia's face. She worked the mild around her mouth, then smiled and nodded. Next, she put the medium to her tongue. She hesitated.

Francis's secretary walked into the room and interrupted. "Kate, there's a call for you. It's Mike. He says it's an emergency."

I tried to stay calm, but my thoughts raced. *If something happened to one of the boys, I'll kill him.* "Excuse me. I'll take it in my office."

I picked up the phone. "Mike. What's wrong?" I asked breathlessly.

"HOME NOW."

"But Mike. I'm in the middle of a tasting. Aunt Cecilia—"

"NOW!" The room reverberated with the sound.

"This had better be good." I hung up, grabbed my purse, and paused for two seconds at the tasting room door. "I'm sorry. There's an emergency at home. I'll be back as soon as I can."

I heard Chuck say, "Women" as I rushed out the door.

A dozen scary scenarios flashed through my mind as I drove, but I forced myself to stay under the speed limit. When I pulled into the driveway, Mike was loading his suitcase into the trunk of the Camaro.

"What?" I demanded. "You're leaving?"

"Kate." He put a heavy hand on each of my shoulders and stared in my eyes. "Can I trust you?"

I stared at him, wide-eyed. I couldn't answer that question. Only he could.

"You can't tell anybody."

"What?"

He squeezed my shoulders. "We're at DEFCON 3."

I knew that DEFCON was short for Defense Condition, the Air Force rating for how close we were to a nuclear war. A five meant that all was calm. The military had been at DEFCON 3 on two other occasions—once during the Cuban Missile Crisis, and once during the Yom Kippur War. If we got to DEFCON 1, it meant the doomsday clock was ticking. DEFCON 3 was a big deal for Mike. For our country. I waited, hoping for more of an explanation.

"I've got to leave. I'm not sure when I'll be back. I don't have time to get the boys to Lindsey's. You're in charge."

He kissed me hard, slammed the trunk, and slipped into the driver's seat. His parting words were, "I will be back."

I stared in disbelief as the Camaro disappeared around the corner.

45.

Molly looked up as I rushed past her open door. "Fred wants to see you in his office."

"What's up?" I leaned on her doorjamb, my hands shaking.

"Chuck's been planting seeds, complaining about you missing work."

"Thanks for the warning."

Fred's door was open, and he motioned for me to enter. In one of the three leather chairs opposite Fred's desk sat Chuck. I plopped in the middle chair. A painting of the Boticelli family home in Naples graced the wall behind Fred's desk. I stared at it, avoiding Chuck's smirky stare.

"Sorry about the emergency." I paused. What excuse now? Finally I blurted, "National security. Sorry, that's all I can say."

"Really?" Fred's voice rang with doubt and awe.

"Mike was home with the boys, and now they're at the sitter's. I'll stay late to make up the time." I scooted back my chair and scanned Fred's face.

"Kate," he started. "I just don't think this department head thing is working out for you. At least not now. You're coming to work with dark circles under your eyes. I heard about your car accident."

I glared at Chuck. *Bastard. Weasel.* The accident happened after work hours. But the less said the better. I nodded in acknowledgement.

"And … Chuck caught an error in your cost estimate for the new salsa." Fred pushed a spreadsheet toward me. Someone had circled the jalapeno cost in red.

I studied the page, then realized my error. Halfway through the project, I had switched from standard-dried to freeze-dried jalapenos. The texture was superior. I'd forgotten to plug in the higher cost.

"I'll fix that." I grabbed the spreadsheet. "I'll have the corrected costs to you within the hour." My head swam. The cost differential was probably cents a jar. But pennies multiplied by a million jars equaled a big screw-up.

Fred eased back in his chair. "Bottom line. I've asked Chuck to continue to sit in on the staff meetings for the next six weeks, until the New Year. That will give us time to evaluate whether you're still up to the department head position."

I hung my head. Everybody in the plant knew there was no love lost between Chuck and me. Eventually one of us was going to go. I was not giving up without a fight. But after everything I'd been through, I wasn't sure how much fight was left in me.

Fred stood. "Chuck, I'll let you get back to the lab. Kate, would you stay a few minutes?"

Chuck shook hands with Fred. "Thanks for your confidence."

Alone with Fred, I waited, my eyes down.

Fred leaned forward. "You were doing so well juggling family and career with one child. When we offered you the department head position, we should have known you'd have another baby." He pointed to the painting behind him. A wedding party was poised in front of the Boticelli ancestral home. "We're a family business. We care about our employees. If this isn't working out for you, with the two kids and Mike's job, then we need to do what's right for everybody. I want to give you a little more time. Let's sit down and talk this through before the end of the year."

Fred stood and held out his hand. "Fair enough?"

I stood and took his hand. It was large and warm. "Fair enough," I nodded. "You said there were two things."

Fred seemed to have forgotten the second thing, then suddenly remembered. "Cecilia wants to take you out to lunch—to eat Mexican. She's still a little confused about this whole salsa thing. I told her that *Tres Margaritas* was as authentic as it gets. She's back talking to Francis about the expansion. She'll be ready at eleven-thirty."

"I'll re-do these costs, and meet her in Francis's office."

Lunch, and alone with Aunt Cecilia. The old woman never went to lunch with anyone except Fred or Francis. Too bad it wasn't happy hour. Nothing like a margarita to capture the authentic taste of Mexico.

On my way back to the lab, I ducked into the bathroom and smudged a little concealer under my eyes to hide the dark circles.

Fred and Francis just thought they ran the company. They handled the day-to-day stuff. As long as Cecilia was alive, she ruled.

46

Aunt Cecilia and I arrived at *Tres Margaritas* before the noon rush.

"Smell the roasting chili peppers," I said.

Cecilia nodded. "Smells inviting."

A brick wall divided the restaurant into two sections, a noisy area with three televisions and a narrow side room. I asked for an end table on the quiet side. The waiter seated us at a table set with tangerine place mats. Strands of dried chili peppers hung from the walls.

Cecilia studied the menu, then closed it. "You order. Italian I know. This Mexican—it's the wave of the future. I see all the Hispanic families in the valley. And the gringos, even Italians, eating Mexican food."

Her eyes scanned the room décor. "It's hard for a *vecchia signora* like me to change her eating habits. But I need to do what's good for business."

A young waitress, dark hair tied back in a ponytail, came over with large plastic glasses of ice water.

"We'll start with chips and salsa," I said.

"Hot or mild salsa?" the girl asked.

"One of each, please. Then bring us each an order of smothered enchiladas."

The salsa arrived. Cecilia dipped a chip into the mild sauce. Her eyes lit up. "This is like your mild salsa. Yours is even better. I like the touch of lime."

"I just want to show you how the product that I developed compares to authentic Mexican," I explained. I spread the mild salsa onto a saucer. "See. The tomatoes are a quarter-inch dice—same as the ones we use in the gourmet marinara. And the green specks are cilantro. We can order it fresh. I've already checked."

The old lady nodded, then took a spoon and poured salsa off the edge. "Kind of thin."

"We'd use a combination of fresh tomatoes and tomato paste, but in a different ratio than the gourmet marinara. That'll give it body. Ours will be thicker. It won't run off the chip like this does." I demonstrated, dipping a chip.

"Now try the hot." I warned with my eyes. "Start off easy."

Cecilia took one taste and then a huge gulp of water. "This is too much for an old lady. You and Chuck work it out."

I chose my words carefully. "I'm trying to work with Chuck. Some days it's a challenge."

"He's jealous of you, Kate. Old school. From a world where men are the bosses. Women do as they're told. But Fred says he has a good head for numbers."

I'd heard the Monday morning banter. Chuck let Fred win at golf every week-end, then filled him with gin and tonic and bad vibes about my performance. Chuck and I had gotten along fine when we were equals. I couldn't wait to get to work on Monday morning—to smell the herbs. Now there was a knot in my stomach every time I walked into the lab. I decided to take the high road, and struggled for words to express my frustration without being a back-stabber. "There's been a lot more tension since I was appointed department head. But, I'll do whatever it takes to keep my job."

Cecilia patted my hand. "Fred and Francis are good boys. Fred has a gift for people, Francis for numbers." She took a long drink of water. "Since my children died, they've been like sons to me. Their wives are nice girls. Okay cooks, but no passion. You have passion, but it's being smothered."

I blinked back the tears. Stay on business. Remember, she's your boss, not your friend. "I try to focus on the product and forget the politics. I love all things Italian. But I'm convinced that Mexican is the right direction for the expansion."

Cecilia looked around the restaurant. Every table had filled in the short time since we were seated. "I see crowded parking lots at all the Mexican restaurants in Sacramento. I think you're right."

The waitress brought our smothered enchiladas. Gradually the conversation turned from work to personal matters. Cecilia produced a photo of a prize orchid, a miniature cymbidium that she had been nurturing for five years. It had finally flowered. "How are the boys, your toddler and the little one that came early?"

"Robbie just had his four-month check-up. He'll blossom in time, just like your cymbidium. I have to be patient." I showed her a picture of Jason and Robbie, sitting in the back yard by the new rose bushes.

"Your husband? He understands? He's supportive?"

Much as I wanted to pour out my heart to her, I held back. "He tries. He was fine with me working when it was just Jason. Now—" I shook my head. "Fred said he'd give me more time."

"You're like the daughter I never had." Cecilia smiled. "I insisted that Fred promote you to department head. Six weeks may be enough maternity leave when everything goes as planned. But when Mother Nature gets screwed up—" She ran her fingers through graying hair, then brightened. "Let's get back to the plant. I've got an idea, but I need to talk to Fred and Francis."

I knew better than to ask. Let it simmer.

47.

With Mike gone, my sleep quality plummeted. I was lucky to get three or four hours a night. I'd toss and turn, drift into a light sleep, then wake, feeling like I'd been jolted with a cattle prod. Thoughts looped—Mike's safety, Sally's visit, Chuck's backstabbing—night after night. I couldn't let go.

Sally had rescheduled her visit for the Monday before Thanksgiving. I'd counted on Mike to run interference. Now I was going to have to ride that one out solo. After the peanut butter incident, and the tricycle accident—what next? I was haunted by Murphy's Law. Something was going to go wrong. I just knew it.

There had been no word from Mike since he left. I'd quizzed Hillary twice during shift changes, for any scoop on the DEFCON status. Since her husband Bruce worked on the flight line, I thought she might have some intel. On Friday I caught her putting on her lab coat. "Any news?" I whispered.

She gave me a strange look, then glanced at her watch. "I've got ten minutes before my shift. Meet me outside."

"Outside?"

"By your car, where there are no ears," she said. "Be nonchalant."

I grabbed my coat and headed to the parking lot. Her Toyota was parked in the row next to my LeSabre. She opened her car door, brought out a brown paper bag, and handed it to me.

The bag contained two packs of cigarettes. "You know I don't smoke."

"Just a decoy. Pretend it's a gift." She surveyed the parking lot. "I pestered Bruce until he broke. I'm sworn to secrecy. Bruce would lose his job."

"I won't breathe a word."

She gave me a long look. "Air force jets are exploding. Two so far, both out of Kadena Air Force Base. Nobody knows how or why. They're being blown out of the sky. The Pentagon is befuddled. They deployed an extra SR-71 to Clark Air Force Base in the Philippines, so they could launch reconnaissance flights from both bases. That's why Mike left. Everybody's on alert. Bruce has a bag packed, sitting in the bedroom closet."

"Shit. What planes?" I held my breath.

"So far only fighters. They can't figure out what's bringing them down. No trace of any subs, surface-to-air missiles, enemy fighter jets. It's a mystery. Mike didn't tell you any of this?"

"He said the Air Force was at DEFCON 3. That's all he had time to tell me."

"They're keeping it under wraps. But word leaks down the line."

This was scary shit. How many times had Mike told me the SR-71 was invincible? He could outrun anything in the sky. If he knew it was coming. But something new. Something Air Force radar couldn't detect. That might be a different story.

"If it got out that Bruce told me." Hillary ran a finger across her throat.

"Your secret's safe."

"Reporters are buzzing around the base and the Pentagon. But the military is mum until they figure this out."

"We'll talk again on Monday. Thanks, pal."

I glanced around the parking lot, then handed the paper bag back to Hillary and got in my car. Hillary headed into the plant.

I drove home, pondering my luck—job on the line, the Gestapo coming on Monday, Jason looking like he'd been abused. To top it all off, Mike was in potential danger. I stopped at a red light. *Lord, could you just throw on something else?*

As if in response, the earth rumbled. A glass of water rested in a cup holder on my console. The water sloshed back and forth. A mini-quake. I had felt them several times since we'd moved to the valley. They usually lasted only a few seconds. *Christ, I was just kidding!*

48.

"An F-4, and then an F-15. Enma would be proud of the way we are punishing the Americans." Akira sat at the small wooden table under the gajumaru tree, poring over a rough map of the base that Kat had drawn. The evening was heavy with humidity. A bush warbler trilled from a branch over their head.

Kat sat across from Akira and wiped his forehead with his forearm. "It's getting more dangerous each time. The MPs have been swarming the flight line. They used to be so lax. I overheard two officers talking. The first time they thought it was just a mechanical issue, but after the second explosion, they're exploring all options. They still have no idea what's happening, but now everyone is on high alert."

"You will find a way, Kat. You have the will."

"My will is weakening," Kat confessed. "I know Enma wants revenge. Our god should punish the actual men who ordered the bomb dropped. These pilots, they are not the ones who should suffer."

"Our mother did not order the attack on Pearl Harbor. Our cousins did not fly the Zeros that dropped bombs on the *Arizona*. But they suffered. Now the Americans must look into the face of Enma."

"One more. Just one more, and then our sworn vengeance will be complete."

"I've been working on these for over three years." Akira held two silvery spheres that shimmered and wobbled in his hand.

Kat's eyes grew wide. "Are you sure they will work?"

"Yes. But getting them on the plane will be challenging." Akira pointed to map. "Here. You must hide in this shed near the fuel tank. When the MPs are not looking, you will find a way to drop the two spheres into the KC-135's fuel tank. You've been watching the tankers leave at dawn. You have to do it around 4 a.m. You have a short window."

Kat sighed and stared into Akira's dark eyes. They were full of wrath, like the eyes on the statue of Enma that stood in the temple. Kat remembered his own mother's eyes. How she stumbled around their home in her final days. How she had cursed the Americans. He tightened his lips. "I will find a way. But this will be the last one. Promise me this will be the last one."

"Watch," Akira said. He slipped the two spheres into a small metal can filled with JP-7, the jet fuel Kat had siphoned from the storage tank over a month ago, when the base was still calm.

The spheres floated at first, but over two hours, the silvery compound that encased the spheres slowly dissolved and the spheres sunk into the jet fuel. The slightest mechanical action would now break the sphere.

They stood ten feet back, behind a low wall that had once been part of a pig sty. Akira pulled a string, releasing the steel flapper, a crude replica of the action that would take place as the KC-135 boom started to retract, while the tanker was still connected to the SR-71.

Akira counted slowly. "One, two ..." At nine, the can burst into a blazing inferno.

49.

I invited Brenda over for some girl time on Saturday night. The boys were in bed. Wally was away visiting his parents. I owed her, after all the babysitting. I bought a bottle of merlot and we sat at the bar on the back porch. I wore a navy sweater to ward off the cool evening air. A pot of chili con queso bubbled over a warmer next to a wooden bowl of tortilla chips. The conversation turned to Sally's pending visit.

"This whole scenario is just stupid," I said. "I would never hurt my boys."

"I would come over for moral support, but I've got to take Wally to the heart doctor on Monday morning," Brenda said. "You'll be fine. Just explain that Jason fell off his trike. It's not like he's the first boy to ever take a spill. He's got a sense of adventure, like his dad."

"I was counting on Mike to be here."

"Face it. You're like a single mom half the time. I admire you for working. A lot of women would just stay home."

"Most of the Air Force wives don't work. I've never been into this whole Officer's Wife thing. Golf and tennis would be nice. There's some great gals, but there's too much gossip and sucking up. I went to a couple of events when Jason was a baby, thinking I'd find a few friends. Not my cup of tea."

Brenda's wine glass was empty, so I poured us both a refill. Brenda swirled her glass. "Your generation has more opportunities. When I graduated high school—thirty years ago—it was teacher, nurse, secretary, or housewife. A few women had more exotic careers, doctors and the like, but most of us were glad to get our MRS. degree."

"I thought I would get my Ph.D. Was smart enough. Spent the summer between my junior and senior year working at Campbell Soup in Philly. I loved the big city bustle, museums, shopping. They offered me a job when I graduated. But then along came Mike."

"How did you guys meet?"

"In a little flower shop in Chancerville. I was home for spring break, just two months before I would graduate college, buying daisies for my mom's birthday. He was on a two-week leave from the Air Force, home to bury his mother." Mike walked through the store with the florist, pointing to all of the flowers that his mother had grown in her garden. He was drop dead gorgeous. Strong, yet so sad. He asked me for advice on the flowers, and then if I wanted to have a beer at the tavern next door. That initiated a whirlwind courtship. He followed me back to college. I kept telling him I wasn't ready to settle down, wanted to work a few years, then maybe grad school. Two nights before he had to go back to his base in Alabama, he filled my dorm room with red roses and produced a diamond ring."

We had made love for the first time, there in the dorm, to the undulating sounds of Etta James' "At Last" and the intoxicating aroma of a hundred roses. A bunch of the girls on my wing clapped when Mike and I emerged from my room the next morning, me wearing a big sparkler on my left hand, him sporting a grin a mile wide.

I looked up from the wine. "Campbell and grad school just faded out of the picture. Mike promised that I could have a career too. I was lucky to find a job with a small seasoning company in Alabama while Mike was an instructor pilot. Learned a lot there. Then I got pregnant with Jason and we moved."

"You had a good balance between career and family, up until Robbie came along. You'll get it back."

"I've got six weeks to prove myself. I can't afford any more mistakes."

"There are other jobs. You could work in a day care or a grocery store," Brenda suggested.

"I love what I do. I'm a whiz at sensory. Hillary marvels at the way I can identify spices in a sauce, formulate the perfect blend of flavors. It's an art. And Marinara is growing. With this new expansion, and the profits from the new line, I'm due for a raise. It's a dream job. I could never replace it."

"There are more important things you can't replace."

Her words stopped me cold. She was right. I bit my thumbnail. "There's got to be a way to juggle it all. Other women manage."

Brenda popped a chip in her mouth. "I wish I could offer more support. But I'm tapped out."

We finished the bottle of wine around midnight. I had hoped the merlot would lull me into a deep slumber. Instead it left me edgy and agitated.

50.

A phrase stuck in my mind from a class for new Air Force wives: "No news is good news." The instructor had told us how proud we should be of our husband's service, but warned that military wives lived with uncertainty. As long as a black car didn't show up on your driveway, it was best to assume all was well. That attitude would keep you sane. I took refuge in the "no news" mantra.

Late Sunday afternoon, Betsy called with the name and address of a woman in Southern California. "This woman, Jane, started a group called PEP, Postpartum Education for Parents. There's an article in *American Baby* magazine. I'm putting it in the mail to you. There's a phone number. Do you have a pencil?"

I took down Jane's phone number, thanked Betsy, and hung up. I picked up the phone to call this woman, then chickened out. Where did I start? Robbie started whimpering, awake from his afternoon nap. I stashed the phone number in the desk at the end of my kitchen counter and scampered down the hall.

After the boys were tucked into bed, I dragged out the bottle of Xanax and read through the prescription information. Xanax was for "anxiety and sleep disturbance." On a scale of one to ten, my anxiety level was at least a twelve. As for sleep disturbance, the sleep fairy had been very stingy with her magic dust. I had read that some preemies took a year to sleep through the night. Could I survive a year of sleep deprivation?

Without Mike as a back-up, I might take the pill and not wake when Robbie screamed for his bottle. That would wake Jason. Sally was due the next morning. I decided to compromise by taking half a pill. I could get by on half a night's sleep.

I carefully sliced the pill with a steak knife, and swallowed half with a gulp of water. I pulled the covers over my head and prayed to the sleep goddess.

I startled from a sound sleep. I had dreamt I was in the SR-71 with Mike. He in the front seat, me riding reconnaissance. The plane exploded.

"Mommy." Jason tugged on my shoulder. "Robbie's crying."

"Thanks, sweetie." I flipped on the lamp by my bed. "I'll get him. Go back to bed."

Jason clung to my nightshirt. "I had a nightmare. Daddy was yelling."

"You too?"

Jason nodded.

That was odd. Jason didn't usually have nightmares. Robbie's cry grew louder. Darn that pill. I shouldn't have taken it.

"Mommy, I'm scared."

"Want to sleep with me? I'll make Robbie's bottle. We can have a slumber party."

"I'll get Woofy." Jason grabbed his stuffed dog and followed me into the kitchen. I warmed Robbie's bottle in a pan of hot water. "Get one of your books. I'll read you a story while Robbie takes his bottle."

Jason brought *The Gingerbread Man*. I decided he didn't need to hear about something being eaten tonight. I propped Robbie on my hip and flipped through the pile.

"How about *The Little Red Hen?*" Baking bread was safe. All three of us snuggled into the new bed. In five minutes, Jason was snoring softly. Robbie finished his bottle. I tucked Robbie back in his crib, but let Jason sleep in our bed. The sound of his steady breath was soothing.

I lay awake. My nightmare had been so vivid, so disturbing. I finally got up and took the other half Xanax, hoping to sleep a couple of hours.

The alarm blared at seven. I could have used another hour of zzzs, but I showered, poured Jason a bowl of Cheerios, and dressed for work. The pill had given me a headache and left me with a loopy feeling.

I scanned the house. Aside from Jason's face, everything looked ship shape. I was rehearsing my explanation to Sally when the phone rang. It was Hillary.

"Kate, do you have your television on?"

"Why?"

"Turn on channel ten."

I picked up the remote with my free hand. Tom Brokaw was talking. There was a photo of an SR-71. "The Pentagon has neither confirmed nor denied that an Air Force spy plane and a refueling tanker exploded over the Yellow Sea, between North Korea and China."

My heart stopped.

51.

I wanted to push rewind. To hear more. But Tom switched to a story about the aftermath of the Mt. Saint Helens eruption.

"Hillary, do they know which crew?"

"No word yet. Bruce is trying to find out. Everything's crazy at the base. I've got to go." She hung up.

I stood there in shock. An SR-71 and a refueler. I thought of the other pilots, their wives. I knew them all. Somehow I managed to place the phone receiver back in its cradle. There were eleven SR's in service, three permanently at Kadena, plus the extra that had just gone over. It could have been any of the crews.

I said my mantra out loud. "No news is good news."

Louder. "NO NEWS IS GOOD NEWS."

"Mommy, what's wrong?" Jason pulled on my shirt.

"Nothing, honey. Sorry I yelled." I reached down and clutched him tight to my chest.

"Go play with Robbie. Give him his rattle." I peeked out the kitchen window, half expecting to see a black car. All I saw was my neighbor Ted, in grey running shorts, out for his morning jog.

I brought both boys into the family room and sat rigidly in front of the television, staring. Jason played with his LEGOs. Robbie amused himself with his newly-found fingers.

I tried to quell the panicky feeling spreading through my body. My hands shook. My breathing was erratic.

My nightmare. It was real.

Mike.

The explosion.

Mike screaming.

The doorbell jangled. I hit mute on the remote control, tottered over to the front door and opened it.

Sally's smile turned sour. "Mrs. Wahlberg. What's wrong?"

I was holding it together, until she uttered those words.

"Wrong ... everything," I said. I could feel the force of the explosion. The fireball. The ejection. Then blackness. Total blackness. I collapsed in a heap on the entry floor, crying hysterically. Sally huddled over me, patting my back.

"Mommy." Jason was at my side.

Sally grasped Jason's shoulders and held him at arms' length. "Jason, what's wrong with your mommy? And what happened to your eye?"

Jason erupted like a volcano. "I fell off the tricycle. Daddy yelled at Mommy. Daddy left. Then Daddy came back. Then he yelled again. Now he's gone."

"Really!" Sally's voice was incredulous.

"Mommy, don't cry." Jason stroked my hair. Robbie started bawling.

"Come sit on the couch. I'll get you some water," Sally said.

She helped me up and onto the living room couch. Jason picked up a rattle and offered it to Robbie. He chewed on it for two seconds, then tossed it, and started wailing again. I was shaking. Sally went over to the kitchen sink, then came back with a glass of water. I took a gulp. It was tepid. I nearly spit it back in the glass, but forced myself to swallow.

"Can you tell me what happened? Where's Mike?"

I calmed enough to say, "An SR-71 exploded."

"Was Mike in the plane?"

"Nobody knows ..."

"Is there somebody you can call? Somebody who can come and watch the boys?"

I tried to think. Lindsey had other kids to watch. Brenda was taking Wally to the doctor. Betsy was always busy. Think. Finally I blurted out, "Mom. I'll call my Mom."

"Your mother is in Kansas, right?"

I nodded.

"It will take her at least a day to get here."

I nodded again. My head was about to explode.

Sally patted my forearm. "Mrs. Wahlberg, are you seeing your psychiatrist?"

"No. I don't see him anymore."

"Are you taking your medication?"

I nodded. I wanted to tell her I was off the meds. My mouth hung open. No words came out.

"Jason, let's go to your room." Sally led Jason by the hand into his bedroom and shut the door. I overheard her quizzing him, but I couldn't make out the words.

After a few minutes, Sally and Jason emerged from the bedroom. Sally went to the kitchen and made a phone call. She came back. "If you don't have anyone to watch the boys—" She hesitated. "We've got a woman who will watch them. At least until your mother comes."

"No," I said. "No. I'll watch the boys. I'll call in sick." My mind was not working. I couldn't focus. "Lindsey watches Jason, at her house."

"I agree. You should call in sick. Until you find out what's going on. Or until your mother gets here. This will just be temporary. I'm sure the judge will be fine with releasing the boys to their grandmother."

"Judge. What judge?"

"We're going to put your boys into protective custody."

"Nooo!"

"You'll have to show up with your attorney. Paul, right? He knows the routine." She put her hands on my shoulders. "You need to go see your doctor. Get some medication. You're very unstable."

"You can't do this."

"You need to cooperate. It will be a lot less traumatic for the boys."

Less traumatic? I wanted to slap her.

I had just enough wits to grab my legs and count to ten, exhaling deeply. When I finished, she was leading Jason back to his room again.

52.

I followed Sally's instructions—stuffed clothes and toys into a duffle bag for Jason, another for Robbie. Sally transferred the car seats to her car. I hugged both boys goodbye, then watched Sally's car disappear around the corner of Butte View Street. Watched my whole world slip away.

I stumbled back into the house. It was empty, not just quiet empty, but soul empty. I stopped to pick up Robbie's jet shaker toy, still damp from his slobber, and put it on the shelf in the boys' room. I poured the rest of Jason's cereal and milk down the drain and turned on the garbage disposal. It whirred noisily. The soggy cereal crisps vanished down the drain. I wanted to follow them, to be shredded into tiny pieces and sucked away. My stomach twisted into a knot, and only sheer determination kept me from throwing up in the sink.

How did this happen?

When would it end?

Why me?

Why? Why? Why?

I turned off the disposal, stupefied. Slowly, I willed my mind back to reality.

I needed to call Paul. His secretary answered and said he was in court. I explained the situation. She promised Paul would call as soon as he was free.

The phone rang. It was Molly. "We heard the news about the explosion. Have they identified the pilots?" Her voice cracked. "Was it Mike?"

"I don't know. Nobody called me. But I have this weird feeling, a premonition."

"Fred said you should take the rest of the week off work. As long as it takes. We're here if you need us."

"Thanks." I was too embarrassed to tell her about the boys. I hung up.

I wasn't sure if Mom was home or at work, but I picked up the phone and dialed the home number. It rang and rang. Finally a breathless answer. "Hello."

"Mom …"

"Kate, what's wrong?"

"Everything." Between tears and gasps, I explained what had happened. "I need you, Mom. Can you come out on the next plane?"

"I'll call the airline as soon as I hang up. Just try to stay calm. We'll get through this."

She called back about forty-five minutes later. "Every single flight is overbooked because of Thanksgiving. Out of Lincoln, Omaha, Kansas City. I've talked to every airline. They all say the same thing—don't even bother to go to the airport or try to get on stand-by. It would be a waste of time. I've got a confirmed seat on the first flight out Thanksgiving morning. It arrives in Sacramento at ten-thirty. That's the best I could do."

"I understand." I felt panicky after I hung up. How was I going to hold it together for three days?

Paul called a few minutes later. I explained about Sally. "She said you'd know what to do."

"They have to hold a hearing within seventy-two hours. But with Thursday being Thanksgiving, we probably can't get in front of the judge until Friday. Judge Steuben handles these cases. I'll stop by his office, as soon as this case goes into recess. Is there someone who can stay with you?"

"My mom's coming. But she couldn't get a flight until Thursday."

"I was planning to be off on Friday, but I'll rearrange my schedule. Make time to cover your hearing. My secretary will call to schedule. Got to run."

I flipped through the channels, hoping for more news about the explosion. But it was all cooking and interior decorating shows. I left the television on low and made a cup of tea to calm myself. I gripped the cup and rocked back and forth on the couch. "No news ... "

There was a knock. I put one foot in front of the other. Finally I reached the door. I bit my lip and opened it.

Snooty Lou and her husband Jerome stood in the doorway, along with a man I didn't recognize. I knew by the look on their faces.

I couldn't breathe. "Mike?"

Jerome nodded. "He's one of the six missing crew members."

Betty Lou smothered me in her arms. "I'm so sorry, Kate. We tried to get here before you heard."

Jerome and Betty Lou supported me over to the couch. One sat on either side of me. Jerome introduced the other man as chaplain Peter Chambers.

The chaplain, a stocky man with deep-set eyes, took the seat next to Jerome. "We know this is a difficult time, Mrs. Wahlberg. Whatever you need. Let us know."

"What happened? How?" I demanded. "The SR was supposed to be invincible."

"The explosion happened during a refueling maneuver over water. We got confirmation this morning of the two crews involved, the tanker and the SR," Jerome said. "Air Force and Navy search teams are combing the area. We assume all four men on the tanker were lost. But you know the SR has ejection seats. If Mike and Robert were able to unlock and eject, there's hope."

"If they ejected, they can find them. Right? With the beacons?" I studied Jerome's face.

"Both ejection seats have a locator beacon. But it's a big ocean. They're trying to track the beacons as we speak. Until we locate the beacons and find the men, we won't know if either Mike or Robert survived. We'll let you know as soon as we hear anything."

I wondered if Mike was alone or with Robert. If they both managed to eject, could they find each other?

Jerome went on. "Based on the location of the planes, and the winds, if Mike and Robert ejected safely, their parachutes drifted toward the Korean peninsula. Chances are they landed in the water. But just in case, we've got ground crews scouring the area south of the demilitarized zone. The State Department is working behind the scenes. If somehow the North Koreans or the Chinese got to them—" He tapped his fingers on his knee. "Both groups are very unpredictable. I wish I had better news, but that's it for now."

"Is there anything we can do for you? Anybody we can call?" the chaplain said.

"I'll phone Mike's brother. Have him go talk to their dad. I've already called my mom. She's coming out on the first available flight, on Thanksgiving Day."

"Do you need somebody to pick her up at the airport? To watch the boys?" Betty Lou asked.

The boys. If Betty Lou hadn't been so concerned about their welfare, they'd be with me now. I tried to reel in my anger. "The boys are with a family." Technically that was true. The Air Force would learn about the custody issue soon enough. For now the only people I'd told were Paul and my mom. "Maybe you could get my mom. I've got her flight number written down in the kitchen."

Robert was divorced and had two daughters. Jerome explained that another chaplain had been dispatched to the house in Alabama where Robert's ex lived. He gave me the names of the tanker crew members. Three of the guys were married. I knew their wives. All lived on base. There were eight kids between the three families. Three widows, eight orphans, for sure. The rest of us were in limbo.

Jerome promised to call the moment he had any updates. Betty Lou offered to spend the night, or take me out to the base to be with the other wives. I thanked her, but said I preferred to be alone.

"Are you sure?" she said. "We can have one of the wives stay with you for the duration."

"I'm sure. My neighbor Brenda will be home in a little while. I didn't sleep well last night, and I'd like to take a nap."

Betty Lou helped me back to the bedroom, tucked me into the bed, and closed the curtains. "If you need anything, call. I'll leave a list with Jerome's direct line, our home number, and the base commander by your phone." Her heavy perfume was making me nauseous. Finally she shut the door.

I lay in my bed, shaking. No boys. No husband. Just my stupid job. Even that was in jeopardy. I had been saving the Xanax for an emergency. This qualified. Maybe I should take the whole damn bottle.

53.

I burrowed in the bed, exhausted. My mind refused to let go of the images—the SR exploding, Mike ejecting, the parachute dropping. So much blackness. How did I get here? Back to work in six weeks? What a pipedream. I was never going to get my life back. Never going to glue together the pieces. There would always be a gaping hole.

Seemed like only yesterday that Mike got the call, asking if he wanted to interview for the SR program. His buddies said he was one of the best instructor pilots on the base. Flew like he was part of the machine. Had a knack for teaching the young guys to relax and fly ahead of the plane. He'd flown the F-4 in Nam, before we met. Didn't talk much about Nam, said it was a lot of stuff he wanted to forget.

He had warned me that it wouldn't be easy. But I saw the gleam in his eye and heard the fire in his voice when he talked about flying supersonic. "It's the chance of a lifetime." How could I say no?

T-38 instructor pilots were home every night. SR-71 pilots were away more than they were home. He'd stood holding the completed application in a brown envelope and asked me, "Are you strong enough to handle it?"

"I'm stronger than I look." My signature line. I hadn't been a lumberjack, like Molly. But back in high school I'd helped my dad and Stevie with the hay. Dad had started me at ten, pushing three bales of alfalfa down the barn chutes to feed the cattle. Never could lift them over my head like Stevie, but I was well-muscled by the time I graduated high school. That was a lot of beer parties, wine, and pasta ago.

Was I still stronger than I looked? Physically, maybe. Emotionally, I used to think so. Now I wasn't sure. What was I really made of? Was I strong enough to be a widow? I wondered—at what point did The Colonel give up? When did she acknowledge that her man was never coming back? Did she still dream about him? Something inside me chipped away at the black hate I felt for her.

I eventually crawled out of bed, went to the medicine cabinet, and pulled out the Xanax. *Whatever you do, don't take it with alcohol. The combination can be lethal.*

I took the prescription vial to the kitchen and reached above the stove, where Mike kept his Jack Daniels. The bottle was three-fourths full. I set the Jack next to the pills. There was some reassurance, knowing I could eject from life. No kids. No husband. No job. Just me and my own emergency escape tools. I stared at the two bottles, the lethal mixture, for twenty minutes. Then I put them both in the cabinet above the stove and headed to the back yard.

The evening air was cool. I lay down on the grass near my peace garden and stared up at the stars. The cascading hum of water was soothing, the grass soft and enveloping. We all ended up back in the earth eventually—hopefully when we were old and gray—not in our prime, not when we had boys to rear and dreams to live. I tried to imagine what it must have been like for Mike. Did he realize what was happening? Did he see the fire coming at him? Did he feel pain? Did he have a chance to pull the D-ring that would eject his seat? If he pulled it, did it work?

So many possibilities. The SR designers went to great lengths to protect the pilots against the unthinkable. Pilots had ejected before and lived. He had explained the ejection procedure to me several times. "If anything goes wrong, I just pull the D-ring, my pressure suit inflates, at 10,000 feet the parachute deploys, and I leisurely glide down to terra firma. Piece of cake. If I happen to be over water, I activate the survival kit twenty-five feet over the ocean, and the life raft inflates. We practice all sorts of emergencies in the simulator, over and over. It's like second nature."

I'd stare at him with skepticism. "If you mess up in the simulator, you get a do-over. In a real emergency, you only get one chance."

He'd smirk. "Honey, have a little faith."

Faith was easy. Survival was hard. Mike had been to ocean survival training in Florida, and land survival training near Spokane. He'd joked about being put in a box for days, told that his wife was a slut. He said he just laughed at his supposed captors and agreed with them. It was our personal joke. He had come back from those two weeks of land survival ten pounds thinner and ten times stronger. I could see the change in him. If he'd somehow managed to eject, there was hope.

Water survival was a bit trickier. There were sharks in the ocean. Not to mention rough seas. Enemy ships. Hopefully the Air Force could trace his locator beacon and reach him before the evil forces descended.

I stared up at the stars. At the edge of the stratosphere, the SR-71 was invincible, the fastest plane on the planet. Whoever had done this knew that the plane was vulnerable during refueling. It was deliberate. Who would hate our government so much? The Russians? The Chinese? The North Koreans? Were those guys waiting in the ocean? An SR-71 pilot would be a trophy, someone to torture and parade in front of the world. Practice torture, like Mike went through in survival training, was one thing. Real torture was another. I shut my eyes to block out the scary images. *Please God. Don't let them torture him.*

After about fifteen minutes of lying in the cool grass, I started to shiver. It must be about daybreak in Korea. Planes would be out searching. I needed to try to get some sleep. Tomorrow would be a new day. I picked myself up off the grass and headed inside.

Mike would want me to be strong—for the boys.

54.

I slept fitfully, jerking awake several times in the night. My dreams were vivid—like I was in the plane with Mike. I lay in my bed the next morning, recalling the events of the previous day. I fought the notion that I had somehow made it happen. Was it real? Were the boys and Mike gone? Or was it all just a bad dream? I needed to fight the scary phantoms seeping into my psyche.

I went and looked in the boys' room. Their beds were empty, the sheets cold.

I brewed a pot of coffee. Caffeine would clear my head. I inhaled the robust aroma, cradled the warm mug in my hand, and curled up on the sofa. I grabbed the remote and turned on the television.

Tom Brokaw was talking about the explosion. There were pictures of all the KC-135 crew members. I recognized all four—Marty, Steve, Jeff, and Richard. Visualizing their families fashioned a gloomy reality to the whole scenario. Brokaw said that they were all presumed dead. Two navy ships, the USS *Avenger* and the USS *Blue Ridge*, were in the area. Pieces of the tanker were being recovered and hauled on board. The Air Force was searching for clues as to why the explosion had occurred.

Photos of Mike and Robert appeared next on the screen. A guest commentator from the Defense Department spoke. "In 1973, the SR-71 set a world record. It is the fastest air-breathing flying machine. Alone, this plane could never be shot down. The explosion occurred during a refueling. The Pentagon theorizes that a piece of shrapnel hit the SR-71." Another guest commentator, this one from Lockheed, talked about the ejection seats. "The pilot and SRO would have had to react instanta-neously in order to eject in time. A split second of hesitation could be fatal."

I sat, numb. The news switched to earthquakes in Italy, wildfires in Southern California, hostages in Iran. The hos-tages were about to spend their second Thanksgiving in captiv-ity. I prayed Mike had not been captured by the North Koreans. Iranians and North Koreans were equally crazy. They hated the U.S. government.

Was Mike strong enough to handle torture? Soldiers had committed suicide to keep from spilling their country's secrets to the enemy. Would Mike? Was that noble?

I had come out of the mental hospital a changed person. Would I commit suicide rather than go back to a mental hospi-tal? I'd never given it serious thought—until today. Would it be noble, or cowardly? What if Jason and Robbie lost both parents to suicide? How would that make a kid feel?

Too many questions. I flipped off the television. Maybe if I moved, my head would clear. I was in no mood to speak to anyone, so I slipped on my blue jeans, Mike's baseball cap, and a pair of sunglasses. Then I slipped out the back gate, hoping no one would recognize me.

No luck. Wally stopped me at the sidewalk. "We heard the news on T.V." His voice quivered. "Ted down the street called. Said he saw the black car at your house yesterday, but was afraid to come over." Wally gave me a big hug. "Is there any-thing we can do?"

I thanked him for asking and started off in the direction of the park. I walked aimlessly, putting one foot ahead of the other, for maybe five miles. Finally I headed home. There was a message from Jerome. He would come by later that morning with an update on the missing crew.

Jerome and Betty Lou arrived in separate cars. Betty Lou brought a casserole. I had barely been able to choke down a piece of dry toast at breakfast, but I thanked her and put it in the fridge.

"The news is good and bad. The Navy spotted one—" he paused, "life raft in the waters of the Yellow Sea. It was punctured, but still floating. They verified that it was from the SR-71. There's a good chance at least one of the men made it out of the plane alive."

"Where did they find it?" I asked.

"About 40 nautical miles south of Haeju, North Korea, and 40 miles northwest of Incheon, South Korea. There's a bunch of islands there. Technically most of the islands are south of the DMZ. But most are so remote, they are virtually a no man's land."

"The beacon?"

Jerome hesitated.

"What? Tell me."

"The Navy thinks they've located one beacon—a thousand feet deep in the ocean. They're not sure. The signal is faint."

"A thousand feet … " I stammered.

"So far no signals from the other beacon. That's the part we don't get."

"One beacon … at the bottom of the ocean."

"They're not sure what that means. The pilot could have dropped it. Not likely, but possible. A Navy battleship is steaming toward the wreckage, and fighter jets are scanning the area. A lot of small fishing boats troll in the area. After the explosion, there might have been a rush to the area. One or both pilots could have been picked up by one of the boats and taken out of the immediate area. Somebody could have found the beacon and inactivated it. Until they send a diver down—we just don't know. For now all you can do is wait and keep the faith."

"It doesn't sound good."

He shook his head. "Betty Lou can stay with you, as long as you need. The other wives have volunteered too."

"I appreciate the offer, but I'd just as soon be alone. I've got some things here to keep me busy. My mom will be here Thursday morning."

Jerome confirmed Mom's flight number and agreed to pick her up at the airport.

Paul's secretary called a bit later. "Your hearing is scheduled for four o'clock on Friday. Paul is planning to explain the situation to Judge Stueben this afternoon and press for permission to allow the boys to come home on Thanksgiving, after your mother arrives. No promises. The court tries to keep children in the family, if at all possible."

Keep the children in the family if at all possible? The realization was sinking in. Mike might never come home. The boys might never come home. Thank goodness I didn't need to see the judge today. I was an emotional wreck.

55.

The hours crawled. Brenda stopped by on Wednesday morning with a pumpkin pie and whipped cream. Any whiff of food made my stomach wrench. But I thanked her graciously. Kimberly from down the street brought a dish of her special cranberry sauce. I put it in the fridge. Maybe Mom would be hungry.

My brain kept reeling through the possibilities. Was Mike dead, alive, hurt? Why hadn't the beacon worked? I mourned every wasted moment, every harsh word, every missed opportunity to show him how much I loved him. Ironically, I didn't *need* to work before. We could have scraped by on Mike's salary. But I'd demanded it all—motherhood, career, two babies. Mike had once taunted that if my career was so important, I should have been content with one child. But I couldn't let Jason be an only child. I wanted everything. Now I risked ending up with nothing.

I hung on every word of the six o'clock news. It was dawn in China. Navy and Air Force crews were searching for wreckage and survivors, giving up their Thanksgiving dinner, hoping to find the two missing pilots before time ran out.

I pulled out our wedding album and flipped through the memories. Me, innocent, primping with the aid of my college roomies. Mike, cocky, posing with his groomsmen—three Air Force buddies from Nam. There was a close-up of us kissing in the park, framed by the branches of a weeping willow. *Till death do us part.* I figured we'd be old and wrinkled.

Next I pulled out Jason's baby album and pored over his pictures. Photo after photo, his first smile, first haircut, first tooth. Even the blurry photos. I kept them all.

There were hardly any photos of Robbie. Maybe a dozen, still in the envelope from the photo shop, waiting to placed in his baby book. I looked a fright, especially in the pictures from the earliest days. My countenance bore what Dr. Falio had termed "Prolixin stare." A blank look. Where was Robbie's mother? Mike's wife?

I dreamt about the explosion, then it happened. There was a force in the universe, something I didn't understand. Was I psychic, or just crazy? Was God testing me?

I put the albums away, got out the Jack and Xanax. My new solace. If the worst happened, when I knew for sure, they'd be there for me. I moved the booze and pills to the top shelf of my bedroom closet. Mom wouldn't find them there. It was reassuring to know that they were within arm's reach as I slipped into bed. Jackie and Zanny. Sleep tight, my friends. I hummed myself to sleep. Jackie and Zanny were lovers ... but he done her wrong.

56.

Thanksgiving dawned clear and windy. I cradled a cup of coffee, searched for warmth from the cup, energy from the caffeine, topped it off and slipped it back into the microwave three or four times. Eventually I poured the bitter brew down the drain.

I didn't want to be in my pajamas when Betty Lou brought Mom. I summoned the energy to slip into sweats, ran a comb through my hair, and slapped on some lipstick.

The doorbell rang. There was a pleasant surprise when I opened the door. "Dad. I didn't know you were coming too."

My dad, a quiet man, smothered me with his leathery arms. "When I heard about Mike, I told your mom we both needed to come. There was one extra seat on the plane."

"The chores?" I said.

"Got the neighbor boy to feed the cattle and the hogs."

"I'm glad you're both here." I turned to hug my mom. Suddenly I felt as if my knees would buckle. "Oh, Mom."

"It's okay, honey." She held me up. I clung to her, shaking.

Jerome stood behind my parents. "I'll get the bags." He went out to the car and brought in two suitcases. I showed him where to put them—in the den with the pullout sofa. Then I phoned Paul, to let him know my mother had arrived.

I invited Jerome to sit in the living room and give us an update.

He rubbed his chin for a long time, then spoke. "They found Robert's body."

I gasped, breathing slowly to fight back the tears. My stomach twisted in a knot. Mike and Robert had been a team for so long. I was counting on them to help each other survive.

Jerome went on. "He ejected, but evidently was hit by a piece of debris from the tanker explosion. He was probably unconscious as he descended, unable to release the survival kit handle. A Navy Seal team found him in very deep water, still strapped to his seat." Jerome shifted nervously. "They've got divers searching the same area for Mike. They found Mike's seat, separated from the life raft. We know he managed to deploy his raft."

"But he couldn't have gone far." Mom put her arm around my shoulder. "They'll find him."

"The Pentagon suspects somebody got to him before our boys and disabled his beacon. Possibly the same ones who shot down the planes. Most likely the Chinese. Could be the Koreans. There's a remote possibility it was a small fishing boat—civilians. All theory at this point. If either the Chinese or Koreans had him, most likely we would have heard by now."

"So we just wait?" I said. "It's so hard. Not knowing."

"That's all we can do. Trust me. The minute we hear anything, I'll let you know." Jerome looked at his watch. "You should be getting a delivery soon. Betty Lou and some of the wives are—" The doorbell rang. "That must be them."

I opened the door. There stood Betty Lou and two other SR-71 pilot's wives, Karen and Sheree, with boxes and casseroles. They filed into the kitchen and unloaded their dishes on the counter. Then they distributed hugs and hushed words of encouragement. Betty Lou had told them about Robert. Both had red eyes. We all assumed our husbands were invincible. This incident evaporated that myth.

Sheree placed several casseroles in my oven to warm. Karen piled the cold food into the fridge, then explained everything to my mom. Food was my last priority. Karen gave me a long hug. "We're going to head out now. Hang in there. Mike's strong. You have to be strong too."

"If there's anything we can do to help, watch the boys. Just let us know," Sheree added.

The mention of the boys made me flush with shame. Thank god she didn't ask where they were. Betty Lou and Jerome slipped out a few minutes later. I leaned on Dad.

Mom went to answer a knock on the door. It was Paul and Lydia, with my precious sons.

"Mommy," Jason ran to me. I swooped him up in my arms.

"Come to Grandma," Mom took Robbie from Lydia. "He's grown so much. I can't believe how he's changed."

Lydia went back to her car and returned with a cornucopia centerpiece, filled with golden mums. I stepped outside to talk to Paul. "Can the boys stay?"

"The boys need to be back at the foster home by seven. Your social worker will stop by around six-thirty to pick them up. You know the hearing is at four tomorrow?"

I nodded.

"You and your mom both need to show up." He paused. "Any word on Mike?"

"They're still searching."

They slipped out, murmuring "good luck" wishes.

Before long the house filled with the aromas of roast turkey and sage. "Shall we eat?" Mom said.

"I haven't been able to keep food down," I said. "But I'll try."

Mom said grace, the Catholic one, and added a prayer for Mike's safe return.

I took tiny bites and chewed slowly. I needed to keep some food down. I'd thrown up or skipped every meal since the news. After a few forkfuls, I pushed the food around the plate. Mom eventually got the idea and took my plate away.

I wondered if Mike was being fed. If he was capable of eating.

57.

Dad spent the afternoon playing with Jason. Mom fussed over Robbie until he went down for his nap. When Sally showed up, I thought Mom would never let go of her grandson. She followed Sally out to the car and tucked Robbie into his car seat.

That evening we sat around the kitchen table. Mom brought out the leftovers and warmed us each a plate in the microwave. I picked at a piece of turkey.

"That all you're eating?" Mom said.

Every time I swallowed, my stomach twisted and coiled into an angry ball. "Maybe I'll have a piece of pie later."

My mother took the plates. "How about a cup of hot tea?"

I nodded. It was nice to be coddled. Last time I'd fought it, but now I just let her take over. I sipped the steamy brew, and found the courage to voice the thoughts that had been running through my mind the past few days.

"I refuse to give up hope. I know the chances are slim, but I believe he's alive. Mike communicated with us. I sensed the explosion in my sleep. Jason did too. We both woke up at almost the exact time it happened." I held my head in my hands. "I guess that sounds crazy. Don't tell anybody. It was probably just a coincidence. Robbie usually wakes up around that time for his nighttime bottle."

"There are things that nobody can explain," Dad said. "Doesn't mean they're crazy."

I smiled and put my hand on Dad's arm. It was as if he'd stored the sun in his weathered skin. "Thanks, Dad."

"I can stay until next Wednesday. We'll see what develops by then. If there's no news, I'll probably head back to the farm. How about you? Will you go back to work at that marinara place, or just stay home?"

"I have no idea. I'll probably take off most of next week. Spend some time with you. Give myself time to calm down. And then—" I tried to think logically. "I'll just take it one day at a time. See how I feel. Right now I can't focus. This could turn from days into weeks." I thought again about The Colonel, waiting forever for her man to come home. "Years even. If I don't go back to work eventually, I'll just sit around and worry myself to death."

Mom finished her tea and took the cups over to the counter. "The hospital hired a temp to cover for me, but they want me back to work on January fifth. Hopefully by then—" I sensed what she didn't say—they'd find Mike, or his body—but she knew better than to voice that possibility. "I'm sure you won't need me that long."

After dinner, Dad suggested a game of gin rummy. "You need some distraction."

At this point, distraction was the most I could hope for. I walked down the hall and retrieved a new deck of playing cards from the hall closet. Thankfully, rummy didn't require a lot of mental acuity.

58

My parents and I arrived at the courthouse fifteen minutes before our docket time. Paul's secretary instructed us to sit in a waiting area. I wore a gray and black plaid blazer. Professional but not over the top. Mom reached over and adjusted my mauve scarf, then slipped her arm around my shoulder.

Paul was nowhere to be seen. I picked tiny bits of lint off my dark slacks. Our hearing was scheduled to start in five minutes. Where was he?

Paul rushed in from a side corridor. "Sorry. My other hearing ran longer than expected." He shook hands with my parents. "We persuaded Judge Steuben to do this in his chambers." He studied me. "You going to be okay?"

I took a deep breath. "I'll do my best."

"Remember, say as little as possible. Let me do most of the talking. We'll let your mom tell the judge about her plans to stay until January."

"Wahlberg," a bailiff called. No more time for coaching.

"Show time," Paul said. "Follow me."

The judge's chambers were paneled with dark wood. A noisy heater clanged, making the room over-warm and stuffy. Judge Steuben, a balding man, roughly sixty, sat behind a walnut desk. Sally was seated in a chair to his right. We took the four chairs opposite the desk. Dad slid into the hot seat, next to Sally. He flashed her a big smile, then balanced his John Deere baseball cap on his left knee.

The judge opened a file folder and read silently. He looked up. "Mrs. Wahlberg, the social worker's report says that your son, Jason, had bruises by his left eye, and scratches on his face. She reported that shortly after she arrived you became hysterical."

It was all I could do not to defend myself. Paul's voice reminded me to keep quiet. "Kate had just heard the news on the television—that a SR-71 had exploded. Given the circumstances, her reaction was to be expected."

The judge went on. "What about the bruises?"

Paul nodded to me to speak. I explained briefly about the new trike and the accident. Sally confirmed that Jason's version of the events matched mine. Paul asked Dad to explain the repairs Mike had made to the concrete. Paul handed two photos of the fixes to the judge. He examined the photos and passed them to Sally. Both nodded their approval.

The judge scrutinized the report, reading a few phrases under his breath. He looked up. "I understand you had a postpartum psychosis."

"Yes." That's all I said—trying to follow Paul's instructions.

The judge leaned forward. "Are you currently under psychiatric care?"

"I was seeing Dr. Falio," I said.

"But you're not seeing him now?"

"No. I'm not sure he's—" I paused, searching for the right word, "the best doctor for me."

Beside me, Paul shifted in his chair. Had I said too much? I bit my tongue.

The judge jotted some notes, then looked up. "I'm going to require that you see someone, a minimum of once a month for the next three months. Maybe a counselor at the base. Does that seem reasonable?"

"Yes, sir."

"And I understand your mother will stay with you until you've stabilized?"

"That's right," Paul said. "Kate's mother, Amanda Bernon, is a nurse. She's planning to stay with Kate through the end of the year, to help her through this difficult time."

"Is that correct, Mrs. Bernon?"

"Yes." Mom patted my knee. "Looking forward to the time with my grandsons."

"Starting in January, I'd like Ms. Sterm to schedule monthly visits to the home, again for three months minimum, to make sure that things are going smoothly. She'll work with you to develop a safety plan—a list of people you can call if you're having any mental health or emotional problems," the judge said.

"The list could include neighbors, friends, maybe some of the Air Force wives," Sally suggested.

"There are people at the church that Kate attends who would be willing to help out. Everyone thinks very highly of Kate and Mike," Paul added.

"Are you agreeable to all of these conditions?" the judge asked.

Did I have a choice? No. Did I want Sally trespassing on my private space? No. I spoke in a low voice. "Yes, sir."

The judge turned to the bailiff. "Bring the boys in."

A side door opened. A woman came in carrying Robbie and his diaper bag. Jason bolted for me.

"Mommy." He crawled on my lap. I smothered him, fighting back the water in my eyes.

Jason climbed off my lap and went to Dad. "Grandpa, can we go home?"

Dad looked at the judge.

"As soon as you select a psychiatrist or counselor, Ms. Wahlberg, give that person's name to Ms. Sterm. We'll schedule a follow-up hearing in January." He closed the file. "I hope they find your husband before then."

Outside the judge's chambers, Paul congratulated me. "You did fine. Take care of yourself." He pressed his hand over mine. "Keep the faith. They've got a prayer chain at the church going for Mike."

Outside the judge's chambers, the dam broke. My body racked with sobs. Dad put his arm around my waist and helped me to the car.

"I'll be all right. Just give me a few minutes." I handed Dad the car keys. "You drive."

We headed across town. Dad noticed an A&W on the edge of town, and suggested we stop for a treat. We all sat around a booth with root beer floats. With a shy look at his wife, Dad taught Jason to blow through the straw, creating a mound of bubbles that overflowed the glass. I remembered blowing root beer bubbles as a little girl, and Mom scolding when I got noisy.

Back at home Mom told me to relax. "I'll put a meat loaf and scalloped potatoes in the oven. You need some comfort food," she said.

Dad came into the boys' room as I finished changing Robbie's diaper. "Wish you could stay longer, Dad."

"I've been thinking about it. Haven't had a real vacation in forty-five years. Always tied to the land, the animals. I'll come back at Christmas."

"That would be the best present."

"I'll stay at least two weeks. If I can take it. Jason may have me worn out." His eyes twinkled.

"He's a handful. Gets all that energy from Mike. I'd appreciate the extra help. Here, play with Robbie for a while." I handed my baby to Dad and slipped into the bedroom for a little alone time.

I was dreading the judge's orders to see a shrink. I didn't want to go back to Dr. Falio. If I told him the truth, he'd insist I go on that lithium—for the rest of my life. What was the point of going to a psychiatrist if you couldn't be honest? I had a sneaky suspicion that the female doctor in his practice was going to concur with Dr. Falio about the bipolar and the lithium. Maybe they were right? But I wasn't willing to give in so easily.

I remembered Jane, the woman who helped women with postpartum problems. I wasn't sure if she could help, but it was worth a try. I needed to work up the courage to call her.

59.

My parents were great at providing distractions. Dad and Jason built endless Lincoln Log forts on the family room floor and sand castles in the backyard sandbox. At lunch, Jason sat on Grandpa's lap and shared a banana. A bite for Gramps, a bite for Jason.

Mom had tuned to a country and western channel on the radio and baked a batch of peanut butter cookies. She smothered Robbie, rushing to his crib at the first whimper. I almost missed getting to change his diapers. "He's starting to look like Mike. The chin, the eyes," she said.

That was too much. I had been holding it together, but I hung my head and sobbed.

"I'm sorry," she patted my back. "If you weren't so big, I'd put you on my lap and rock you."

"I probably just need a good cry." I headed for the bedroom. I hadn't let myself fall apart since the day Sally showed up. I'd tried so hard to think positive. But with each passing hour, and no news, my hopes sunk. Now that I didn't have to be the strong one, I could let the tears flow. I shut the door, crawled under the covers, and pulled Mike's pillow over my head to muffle my sobs.

Afterward I got up, my head all stuffy from the cry. Mom made me her special recipe of tea, with little broken pieces of real cinnamon stick, cloves, sugar, and a little milk. It was her special treat, a drink she used to make when I was a little girl and scraped my knee, or came down with strep throat. She called it medicine. I knew the secret ingredient was love.

Jason came over and sat on my lap. "What's wrong, Mommy?"

"I miss your dad," I said in a soft tone.

"Me too. When's Daddy coming home?" he asked.

I searched the air for an answer. How do you explain the words "maybe never" to a three-year-old? I said, "Your dad has a dangerous job. Nobody knows when—" I couldn't add "or if."

"Can I make a tape for Daddy?" Jason asked.

For Jason's third birthday Mike had bought matching tape recorders. Jason made tapes for Mike to take on his trips, and Mike made tapes for Jason to listen to when he was away. So he wouldn't forget his dad's voice. I still had two tapes Mike had made just prior to the Mildenhall trip. One I let Jason listen to in the evenings, as he was getting ready for bed. The other I kept tucked away in my top bedroom drawer—just for me, just in case. I trembled at the thought of having to bring that one into play.

"Sure," I said. "Maybe you can make one for Grandpa too, to take to the farm."

* * *

Jerome stopped by on Saturday morning. He asked Mom and Dad to take the boys for a walk while we talked.

He always sat in the same spot on the couch. "A navy ship will stay in the area for weeks, pulling pieces of the two planes off the ocean floor. The pieces will be flown back to Okinawa. A special team is working to fit together the wreckage and determine what brought the planes down."

He sighed deeply. "Fighter jets are still scanning the area. But, Kate, it's been four days. The mission has officially changed from rescue to recovery."

"They can't give up."

"It's policy. They have to be realistic. The chances of finding him alive at this point are slim."

"I haven't given up." I said it adamantly. But each day hope was slipping from my own white-knuckled grip. "They are still searching?"

"Yes. If I were in your shoes, I wouldn't give up hope either." He stood up to leave. "It makes no sense. No pilot. No beacon. He's simply vanished without a trace."

60.

Hillary called later that morning. "Are you coming back to work?"

"I want to show up on Monday and talk to Fred. I'm going to try part time for a while. There are a few things I've got to get under control on the home front."

"Good for you. Chuck's already talking about redecorating your office."

"Tell that S.O.B. to hold off calling the painter." I wasn't giving in that easy.

"Everybody in the plant is rooting for you, and praying for Mike."

"I'm trying to keep all my options open. Maybe I can work part time, until this mess gets straightened out."

"I wasn't sure if you'd heard," Hillary's voice dropped. "There's going to be a service on the base for the guys who died. Tomorrow, at two o'clock."

"It's hard for me to face people now. But I need to go—for Robert's family."

By Saturday afternoon, the boys had bonded with their grandparents. Jason followed Grandpa around like a little soldier, matching his gait and wearing a miniature John Deere baseball cap. Robbie gurgled and cooed at Grandma. Grandma "ga-gaed" and "goo- gooed" right back.

After the boys were asleep, we sat in the family room. Dad perused the local newspaper and Mom leafed through *Better Homes and Gardens*. I picked up one of my food journals, and stared at the pages, unable to absorb a thing. My mind kept jumping to Mike. I gave up and tossed the magazine back in the pile.

"I think I should go back to work," I said.

"It's too soon," Mom draped her arm over my shoulder. "Give yourself time to mourn, to heal."

"He's not dead. Just missing. They'll find him. If I sit around all day and muse over the possibilities, I'll go crazy." I needed some activity where I could take control, or at least have an impact. I thought about The Colonel, petrified into stone after waiting for thirty years.

"The important thing is for you to take care of yourself," Mom said.

"Work will give my thoughts a purpose. Maybe I'll be able to keep my job. Without my work—" I slumped back on the couch. "It's going to be lonely staying at home with the boys. Next year Jason will start day care. I'll mope around all day and stare at Robbie's face. And all I'll see is a miniature Mike."

"It's your choice," Dad said. "That's why your mom is here."

"I'm worried that you're pushing yourself too hard. Too soon," Mom said.

I was worried too, but I felt the need to escape. My mother was both comforting and smothering. She was constantly doing things for me, holding the door open for me, pulling out my chair, folding my napkin. As if I were half invalid.

On top of that, everything in the house reminded me of Mike, from the new blue paint on the bedroom walls to the little fountain trickling away in the back yard.

Work would be an escape. My other world. I knew it was too soon, but I needed to show up a few days next week if I wanted to keep my job.

61.

Dad drove me to the base chapel on Sunday. Mom stayed home with the boys. We purposely arrived just before the service started. The chapel held about three hundred people, but there was an overflow crowd. I wore sunglasses and stood in the back, leaning on my dad. One of the airmen recognized me and brought a folding chair.

There were no caskets, just photos of each man on a long table draped with a purple cloth. Private ceremonies would be held for the individual servicemen in their home communities. The chaplain who had visited my house opened the service by reading the names of the five crew members who had been lost. The base commander spoke of the debt our country owed these men. I kept seeing Mike's face, recalled photos of him and Robert standing proud in front of the SR-71, their arms wrapped around each other.

The choir sang the Air Force ballad, "Off We Go, Into the Wild Blue Yonder." When they got to the words—*We live in fame or go down in flames*—loud sobs erupted throughout the chapel. I hung my head and breathed in deep gulps. Dad kept patting my back.

Dad supported my elbow as we walked through the condolence line. I'd met Robert's two daughters once when they were visiting from Alabama. Cute girls, maybe twelve and fourteen, with their dad's hazel eyes and jutting chin. This was my first time to meet the ex-wife, a short woman who stood with an arm wrapped around each daughter.

"Any news about Mike?" She spoke with a deep Southern accent.

I just shook my head. I tried to speak but couldn't. I managed to eke out the word "Sorry" over and over as I moved through the line, shaking hands with each widow, hugging each orphan. The Air Force could be cold and regimental. But at times like this, we were one big family, united in our common grief.

We went outside for a twenty-one gun salute. The sound of each gun discharge pierced my heart. Then the Air Force Thunderbirds flew over. I knew they would do the missing man formation. Six planes zoomed overhead in a v-formation. Then one plane pulled up and out, to symbolize the fallen pilots. Today the "missing man" maneuver took on a new meaning. I was certain most of the crowd was thinking about the fate of the missing SR-71 pilot.

I needed to use the restroom before we headed home. From the stall I overheard two women talking.

"They say Carter's pulled in Kissinger, got him jetting all over Asia. If somebody's got him, he'll negotiate a prisoner swap," a voice said.

"The C.I.A. says nobody's talking. At least not yet. Somebody's just waiting to embarrass Carter."

I thought the second voice was the base commander's wife. I wasn't sure.

"Just like Gary Powers and that whole U-2 debacle," the first woman said.

"You know Gary's wife Barbara took to drinking while Gary was in prison. They ended up getting a divorce."

I waited in silence until they left.

Gary Powers, the U-2 pilot, was put on trial in front of the whole world. It was quite a spectacle. Gary was criticized for not committing suicide, for not blowing up his U-2. Instead of a hero's welcome, Gary got a cold reception from the American people on his return from captivity. This was the first time I had heard about Barbara drinking. Can't say as I blamed her. Nobody said being a spy pilot's wife was easy.

If they did rescue Mike, I realized he would never again be the same man who had charged off in his Camaro just sixteen days ago. Not after being imprisoned, possibly tortured. Would I even recognize the man that might return from this ordeal?

And if he was okay, how could I ever let him leave again? How would I feel when he packed his suitcase, when he backed out of the driveway?

I emerged from the restroom and looked for Dad, feeling as if I would collapse without his support. I found him, chatting with Jerome and another SR-71 pilot.

"Dad, I'm—"

He turned to me. "Let's get you home."

62.

Television trucks had been cruising our neighborhood ever since the news broke about the explosion. Jerome gave me strict instructions to ignore them. "Look through the peephole before you open the door. If any reporters bother you, give me a call." That was a relief. I was in no condition to appear on camera. The wives on the base were insulated from the press. I was supposed to be off-limits too, but it was a free country. A missing SR-71 pilot was hot news.

Despite my parents' misgivings, I went to work on Monday morning. A television crew from KCNU, the local Sacramento station, waited outside The Marinara Factory's front door. I drove around to the back parking lot and slipped in the side door. I grabbed my lab coat from the locker room and headed into the lab. Nitin, our microbiologist, was there. "Any news?"

"They're still searching. Frankly, I don't know any more than what they say on the news."

"We all saw it on the television. We were hoping it wasn't Mike," he paused, taking my hand in his, giving me a warm squeeze. "Then we saw his picture. We're real sorry."

"I appreciate the support." I ducked into my office.

Nitin was a loyal colleague. He knew every nasty microbe that could grow on food and how to keep them out of the Marinara line. I'd heard Chuck yell at Nitin over ridiculous things, trying to push product out the door before all the micro was complete, thinking it would save a dime. But Nitin always stood his ground.

I grabbed my notebook and headed for the conference room. Molly intercepted me in the hall. "You don't have to be here. Under the circumstances, nobody expects you to be here."

"I wanted to talk to Fred. Work out something so that I can show up a few days this week, and still spend time with my parents. It actually felt good to get dressed and come to work. Something to focus on besides the search, the waiting. The Air Force will contact me if there's any news."

"Did you see the television crew?"

"Sorry about that."

"Fred made a statement. Said that the thoughts and prayers of the entire company were with you and your family. He said you would be on leave for the foreseeable future. Figured that would keep them away."

"Reporters are like sharks."

I slipped into my usual chair in the conference room. Chuck sat across from me. Fred opened by saying that Aunt Cecilia insisted I have a flexible schedule until the end of the year. He left the rest unspoken. In January everything would change. My grace period would be over.

Chuck volunteered to double-check my work, in case I was distracted. I started to say that wouldn't be necessary, but held my tongue. Molly passed out a chart, indicating who was primary and secondary on each responsibility for the expansion. My name was first on the formulas, Chuck was to take the lead on costing. "Does this work for everyone?" Fred said, looking me square in the eye.

I nodded, willing myself to focus on the tasks at hand.

Jennifer in Human Resources announced that she had finished the job description for "the new position." She was somewhat vague. I noted furtive glances between Fred and Jennifer. Something was amiss. I could sense it. Molly looked down, unable to meet my eyes. I knew better than to blurt out "What new position?" in the middle of the meeting. I'd worm it out of Molly later, when she was alone.

At lunchtime I found Molly nibbling on a sandwich at her desk.

"What's with this new position?" I said, trying to sound nonchalant, but not succeeding.

She set the sandwich on a zip-loc bag. "Fred wants to discuss this with you. But not this afternoon."

"Before I even get a chance to prove—"

"They're just covering themselves. Fred and Francis have a business to run. They need to be able to count on the staff, especially the department heads."

Molly sipped on her Dr. Pepper. "If it's any consolation—and don't you breathe a word of this to anyone—"

"Scout's honor." I raised my hand and rolled my eyes.

"They know Chuck's not department head material. Nobody in the department likes him. They're thinking about bringing in a new person for a year. Then they'll make permanent changes."

"So when does Fred want to talk to me?"

"Thursday."

"Let me know if there's any more scuttlebutt."

A new person. Another competitor for my job. Might as well give up and start packing my box. At least I'd show up on Thursday and hear Fred out.

63.

That evening I found the number Betsy had given me and worked up the courage to call. The phone rang and rang. I was about to hang up when a cheery voice answered. "This is Jane. How can I help you?"

I explained that I had read the article from *Parents* magazine. "I need help. I'm having some postpartum issues."

"I'm sorry to hear that. Tell me a little bit about yourself."

I told Jane who I was, and that Mike was missing in action.

"You're the wife of the pilot who was shot down. I'm so sorry. Any news?"

"It's been a week now. They're still searching."

"My husband's a pilot too. Little planes. None of that fancy supersonic stuff. How are you holding up?"

We exchanged small talk for a while. Jane explained that she had two children, ages eight and five, and she had experienced some postpartum issues herself. That's why she was helping other women.

I took a deep breath and started in. "I had a postpartum psychosis, after my second baby. I was getting better. But now, everything feels so chaotic. My kids were taken into protective custody. The judge insists that I see a psychiatrist. The one I was seeing wants me to go on lithium. My friend Betsy suggested you could help."

"Wow!" Jane said. "Did you have any problems with your first baby?"

"I didn't have any problems with Jason. I was happy, a good mom."

"First of all, you are not alone. There are thousands of women out there struggling with mental health problems after they have their babies," Jane said.

"Thousands? My mom told me about one woman from our home town who had twins and spent some time in the state hospital. But that's the only other situation I've heard about. I'm the last person any of my family or friends would expect to go crazy."

"It's also important for you to understand, you are not to blame for what you're feeling."

"Thanks," I mumbled, despite the fact that I was drowning in guilt.

"Most women don't talk about it. There's truly an epidemic of silence. But gradually I'm connecting with lots of them."

"Do they get better?"

"Most do get better." She paused. "You need to believe that you will be well and feel like yourself again. We're trying to build a support network in every community. It's slow. Do you have a paper and pen nearby? I want you to write down a few things."

I already had a notepad and pencil, so I told Jane to start in.

First she had me write "**Mothering the mother,**" then three simple sentences.

I'm not alone.
I'm not to blame for what I'm feeling.
I will be well and feel like myself again—this is treatable.

"Make this your mantra, read it over and over," Jane said.

"I'll read it every day." I set the notepad on the nightstand. "Everybody's telling me what to do, but not allowing me to feel." I paused to catch my breath. "Until I talked to you, I didn't think anybody understood." I finally let out the truth. "At this point, I don't know if my mind will ever be right again. It's scary."

"Do you have a psychiatrist that has worked with women with postpartum mental health problems?"

"Not yet. The first doctor had me held down and medicated against my will. He wasn't very sympathetic."

"I'm sorry that happened."

"I've been seeing another doctor. Much nicer, but I don't think he has any experience with postpartum women."

"You said you live near Sacramento. We don't have anybody there, but there is a group in San Francisco called Bananas. They can recommend a psychiatrist who has worked with women like you. I'll get in touch with them, then call you back with some referrals. Would that be okay?"

"Please. I will go see one. I don't have a choice. I have to report back to this judge and let him know that I'm seeing somebody. The Bay Area is ninety miles away, but I can get there."

Jane and I chatted on. She was down to earth, full of practical ideas. She made me write down a plan of action. I took another piece of paper from the notepad and wrote:

Steps to Wellness:
· **Education**
· **Sleep**
· **Nutrition**
· **Exercise and Time for Yourself**
· **Nonjudgmental Sharing**
· **Emotional Support**
· **Practical Support**
· **Referrals to Resources**

She gave me a few ideas on each, made it all sound like a formula. As easy as making marinara sauce. But I knew from experience, that even with a formula, things could go wrong. "I'm just trying to hold myself together until they find Mike."

"That must be difficult. Take care of yourself. If you're having scary thoughts, you should get immediate help. Call 911."

I sat there holding the phone. "I'm going to be okay," I said.

"Kate, promise me you'll call 911 if you start having thoughts about self-harm."

I was silent for a moment, thinking of Jackie and Zanny. "I appreciate everything you've said."

"Please call me any time. I'm concerned about you. Is there someone there with you now, someone I can talk to?"

I didn't want my mom or dad to worry, so once again I lied. "My mom is here, but she just fell asleep. I don't want to wake her." I felt guilty. Jane had been so nice.

"I'll get back to you, soon, with the names of some doctors. I want to hear that you're getting better."

I thanked Jane and hung up. Now I had a plan—and a back-up plan, just in case Jane's formula didn't work. I opened the closet door and checked that my two friends were still on the top shelf behind Mike's sweatshirts.

64.

Jane was prompt with the referrals. I settled on a Dr. Stone, who agreed to see me on Friday afternoon at two o'clock. Her office was in a four-story medical building, two blocks from the Oakland Medical Center. Dad had gone back to the farm, so we left the boys with Lindsey, and Mom came along to give directions and moral support.

Dr. Stone greeted me with a firm handshake and a big smile. She was tall, maybe five-ten, and thin, with salt and pepper hair. Her hazel eyes sparkled above half-rim glasses.

She escorted us into her office and nodded to a turquoise loveseat. The office smelled of lavender, and was decorated with mother and child photos. Happy photos. Most of the kids were toddlers. All wore big smiles. It was amazing how closely each baby resembled its mother. If you'd have torn all the pictures in two, and told somebody to match each baby with its mom, it would have taken about two seconds per match. I felt more indelibly bonded to my returned sons. She noticed me staring at the photos. "My husband is a photographer. These are his customers. He gives them a little discount if they let me display a copy. He picks the best," she said.

"They all seem happy." I slumped in the chair.

"Every family has both its happy moments and its struggles. My job is to help families through the tough times, so they can have more of the happy times."

"Jane said you specialize in postpartum moms," I said.

"So you were referred by Jane Honikman?"

I nodded.

"That woman is a jewel. We need an army of Janes." Dr. Stone smiled. "Right now postpartum is about a fourth of my practice. I also deal with other women's issues. But let's talk about you. I'd like to start by asking some background questions."

We spent about ten minutes talking about my childhood, my education. When we got to the part about my marriage, I had to grab a Kleenex. Mom wrapped her arm around my shoulder.

Dr. Stone gave me a few minutes to calm down. I explained that Mike and I had just been through a little bump in our marriage, but I felt positive about our relationship before he left. We were planning to see a counselor, to work on some issues, but Mike got called overseas before the appointment. Then we moved on to Jason's birth and how I handled that. Next she asked me about Robbie's birth. I tried to keep the anger down, but when I got to the part about not sleeping for ten days, I could taste the bitterness in my voice.

She took notes, prompting me every so often with "How did that feel?" or "How did you react?" Her voice was calm and reassuring. Then she explained that she was going to ask me some questions to establish my concept of reality. I knew the drill and easily answered the questions. When we got to the president question, I said, "Jimmy Carter is now president, but since he lost the election Ronald Reagan will be the new president in January."

Much as I hated having to answer the questions, I could count backward by sevens from a hundred. I knew who I was, where I was, and above all why I was here—to get better. So far I liked Dr. Stone. I relaxed a bit, knowing that I was still treading on the magic carpet of sanity.

Next we moved on to the medication history. I had written down a list of the pills I had taken after the hospital. "Are you taking any medications now?"

"No." I purposely didn't mention the Xanax. I knew that I was becoming obsessive about my emergency escape plan. I found myself humming little variations of "Jackie and Zanny" way too often.

She gave me a look, like she knew I was holding something back. Maybe my face gave me away. Mike had warned me never to play more than penny-ante poker. She waited. There was a long awkward silence. Dr. Stone seemed nice, but I remembered Dr. Falio and the needle.

"Eventually you're going to have to trust me," she said.

I nodded. Eventually. "The pills made me a zombie. It broke my heart when Robbie wouldn't breastfeed. With Jason I felt indispensible. With Robbie, anybody could warm his bottle. Maybe that's why I wanted to go back to work, to feel needed. But with all the stress of work, occasional second shift, Mike missing—I'm constantly on edge. I can never relax."

"There are some other medications we could try. We could start with a lower dosage. Medications help so many of my patients to stabilize their mood."

"Would I have to be on them for the rest of my life?"

"That all depends on you. Your baby is—" She glanced at her notes "Only five and a half months. Have your periods started back?"

"They started around four months. When I was finally off all the meds."

"And did you notice any changes in your mood or your sleep patterns when your period started?"

"I can't remember. Does it matter?"

"We don't understand it fully. But we're beginning to realize that women's hormones have a big effect on their mood."

"The sleep problems got worse when I sold my bed. After that I didn't sleep regularly for over a month. I knew I was—" I stopped myself mid-sentence. I wanted to say a walking time bomb, but I didn't trust Dr. Stone fully yet. I had to be careful with my words. "If I didn't get enough sleep, my brain was fuzzy. But at least I knew it was fuzzy. I tried to explain to Dr. Falio, but he jumped right to the medication thing. If I'm running on minimal sleep for over a week, I just don't trust myself."

"So for this visit, let's just focus on sleep. I'd prefer to start you on medication, but since you're reluctant, we can try some alternative strategies, at least for a few weeks. I have a project with some women who are going through perimenopause. Both menopause and the postpartum year are periods of tremendous changes in a woman's hormones."

"Like PMS on steroids."

"Interesting comparison. For the past sixteen months, we've been working on a sleep project. Twenty women come together every two weeks. We've been exploring techniques to help them sleep, and the leader—just a volunteer—has typed up this list of what works and what doesn't. It's far short of a clinical trial. But without funding, it's a start. Most of the women have found these techniques helpful." She walked over to her desk, pulled out a file folder, and handed me a sheet of paper.

I studied the list, which was broken out by section. The strategies seemed sensible. This was good. I felt encouraged that Dr. Stone didn't insist on drugs, at least not yet.

I scanned the list. Might as well be in a nunnery. But it was worth a try. Anything to avoid drugs.

"Do you have any questions about the sleep sheet? Anything you want to go over?"

"This part about no alcohol—sometimes a glass of wine helps me fall asleep."

"It does, but then most people wake up when the alcohol wears off. What you need is deep sleep."

I'd buy that. Drinking wasn't as much fun with Mike gone anyway. Before all this, a glass of wine helped me unwind and feel in the mood for sex. Now it just reminded me that there was a big empty spot in the bed where Mike used to sleep.

Dr. Stone sat forward in her chair. "Here's the score. You've already got two strikes against you—the psychosis and the subsequent manic period. You can't afford to get out of control again. If you do, then I'm going to ask you to give medication a try."

I nodded, but in my heart, I knew that was not going to happen. I glanced at the list again. Absolutely no alcohol when you're in crisis mode. *Jackie and Zanny were lovers. They swore to be true to the end. And he done her in.* Let's hope the sleep ideas worked.

The Sleep Project – Ideas From Women For Women

Sleep Habits
Avoid naps if at all possible, or limit them to 15 minutes.
Go to bed every night at the same time.
Wake up every morning at the same time.

Diet
Limit caffeine to one cup of coffee per day or one caffeinated soft drink.
Eat three balanced meals and two snacks per day.
Try warm milk before bed.
No sweets—fruit for dessert.

Exercise
Walk at least 15 minutes every day.
Don't exercise in the hour before you go to bed.

Alcohol
Absolutely none when you're in crisis mode.
At a party, fake it with virgin cocktails, try a tonic water with a twist of lime.

Sleep Environment
Establish a bedtime ritual. Take a shower. Listen to soothing music.
Avoid television.
Use a ceiling fan for white noise.
Lower bedroom temperature to 68 or below.
Use room-darkening shades.

65.

I woke Saturday morning feeling positive about Dr. Stone. I forced myself to stop after one cup of coffee, then went for the prescribed fifteen-minute walk. The Sleep Project gave me hope. I wasn't sure that what worked for menopausal women would work for a slightly psychotic mom, but it was worth a try.

After my walk, I found Mom in the kitchen.

"Waffles with chocolate chips for breakfast," she said.

"Just like when I was a little girl. More comfort food." The kitchen radiated aromas of baked chocolate and vanilla. "I'm not supposed to have sweets. Three balanced meals, remember?" I held up a waffle and inhaled the sweet aroma. No calories in a whiff. I broke off a piece and stuffed it in my mouth. At the moment, willpower was not my strong suit.

"I made you an egg, on the side." She poured a tall glass of milk for me and a squatty one for Jason. Next she cut a fresh orange, which she arranged in sections on the side. Mom proudly set the plate in front of me. "Now you've got a balanced meal."

Jason sat in his booster seat, and insisted on pouring his own syrup, a huge dipping pool that covered half his plate. Mom cut his waffle into pieces, and Jason dove in. After two bites he paused, syrup running down his chin. "Is Daddy coming home this morning?"

I looked at Mom. She looked at me. Both of us struggled for words.

"Mommy always makes waffles when Daddy comes home." Jason grabbed an orange slice from my plate and stuffed it in his mouth like an orange smiley face, sucking loudly on the fruit.

The waffle stuck in my throat. I downed it with a swig of milk and pushed my plate back. My stomach did that churning thing. If I took another bite, I'd throw up.

Mom looked disappointed. She had worked hard on the breakfast.

Jason was smart for a kid going on four. He had seen his dad's picture on the television screen, had overheard enough of the conversations. I kept telling him they would find Daddy. It was now twelve days since the explosion. With each passing day, I felt more like a liar.

Robbie was sitting in his high chair, playing with his little jet rattle. He dropped it and let out a wail. Mom looked like she was going to cry. I picked up Robbie's rattle and handed it back to him, then grabbed an orange section and sucked on it, trying to get us back to where we had been before Jason dropped the "D" word.

Was this what it was going to be like? Forever in limbo. The most we could hope for, a constant string of distractions. What was it going to be like when Mom left? At the moment, she was the glue holding the family together.

Mom cleared the table. "I was wondering if you wanted to get a Christmas tree?"

Another distraction. I bit my lip. "Not this week. It's too soon." I reached over and grabbed the day planner next to the phone. Christmas fell on a Thursday. "Maybe on the 20th, the Saturday before Christmas."

"Jason, have you written your letter to Santa?" Mom asked.

"Santa." Jason climbed down from the table and ran over to the fireplace. He pulled back the wire mesh that covered the firebox and peered in. "Grandma, Santa comes here."

Mom nodded.

I wiped up the syrup that Jason had dripped on the edge, and found a lined Big Chief tablet. Mom sat at the kitchen table. Jason crawled onto her lap. She wrote in big block letters, DEAR SANTA.

"What would you like Santa to bring you?" She poised the pencil.

"Can I draw it?" Jason took the pencil.

"Santa would love that," Mom said.

I put the dishes in the dishwasher, then looked over my shoulder. Mom's eyes were wet.

Last summer, when I was drugged up, Mike had spent time teaching Jason to draw simple houses, airplanes, and parachutes. Jason had drawn a tall figure with a big grin, parachuting down to a house.

"Look, Mommy." Jason was all smiles. "Santa will bring Daddy home."

I nodded and tussled his hair. "Santa will bring you lots of surprises. You never know for sure what you'll get."

Any other year, I would be excited about the holidays. Now I was dreading them. A small holiday get-together for the SR crews was scheduled that evening at the Officer's Club. I had declined, even though Betty Lou called three times to encourage me to attend. Next week was the annual Marinara holiday bash, a big feast at an Italian restaurant in Sacramento. Mike and I had always relished the event. Hillary offered to pick me up, but I said no thanks. The neighborhood Christmas tea and cookie exchange would be on Sunday. Brenda made the best walnut fudge on the planet. I told Mom to go in my place. I'd watch the boys.

Getting through the holidays was going to be tough. No alcohol. No sweets. No sweetheart.

66.

I crossed one more item, salsa scale-up formula, off my To
Do list. Each day was a struggle. Go through the motions at
work, try to focus on each task at hand. It was officially fourteen days AE—after explosion. Twenty-eight days until I had
to shoulder work alone. I kept telling myself, one day at a time.
Just manage to get through today.

I hoped Aunt Cecilia would come in this week to taste the
salsa. She always cheered me up with her stories of the old
country, the restaurant start-up, her first attempts at bottling
the extra marinara sauce. She never spoke of her husband and
sons, at least not to me. But occasionally, in the middle of a
conversation, she would grow silent, and her eyes would get
that far-off look.

Now I understood. You cope with tragedy. Life goes on. But
sometimes the littlest thing—a word, a song, a smell—takes
you back to a moment with your loved ones—a moment before
the world inexorably changed. And you have to pause and
gather the strength from within yourself to get back to the here
and now, the new reality.

Chuck stepped into my office and tossed a formula in my
in-box. He was in a particularly cheery mood. "Going to be
ready to pull a full load come January?"

I smiled and grabbed the formula. That remark didn't
deserve a response. When Mike was in the States, he could
cover some of the parent things—stay home with the boys when
they were sick, occasionally take them to the doctor. I couldn't
imagine how I was going to handle the load when Mom left. On
January 5th it would all hit: single mom, full-time job, plus all

the things that Mike used to do—taxes, yard work, car repair. Mission impossible.

I kept telling myself that there were lots of single moms who worked full time. They managed. They probably thought life was crazy a good portion of the time. They just lacked the little piece of paper that documented their insanity. I decided that I should pull my ace in the hole and ask Aunt Cecilia out to lunch. I phoned her on my lunch hour and suggested lunch on Thursday. She asked about Mike, and I gave her my memorized statement.

There was an awkward silence. Then she said, "I can't come on Thursday. I'm scheduled to be at the plant on Friday. They haven't told you?"

"Told me what?"

"Fred and Francis. Those boys. They're bringing in a candidate for the job opening. I'm sorry. I thought you knew—" Cecilia stopped short.

I hadn't expected them to find someone so quickly. That explained why Molly had avoided chatting in the hall. "So does that mean they're going to let somebody go?"

"Not you, *Piccola Stella*. Not our little star. I told them 'over my dead body'. We're just not sure you can handle full time. We're going to look at the budget, the fit. With the plant expansion and the new equipment being installed, there's going to be a lot of work in January."

I hung up, stomped over to Molly's office, and rapped on her door. She looked up from her typewriter.

"So when were you going to tell me about the candidate?" I asked.

"Fred told me not to mention it until Thursday. We'd like you to meet with Rosalyn from ten to eleven on Friday morning and give her a tour of the lab."

"Rosalyn, a woman?"

Molly nodded.

"Where's she from?"

"Campbell."

"Can I see her resume?"

Molly hesitated. "Can't see the harm. I was going to show it to you on Thursday." She reached into her desk, pulled out a file, and handed me a three-page resume. "You can look at this, then give it back."

I scanned the neatly printed resume. Rosalyn M. Giovani. Italian name. This woman had a master's degree and nearly thirty years of experience including long stints at Heinz and Campbell. My heart sunk. This was not someone who would work under me. This woman was qualified to run the company. And just when I had worked so hard to get back to full time, to keep my job.

I moped around the office the rest of the week. On Thursday after work I got a haircut. Mike liked long hair. Short was more professional. I told my hairdresser to take off four inches. She asked me three times if I was sure, then snipped away until I had a cute bob that fell just above my chin. I liked the new look.

I tossed and turned on Thursday night, dreading meeting this new person. Why would anyone from Campbell, with all that experience, want to transplant themselves to this little town? Marinara didn't exactly pay top salaries. Something didn't add up.

67.

On Friday morning, I dressed in my most professional blazer, and strode into work sporting a smile of fake confidence. I was determined to wow this new woman, and to have at least fifteen minutes to bend Aunt Cecilia's ear before I had to leave for my two o'clock appointment with Dr. Stone. I sat at my desk and tried three times to check the hot salsa formula, but my mind refused to focus. Finally I gave up and put the spreadsheet back in the To Do pile.

Later there was a rap on my office door. Fred beamed. "Kate, I'd like you to meet Rosalyn Giovani."

When I saw the woman my heart stopped. Rosalyn could have been Aunt Cecilia's daughter, or at least a niece. She had the same short round body, the same fiery dark eyes. But the deal sealer was the crucifix she wore around her neck. It was a slightly smaller version of the one that Aunt Cecilia always wore—Jesus hanging against a dark ebony background. It looked elegant tucked just above a white shell, accenting a black tweed suit with simple lines. I figured I might as well grab a box and start cleaning out my desk.

I rose to shake the candidate's hand.

"I saw the story about your husband on the news," she said. "I can't imagine how difficult it must be for you."

Her hand was warm and moist, her handshake firm. She put her other hand over mine and I felt her strength. I looked down and counted to three to compose myself. "Thank you. My mom is here. She's helping a lot."

"Family is good. My son and his wife moved to the Bay Area last year, and presented me with my first grandchild this past summer, so when I saw this job—"

Aha! Now I understood why she would leave the East Coast and come to the middle of nowhere. "Girl? Boy?"

"Girl. They're spoiling her rotten." In that moment I saw in Rosalyn the same pride that Mom exuded when she talked about the boys. Rosalyn seemed genuine. Time would tell.

"I'm jealous. I have two boys. But you're here to see the lab and hear about our work," I said, struggling to maintain a professional aura.

"I'll leave you two to chat," Fred said. "At eleven, bring Ms. Giovani to the office. I'll give her the plant tour before lunch."

Rosalyn sat and we started to talk tomatoes. Rosalyn asked about our product development process and the plant expansion. I told her about my internship at Campbell. I didn't remember meeting her, but it was a big place. "Campbell has nearly fifteen thousand employees worldwide. You can get lost in the corporate maze," she said. "I'm excited about the prospect of working in a much smaller environment."

I imagined her figuring out where she'd hang the pictures of her grandchildren in my old—make that her new—office.

"I am going to miss Philly," she sighed.

Philly or grandchildren. As if there was any question what her choice would be. Business was good, so I assumed Fred and Francis could cough up enough money to compensate this woman. I gave her the tour of the lab, showing her the quality control workbench and the sensory room. I introduced her to Chuck, Hillary, and Nitin. Chuck said that he was scheduled to spend time with her after lunch. That was news to me. Not good news. This woman was about to take everything I had worked for three years to build, but somehow I found it hard not to like her. I wished her well—whatever her decision about the job.

68.

By now I had figured out my way to Alameda, so I drove by myself, leaving Mom home with the boys. By the time I got to Dr. Stone's office, I was in a real funk. There was a little Christmas tree with blinking white lights in the waiting room, and Christmas songs wafted from the stereo. All the holiday trappings just added to my misery.

I poured out my heart to my new shrink. It had been eighteen days since the explosion, and with each passing day, I had to scrabble farther to find hope. Jerome no longer called every day. Now my job was in limbo too. I felt like I'd made a good impression with Rosalyn, but Francis was such a penny-pincher. Surely the company couldn't afford three full-time product developers. And I still had the shadow of the court looming over my children. "I feel like a prisoner of war." I ran my fingers through my hair, still getting used to the short do. "My mom is the best. And I really appreciate her being here for me. But occasionally she gets on my nerves. She treats me like one of the kids, trying to get me to eat, telling me it's time to go to bed."

"Have you talked to her about how you feel?"

"It's like talking to a brick wall. I remind her that I'm an adult, and fifteen minutes later, she's trying to force feed me." The conversation shifted to the eating disorder I'd developed after the psychosis.

"A lot of my postpartum patients struggle with weight problems. Every medication has some side effects. But we have to balance those against the possibility of your mood disorder worsening," she said.

Somehow it made my lot easier to bear, knowing that other women wrestled with the same issues. "Were any of your other patients afraid to sleep in their own bed?" I explained about selling the bed and redecorating the bedroom.

"There are a wide variety of perinatal mood disorders. Yours sounds a little like a post traumatic stress disorder, which we call PTSD. They're not very common in postpartum women, but we do see them."

"PTSD. Like the military guys after Nam?" I said.

"Similar. We should probably devote at least one session to talking about those experiences." She pulled out a brochure. "This has some breathing techniques. It might help if you get scary feelings or flashbacks."

"I know it sounds weird, but I dreamt about the explosion, the night Mike's plane went down. It was so real. And now it's like he's calling to me, from this dark place. And I can't get to him, can't help him."

"I know it's not easy," she shifted in her chair. "But maybe you need to start thinking about letting go. After eighteen days. With no word."

"No!" I sat shaking. "Sorry, I didn't mean to yell. But I keep thinking one day he's going to walk through the garage door with that big 'I'm here to take you to bed' grin on his face. I'm not ready. Not yet." I squeezed my two hands together to stop the shaking.

"Letting go is a gradual process. But one I think you need to work through." Dr. Stone's lip jutted out. "Maybe we can talk about it more after the first of the year. The holidays are tough."

Would I really have to let go? Could I ever let go?

69.

I ambled into the lab and realized there was only one work week left before Christmas. Hillary had set out twelve beakers, filled with alternating red and green waters on the counter on the right side of the lab. She claimed it was a light stability test for various natural and artificial colors. But I knew it was her way of decorating the lab for the holiday. On a typical year, as the days drew close to Christmas, I would be singing carols under my breath, counting down the days. This year each passing day was one more hash mark on the calendar of doom.

Over the week-end, I had typed up a proposal for a thirty-hour week, starting in January. I could be in the plant every day for six hours, come in early on Monday, Wednesday, and Friday, and stay late on Tuesdays and Thursdays. That way I wouldn't miss anything. The proposal was addressed to Cecilia, Fred, and Francis. I figured the old woman would be on my side. Francis was the penny-pincher. He might agree, because I was suggesting a lower salary. Fred was going to be the hurdle.

I had proposed that I keep the role of department head. That was a long shot, but if the Boticellis nixed that part of the deal, so be it. All of the other department heads worked at least forty hours a week, some as many as fifty. Chuck was always the first one in the office in the morning and the last to leave at night. Easy for him. He had no one to go home to.

Chuck stood in the center of the lab, just to the right of the holiday beakers, with a strange expression on his face. "Did you hear the news?" he asked.

The tone of his voice alarmed me. "No."

"Cecilia had a heart attack. During the night. She's in intensive care."

I slapped my hand over my mouth, remembering her words from the week before—*over my dead body.* Was Chuck distressed or delighted? I nearly sprinted to Molly's office.

Molly, who was always calm and collected, was clearly frazzled. "She's at Sacramento General. Both boys were with her late into the night, then Fred went home to get a little sleep. He left a message that he'd be in around ten. Francis is with her now. Poor woman. She was stressed out over the expansion." I hadn't realized it before, but Molly obviously had a deep fondness for the company matriarch.

"Will she be okay?"

"Nobody's saying. I'm not sure they know yet. But the lady's seventy. Even if she makes it, I suspect that Fred and Francis will insist she let them take full control."

"That means a lot of things will be done differently."

"You were always her favorite." Molly sniffed and blotted the corner of her eye with a tissue. "But you're right. Things will change."

I went back to my office and brooded, my worry for Aunt Cecilia exacerbating my job anxiety. Part time job. Keep my role as department head. Fat chance.

I crumpled up my proposal and tossed it in the trash.

70.

Friday was my last visit with Dr. Stone before the New Year. She was going to take two weeks off for the holidays. She wore a cherry red blazer with a little Christmas tree pin. A humongous poinsettia wrapped in silver foil adorned her desk. She was in a particularly good mood. I guessed that the prospect of two weeks of vacation would make anybody cheery. Anybody except me.

She picked up her notebook. "How are things going?"

"This is the most depressing holiday I've ever had."

"The holidays are especially hard when our loved ones aren't with us."

"My dad is coming out tomorrow. He'll stay until New Year's Eve. We'll get a tree on Sunday. Mom's been wanting one. She's been shopping with the boys. Took them to get their pictures taken with Santa at the mall. I just can't get into Christmas this year."

"Not even for the boys?"

"Jason gets Christmas. But he thinks his dad will be home for the holidays. That's what he asked Santa for. No toys. Just his dad."

"How are you coping? Are you having any success following the sleep suggestions?

"The exercise thing is great. And I do think it's helping. I'm just not sure how I'll find time to walk or run once Mom is gone. Maybe I can take the boys to their sitter early and walk around the plant for fifteen minutes."

"Sometimes you have to be creative."

I explained about Aunt Cecilia's heart attack, and how that jeopardized my hopes for a part-time schedule in the coming year.

Dr. Stone made some notes. "Anything else new?"

"I'm going to make a will. If anything happens to me, Mike's brother will take the boys. I've already asked him, and he agreed. He and his wife have one daughter. If I'm not around, at least the boys would be close to two Grandpas and one Grandma. I'm meeting with Paul, my attorney, next week to get everything signed."

"A will? That makes practical sense with Mike missing." She hesitated. "Of course you're healthy. Chances of something happening to *you* are slim. Tell me more about this. What do you think might happen?" She sat and stared at me for a long time.

Dr. Stone was nice, but I knew she would be making a report to the judge. My little escape tune ran through my head. On my walks I sometimes added verses. *Jackie and Zanny were lovers. She stood on the bridge and asked him to shove her.* I said in a low voice, "Life is unpredictable. You never know what might happen."

She jotted more notes in her book, then closed it. She gave me a lecture, similar to the one from Jane, about calling 911. She also handed me a card, with a number for her answering service that I could call in an emergency. "Tape this next to your telephone. You can call this number, any time of the day or night."

I took the card and tucked it in my purse.

"In the New Year I'm going to start a support group for women with postpartum depression," she said. "It'll be the first Wednesday evening of the month, from six to eight. I think you would find it helpful to talk with other women who've been through similar situations."

"It won't be easy to get here. But I can talk to Lindsey, see if she'll keep the boys late."

A support group, talking to other women who'd been through what I'd been through. Surely no other woman had suffered as much as I had. Or had they?

I left Dr. Stone's office with a heavy heart. I wasn't a hundred percent sure if I'd be around in the New Year.

71.

When Dad arrived from Kansas, the Christmas preparations kicked into high gear. He insisted on a real tree, so we all went together and selected a seven-foot white pine. Before long the whole house smelled like a conifer forest. I was a clear light person, but the Bernon tradition was colored lights, so Mom purchased three new strands of multi-color lights, and Dad hung them on the tree. Ever since Jason was born, Mom had been making little cloth ornaments for our tree from pre-printed cloth that she sewed together and stuffed. She had been busy stitching in the evenings after the boys were tucked into bed, and this year there were a dozen new cloth ornaments, including a little drummer boy, several shepherds, and a smiling toy train.

On Christmas Eve, Mom set Robbie's infant seat next to the tree, close enough that he could kick the lower branches with his foot. His eyes got big as he watched the tinsel shimmer. He waved his little arms and squealed. If he could talk, I knew he'd be saying, "Look what I can do." With each passing month, his emerging personality reminded me more and more of Mike. That same determination, that innate lust for adventure. If only Mike were here to guide that vigor, to channel the boys' energy into positive ventures. At least the boys had two grandpas and three uncles to provide that male influence. Not the same as a dad. All lived in Kansas, half a continent away.

Mom's Christmas Eve tradition was a vegetable cheese soup, an indulgent hearty dish that she served with crusty parmesan bread. I peeled potatoes and carrots, then grated them into a huge glass bowl until I had eight cups total. Next I diced an onion. Big salty tears flowed, only partially caused by the onion. Before long the odor of sautéing veggies filled the room. I tuned the stereo to a channel playing Christmas carols, and tried to put on my best holiday face.

We ate an early dinner, then bundled up the boys to go to the seven o'clock service. Midnight Mass was out of the question. We had just buckled the boys in their car seats when Mom realized she was missing her gloves. She went in the house, and emerged five minutes later. "I looked all over for those gloves," she declared.

I winked at her. She'd been playing that same trick as long as I could remember. When we got home there were dozens of elegantly decorated gifts under the tree. No wonder it had taken her so long to find those gloves. Each stack was wrapped in a different holiday paper, each paper matched to the personality of the giftee. Mine were in a shiny silver and mauve wrap, Dad's in John Deere green, Robbie's in baby's first Christmas paper. Where in our tiny house had Mom been hiding them all?

"Santa came. Santa came." Jason ran to the tree. He pulled on my arm. "Can I open mine?"

"Give your grandparents a few minutes to relax while I set up the camera," I said.

I got out Mike's tripod, and the movie camera, painfully aware that our regular family photographer was not here to take the traditional Christmas movie. After a little struggle, Dad and I managed to attach the movie camera to the tripod. I turned on the camera and gave Jason the okay to start ripping paper.

"Look Grandpa, Santa brought me another tractor." Jason held up a shiny metal John Deere.

"And this is a hay baler," Grandpa explained. "You drive over the field. The hay goes in here. The bale comes out here."

"Can I drive it in the grass?"

"Tomorrow," Dad said.

Jason tore open a box with a bicycle helmet. He tried it on, then tossed it aside.

Robbie happily crumpled the paper. Presents were not really necessary at his age. Mom opened a package for him, a stuffed puppy on a string that barked and wagged its tail. Mom handed him the puppy, and he gummed the dog's face for a while, then dropped it and went back to the wrapping paper.

When the boys had opened all their gifts I turned off the camera. "This is for you, Mom." I handed her a small box. "Thanks for all you've done."

"You shouldn't have."

"I wouldn't have survived the last month without you. It's the least I could do."

She tore off the silver paper to reveal a velvet ring box. She opened it, then gasped when she saw the gold mother's ring, with five semi-precious stones, one each for Jason, Robbie, uncles Stevie and Peter, and me. Dad wasn't very big on jewelry. She had noted when Jason was born that several of her friends had mother's rings that included stones for the grandchildren. I took that as a hint.

"It fits perfectly." She held it up to Dad to admire, then turned to me. "How did you know my size?"

"Remember when we stopped at the jeweler in the mall and had your rings cleaned?"

She nodded.

"That was on purpose." Mom wasn't the only one who had tricks up her sleeve.

Dad opened a shirt box containing a new flannel shirt and some work gloves. "Just what I need to get the chores done this winter. Much appreciated." Every other Christmas he'd insisted that he didn't need anything, but this year he was going along with the festivities.

I opened a huge box. A slow cooker and cookbook with easy meal recipes. "This is great. I can come home to dinner on the counter." After the last present was opened, I stood. "I guess we should clean up the paper."

I grabbed a black trash bag and started scooping up torn paper and bows. The doorbell rang. I suspected it was one of the neighbors with a holiday treat. I opened the door. There stood Santa and three very large elves—all wearing blue jeans, red flannel shirts, and red Santa hats. The three elves I recognized as Joe, Sam, and Doug, three SR-71 pilots. Santa I did not recognize.

"Ho, Ho, Ho!" Santa said.

Suddenly I knew who was in the Santa suit. I would recognize Spencer's voice anywhere. I could sniff that Santa and the elves had already been nipping the holiday cheer.

"Santa." Jason jumped up and ran to him. "Did you bring my daddy?"

Santa shook his head and wiped his cheek with his red coat sleeve. "Santa's still looking for your dad. But we did bring you some toys."

One of the elves, Joe, stepped forward. He took the large red bag from Santa Spencer and led the troop into the living room. "We heard you've been a good little boy, and so has your brother."

Santa recovered his composure, reached into his bag, and pulled out a humongous teddy bear, three times bigger than Robbie. He set it next to Robbie in his infant seat. "There you go little guy." Next Santa pulled out a red towel, which he unwrapped to reveal a carved wooden T-38 jet. "Your daddy flew this airplane."

Jason's eyes lit up as he took the plane. He ran around the room, holding it in his hand and making engine noises.

"And there's two more." Joe unwrapped an F-4 model, and Sam unwrapped a SR-71.

The last one brought tears to my eyes. I held my fingers over the bridge of my nose to force them back and managed to whisper, "Thanks."

"Each one comes with its own stand. We had plane numbers painted on them." Joe pointed out the numbers on the planes to Jason. "These were the planes your daddy flew. He wants you to practice flying them." He swallowed. "Until he can come home and help you."

I forgave the guys for nipping. This wasn't easy.

There was an emerald green silk robe for me. "It's called a happi coat," Spencer said. "Japanese women wear them on holidays."

I tried it on. The silk felt elegant. I doubted I would ever be happy again, but I appreciated the gesture. These guys had taken time from their families or girlfriends to bring a bit of cheer to us on Christmas Eve.

"Would Santa like some milk and cookies?" Mom asked. "We were going to set some out for you."

That helped break the tension. Dad introduced himself to Santa and the elves, and Joe admired the John Deere tractor and bailer. After Santa and his elves had downed the milk and cookies, I walked them to the door.

"Any word?" I asked.

Spencer shook his head. "I wish I could say no news is good news. The Air Force is befuddled. It's now a CIA thing. They may know more than they're letting out. They've got people on the ground asking questions. The base commander talks to the Pentagon every day. The Pentagon talks to the CIA. But so far nothing." He gave me a big hug. "If you get lonely, let me know."

I recoiled from his alcohol breath. "You've got Mandy and Candy to keep you company."

"They left me a week ago."

"Come on. Leave her alone." Joe grabbed Spencer's elbow. The elves headed for Spencer's white Corvette. I noticed that Sam was the designated driver. Spencer crawled in the back seat.

Back in the house. Dad stuffed wrapping paper into the trash bag. Mom filled the bathtub for Jason and Robbie. I picked up the SR-71 and felt the smooth painted wood. Closed my eyes and pictured the explosion. The memories of my dream that night were still so vivid. I imagined Mike ejecting at the last minute, drifting down close to the ocean, cutting the cord on the life raft.

Then it all went blank.

72.

I woke up in a post-Christmas funk. Mom cooked oatmeal for breakfast. I couldn't eat. She was starting to feed Robbie spinach. She teased and cajoled. Robbie swallowed some, and spit out more. Then she picked up a spoon of oatmeal, and pushed it to my mouth, just like she was spoon-feeding Robbie.

"I'm not a child," I yelled.

Hurt registered in her eyes. She threw the spoon down, turned her back to me, and focused on Robbie.

Guilt overwhelmed me. "Sorry, Mom." I wished I could take back the harsh words.

Later that morning, she called the airline. There was one seat left on the flight that Dad would take on the morning of the 31st. She changed her booking. If she left early, she'd have a few days to relax before she started back to work. She started packing her suitcase.

I apologized over and over until she finally told me to stop. Then I went to my bedroom with a tin of sugar cookies that Brenda had baked. I nibbled very slowly, but within an hour, the tin was empty. I opened the bathroom cabinet and stared at the bottle of ipecac for the longest time. I shut the door. Not today. Not going back down that route. I had other friends in bottles.

Dad took down the tree and hauled it out for the trash company to pick up. Mom packed the decorations into old shoe boxes. All that remained from the holidays was one limp poinsettia, parked on the kitchen counter. Every day it had dropped another leaf, until all that was left was a green stem and two humongous red leaves. I tossed the plant in the trash can.

Enough things were slowly dying around the house. I needed to put it out of its misery.

On the morning of the 31st, I drove them to the airport. We exchanged tearful goodbyes in the parking lot, so I didn't have to haul the boys into the terminal. I stayed in the parking lot long after Mom and Dad had disappeared, wishing that Mom would come running out, praying that she'd open the car door and say, "Honey, I knew you weren't quite ready yet. I'm going to stay another week, another month, as long as you need me."

But I knew that wasn't going to happen.

She was gone.

It was all up to me now.

The drive home was forlorn. Jason and I sang "Jingle Bells" for a while. Eventually he fell asleep in his car seat. I tuned the car radio to a news station, imagining that the announcer would say, "We've just found the missing SR-71 pilot, alive and well." But the news was of a Jewish-owned hotel in Nairobi being bombed. Eighteen had been killed. There was a coup in Ghana. War, death, destruction. I punched the radio off. I had enough trauma in my own life.

Molly called to check in on me. She also let me know that Rosalyn had accepted the job and would start on Monday the fifth. I was too depressed to ask for details. I would probably be banished to a cubicle, have to take a big cut in pay, and be on probation to keep my job. I prepared myself to go back to work on the day after New Year's, pack up my office, and make room for Rosalyn.

I tried three times to rewrite my proposal to the Boticellis. If I was going to take a demotion, I might as well negotiate for a lighter schedule. I tried to put all my strengths into words, to explain why I was fit to run the department. After the third try I gave up. Maybe I'd get inspiration in the New Year.

73.

I bathed Jason and Robbie, then nestled both in the large round papasan chair and started reading books. I finished *Johnny the Tractor Finds a New Home*, and *The Cat in the Hat*. I closed the latter and said, "Bedtime."

"But Grandma reads us *Jack and the Beanstalk* too," Jason said.

"Grandma's not here," I snapped.

Jason burst into tears. Robbie cried in chorus. I had to read two more books to calm them down. It was long past their regular bedtime when finally I tucked both boys into bed and closed their bedroom door.

With both boys asleep, and Mom and Dad gone, the house was eerily quiet. No gin rummy for distraction. No banter about the day's events. I got out the cards and dealt a game of solitaire on the kitchen table. It was only seven-thirty. I didn't want to go to bed before my standard nine o'clock. I knew if I did, I'd just toss and turn half the night.

Bored, I decided to turn on the television and watch the live coverage of the New Year festivities in New York. This year the Times Square ball was decorated in red and green to look like an apple, in honor of the *I Love New York* campaign. Times Square was filled with college kids and happy couples. John Cougar performed "Hurts So Good." I could feel the "hurt," but none of the "good." The revelry depressed me.

On a typical New Year's Eve, Mike and I would get a sitter and go to a party. Last year I was pregnant and drank virgin cocktails. Mike had decided that since I was the designated driver, he could tie one on. He played his party photographer routine, a holdover from a college job, convincing several of the wives to lift their skirt and show a little leg, and the husbands to pose macho with cigars. Face it, Mike was the dynamic one in the marriage, the life of the party. I was the serious scientist. Life was boring without him. After fifteen minutes, I turned the television off. I was alone in a hick town with two sleeping kids. Happy New Year.

What did I have to look forward to in the New Year—limbo, isolation, despair. That was next year. Tonight, my two special friends, Jackie and Zanny, could cheer me up.

One small nip of Jack couldn't hurt.

Dr. Stone had said no alcohol. But Christ, I wasn't dead—yet.

I got out a whiskey glass and added just one ice cube. I poured half a shot and swirled the whiskey in the ice. Took one sip. Gulped the rest. Good old Jack burned all the way down. Mike had trained me in the fine art of drinking. *Always eat a few greasy appetizers.* The thought of greasy food made my stomach tighten like a noose.

I hadn't drunk in a while. The buzz felt great. Liberating. It was fun to be up for a change. I started dancing around the kitchen, a friend in each hand, singing, "Jackie and Zanny were lovers. Best friends to the crazy mother."

I stopped in my tracks. *Crazy mother.* That's exactly what I had become. Crazy. Alone.

I had been so proud to tell people "I'm the Head of Quality Assurance at The Marinara Factory." And then, if they asked what my husband did, I would casually drop, "Mike flies the SR-71, you know, that supersonic spy plane." Slam-dunk!

But I wasn't satisfied. Had to have two kids. Had to be department head. Had to have it all. The perfect life. Before Robbie, I was at the top of my game. Now I was at the bottom of the heap.

I grabbed two ice cubes and poured another shot, this time a double. I liked the way Jack warmed my tummy. This time I'd sip. Might as well include my other best friend. "Come on out Zanny. You need to join the party. Happy New Year!"

I opened the pill bottle and poured my friends out on the kitchen table. I counted them. Thirteen cute white ovals remained. I arranged them into an M for Mike.

"Well friends, what shall we do next?"

Maybe one would help me get through the night.

Just one.

What could it hurt?

I grabbed a glass of water, and picked up a pill. I contemplated.

Maybe I should take two? For good measure. Get a night of deep sleep.

No. Mom was gone, and tonight I needed to wake up with Robbie. I set the pills back on the table.

I felt rotten that Mom had left on a sour note.

After all she'd done for me. Damn it. Why did I yell at her?

Dropping everything three times and flying out here. I couldn't let it happen again. Couldn't go crazy again. If I did, they'd lock me up and throw away the key. But my two friends were here to prevent that. My thoughts were all a jumble. From the drink? Perhaps. But the beauty was—I didn't care.

I envisioned myself stabbing that asshole Chuck. Of course, I wouldn't do that. Or would I? Some days I wasn't sure what I was capable of. Maybe I could hire a hit man to do it for me. That was the Sicilian way. How a Boticelli would get the job done. A hit man. I liked that idea.

What if I did something to hurt the boys? In a moment of temporary insanity. Trying to protect them. Somehow injuring them. The closet incident had left me quaking in my stilettos.

Christ, what was I thinking?

74.

Good thing I had made a will. Mike's brother Terry and his wife Julia both loved Jason. She hadn't even met Robbie, but she adored babies. Terry was a preacher. They took their Bible literally. People could have worse faults.

They would provide a safe life for the boys. Jason would never play competitive sports. Terry still walked with a slight limp from an old high-school football injury. Robbie would never sit in a cockpit. Couldn't let him follow in his old man's footsteps. Get himself blown up.

Was that the life Mike would want for his boys? Safe—from a crazy mom, from anything courageous or foolhardy. The boys would be encouraged to marry conservative women, stay-at-home-mom types. To keep their distance from women who wanted it all and ended up with nothing.

I rearranged the Xanax into an L for loony. The second shot of Jack had gone down like silk. Maybe I should have three for good luck.

What had Dr. Stone said? "Three strikes, you're out." I was so close.

Better quit while I was ahead, while I still had the will power. I set the bottle of Jack in the cabinet above the stove. With Mom and Dad gone, I didn't have to hide it in my bedroom. I slurped the last gulp of Jack, diluted with melted ice, and rearranged the pills back to an M.

The big question was, did I want to go on living without Mike? Could I go on living without him? I wanted to be with him. If I took the pills, and didn't wake up on this earth, would I wake up in Mike's arms in heaven? I had this eerie sensation—Mike was reaching out to me, calling to me, waiting for me to … to what? That part was still dark and fuzzy.

I had gone on faith for so long. But Christmas had punched a big hole in my faith card.

Maybe I should check on the boys. I slowly twisted the door handle and walked in. First I peeked at Jason, sleeping in his captain's bed, his arm around Woofy, his hair all crumpled up. Next I peeked at Robbie, his little lips inhaling and exhaling softly, his body curled up in a ball.

Dad had made a shelf for Jason's three airplanes over the head of his bed. I took the SR-71 off the shelf and stroked the smooth wood. What would Mike want me to do? Much as he liked Terry and Julia, did he want his boys growing up as safe and boring Bible thumpers?

Suddenly it was clear, crystal clear. I put the plane back on the shelf, tiptoed out of the bedroom, and closed the door. I went to the kitchen table and swiped all the Xanax into my hand. Walked over to the kitchen sink. Grabbed a glass of water.

I held the pills in one hand, the water in the other. This was so much harder than I had imagined.

All the times I had thought of taking those pills. Of ending the nightmare. I'd told Molly, *I'm stronger than I look.*

Was I strong?

Or was I weak?

Jackie—give me courage. Let me end it.

Zanny—let me go to sleep and never wake up.

Mike—what should I do?

It was as if he was speaking to me, across the miles. *Kate, you know the right thing.*

If I kept these pills, sooner or later … in a moment of weakness, a moment of anger, a moment of desperation … I'd use them.

I went to the phone and stared at the number Dr. Stone had given me. If I called that number, would she report back to Sally? To Judge Steuben?

What had Jane said, "Promise me, you'll call 911." If I called 911, they'd know I was crazy.

I looked at the clock. Two minutes until nine, west coast time, almost midnight in New York. Would Jane be up? Would she be at a party? She had said I could call her. But at this hour? No. That was more crazy.

What else had Jane said? I set down the water, and got the first piece of paper with my mantra.

I'm not alone.

I'm not to blame for what I'm feeling.

I will be well and feel like myself again—this is treatable.

I said it out loud, "I will be well." Jane was right. I needed to believe in myself, to keep seeing Dr. Stone. I needed more time.

The second hand on the clock ticked toward the twelve, toward a new year, a fresh start.

I turned on the faucet, then the garbage disposal.

I turned my hand over and watched the pills fall one by one into the sink. As each one hit the disposal, there was a loud whirl. *Sorry Zanny.* The disposal crunched and sucked away my escape route.

Next I went to the cabinet above the stove and got the Jack. *You've got to go too, buddy.*

I tilted the bottle and watched the expensive brown fluid mix with the water going down the drain. Finally I turned off the disposal. The house was quiet as a graveyard.

I could turn the television on. By now the ball had dropped in New York City. But I couldn't bear to see all those happy people, kissing and singing "Auld Lang Syne." I headed to bed.

Ever since he left, I had not washed Mike's pillowcase. For a while the scents of his sweat and cologne had lingered. I curled up in a fetal cocoon and buried my nose in the pillow, struggling to catch a whiff of my sweetie. But even his scent was gone.

75.

The phone jingled. I woke with a start and glanced at the clock on the nightstand. Two-fifteen. What idiot would call me at this time of night?

Probably Spencer. Probably drunk.

I was pissed. I picked up the phone and uttered an irritated, "What?"

"Kate." A pause. "It's Jerome."

"Jerome?" His voice sounded strange—giddy and breathless. Surely Jerome wouldn't call me drunk.

"We've got Mike. The Navy Seals just plucked him out of North Korea."

"Really?" My heart pounded. I clutched the phone so hard I thought it would break.

Jerome didn't have many details. "Don't speak to anyone about this."

"Not even my parents?"

"No one. Not until he's back in the States. That might take a day or two. Understand?"

Now I was the giddy one.

* * *

Early the next morning, Jerome called again. Mike would need a thorough medical exam and a series of debriefings before he was released to return to the States. He could have no communications with me until after the debriefings. I nearly pinged off the walls in anticipation, but tried to keep myself occupied cleaning the house, and prettying up for the homecoming.

Finally, Jason and I stood on the edge of the flight line, along with most of the SR-71 squadron. Maybe three hundred people had come to welcome Mike home. I scanned the horizon, searching for the KC-135 tanker that was scheduled to land any minute. The sun was just setting, leaving the sky awash with waves of mauve threaded through a few dark clouds. The winter wind was sharp, and I had wrapped a thick black sweater over my red dress. Despite the chill, I was happy that I had decided on nylons and black heels for Mike's homecoming.

Betty Lou stayed in the car with Robbie, who napped through all the excitement. Jason played tag with a couple of other little boys. I hadn't told him about Mike, only that we were going out to the base to watch an airplane land. I didn't want to disappoint him—just in case something happened on the flight home.

The reality that Mike was alive was still sinking in. So many bizarre things had happened in the past six months. When I held my man in my arms, I'd know it was all real.

"There it is," somebody yelled. I saw the red and green wing lights as the plane approached. I held my breath until the tanker's wheels touched the concrete. It seemed an eternity as the plane slowed at the end of the runway, turned around, and taxied to the spot outside the hangar where we all waited. A ground crew wheeled mobile stairs to the plane.

A red line ran along the runway and out from the hanger. Civilians were never allowed into the area. The words: "WARNING RESTRICTED AREA – USE OF DEADLY FORCE AUTHORIZED," had been painted across the concrete. I never understood the line. After all, it was the families of the flight crews who gathered to welcome their warriors home. But in all the times I had come out to the base to meet the returning crews, no civilian had ever crossed the line. Everything to do with the SR-71 operations was top secret. Four MPs guarded the line, armed with assault rifles to ensure that the runway boundary was not breached.

Betty Lou came over with Robbie. He had woken from his nap and cried hungrily.

"I'll take him." I balanced Robbie on my hip, and plopped a pacifier in his mouth.

The passenger door of the plane opened. Mike appeared in the jet doorway. A big cheer went up from the crowd. When I saw him, my heart pounded. He looked like he hadn't eaten in a month. He was wearing a green flight suit, obviously borrowed from a tanker pilot. It hung on his thin frame. But there was that assured grin. I waved. He spotted me and started down the stairway. I shifted Robbie onto my left hip, then pointed with my right hand, "Look who's here, Robbie."

Jason played a few feet away. He looked up, recognized the man on the jetway. "Daddy." He sprinted toward the plane, darting across the red line of death. Spencer lunged to grab him, but missed.

Suddenly four M-16 rifles were aimed at Jason.

"Nooo!" I screamed.

76.

I dashed toward the line, as fast as I could in high heels. One of the MPs stepped in front of me. The other three kept their barrels beaded on Jason.

"At ease," the base commander yelled.

The armed guards relaxed. Thank god none of the guards had a trigger finger.

Jason started up the jetway. Mike caught him on the fourth step. He lifted our son in his arms and engulfed him with a huge bear hug, then shifted him to his hip. Jason was all smiles as he hugged his dad.

Mike was immediately surrounded by the other SR-71 pilots, slapping him on the back, shaking his free hand. I decided that since I could read, I'd obey Air Force protocol and wait for Mike to cross the line.

Mike pushed through the crowd and made his way to me. He set Jason on the ground, and held out his arms. We hugged like two ghosts reunited, clinging to each. His lips were on mine, his taste, his smell. I drank them in like a starving child.

Then he took Robbie off my hip, tossed him in the air, and whispered, "Daddy's home. What do you think of that?"

Robbie gurgled, then started whimpering.

"It'll take time," I said.

"He's at that 'who's this strange person with the deep voice' stage." Mike rubbed noses with Robbie, then handed him back to me.

Jerome gave a short speech, followed by the base commander. Both praised Mike and the Navy Seals. Then the base commander said Mike needed to go home and be with his family.

Mike asked me to drive. He would need to go back to the base the next day for more debriefings, but tonight was ours. Jason fell asleep ten minutes into the drive. We drove past the stone gate that marked the entrance to the base and Mike filled me in on the saga.

"The Air Force thought its planes were being shot down, but it turned out to be a sabotage of the fuel systems. They caught the guys behind it—two Japanese brothers. One confessed. We had just finished our refueling, and I had pulled up along-side the tanker to give them the thumbs-up. I saw the tanker explode and knew that the SR might be hit by pieces of shrap-nel. I yelled, 'Eject' to Robert." Here he stopped, choked up.

I reached over to caress his thigh. "I'm sorry about Robert."

We drove in silence for a few miles. Mike resumed his story. "When I saw the explosion, I knew everybody in the tanker was a goner. I had hoped Robert made it. Didn't know for sure until yesterday. Robert probably ejected two seconds after me. Too late. The SR exploded under me. The force was horrific. I searched for his raft, but couldn't find it. I'd been in the raft maybe ten minutes when a small fishing boat approached. I debated whether or not to try a shoot-out. Three guys had rifle barrels pointed at me. At that point I was still dazed from the ejection. My eyes were still burning from the explosion. I was afraid my aim would be off. I figured I could easily kill two. But the chances of getting all three before one got a shot off were too slim. I was thinking about you and the boys. I needed to play it safe."

"They took me onboard and slit my life raft. Then they searched me and took my gun. Took my personal locator beacon and stomped it. They were speaking Korean, so I had no idea what they were saying. I could tell they were scared, and arguing about what to do with me. One guy kept pointing to the ocean. The taller guy, the one that looked to be in charge

of the boat, kept shaking his head. Lucky for me, he won out."
Here Mike paused.

"The next morning they turned me over to the North Koreans, and I was taken to a prison camp in a remote area of the peninsula. Huge place. Three generations of Korean families rotting away there."

"Did they—" I couldn't say the word, torture. Mike read my mind.

"The North Koreans have some interesting interrogation techniques. I don't want to talk about it. Not to you. I learned later that they were planning to trade me for a group of five North Korean spies, so they kept my capture hush-hush. They needed me alive and in one piece to use as a bargaining chip. But they wanted some intel first."

"You didn't—"

"I fed them a lot of garbage. Just enough to make them think they were getting intel. But that's just for your ears."

"You've lost so much weight. Did they feed you?"

"We had a daily ration of chimchee, nasty fermented cabbage, sometimes with a rotten fish head thrown in. I swear, Kate, I'll never put another piece of fish in my mouth as long as I live."

"How did you escape?"

"There was this old guy. F-86 Sabre pilot. Shot down way back in '52. He had learned to speak Korean and had hooked up with a young Korean dissident, brilliant electronic genius. Kid had only been in the camp for a few months. We talked in the prison yard during the day and whispered in our cells at night. The kid had friends on the outside and had pieced together a small two-way radio. After several failed attempts, he eventually got word, via his buddies, to our government. The Seals were air dropped into the camp at night and found me. I refused to go without the old guy and the kid. The Seals helped us all slip under the fence into a remote area. They radioed for a chopper. It was there in minutes." Mike got choked up again.

"A perimeter guard got off a shot—the old guy stepped in front of the kid and took the bullet. The Seals killed the guard, but there was no saving the old guy. We brought his body back. I have letters for his old girlfriend. The old guy made me promise, if he didn't make it out alive, that I'd deliver them."

We drove on in silence. Mike yawned. "The chopper flew us back to the *Avenger*. You should have heard the cheers of the sailors when I stepped onto the deck of that ship. We've got one hell of a military, and I'm proud to be part of it."

Mike reclined the seat and relaxed. "Nice car. I had a lot of time to think while I was holed away in that prison. I'm sorry about a lot of things. We can talk about all that later. Tonight I'm tired, Kate."

We drove the rest of the way home in silence.

After tucking the boys in bed, Mike and I showered together. He ran his finger over my ribs. "I've been subsisting on about a tenth of what I'd normally eat. What's your excuse? Aunt Cecilia quit making sauce?"

"Aunt Cecilia had a heart attack. I've been so worried about her. She's out of the hospital, but probably won't be coming back to the plant very often. I'm not even sure I'll have a job on Monday. It's a long story." I exhaled deeply. "But it can wait." I didn't want to think about work. Tonight my world was complete.

Mike nodded, then turned off the water. We snuggled under the same towel, cuddling. Then Mike tossed the towel to the floor, sat me on the edge of the bed, and dropped to his knees.

"Kate, can you ever forgive me? I'm so sorry for leaving you alone. I thought you were milking this whole crazy thing. I thought you could just will the nightmare to go away. That you could be the person you were before the psychosis. Now I realize—"

He started sobbing. "I'm so sorry, Kate. I realize you'll never be the same person again. I'll never be the same person again. The memories of the explosion, the wretched loneliness, not knowing if I'd ever see you or the boys again."

I pulled Mike up into the bed and held him tight.

"I knew you didn't understand. Nobody knows, until they go through it." I touched his hand to my heart. "It's okay. I forgive you." Now I was the one who would have to be patient and understanding.

"Please, tonight. Just hold me," he whispered. "And I'll try to spend the rest of my life making it up to you."

77.

I made waffles. Offered to make eggs and bacon too, but Mike said that his stomach had shrunk. It would take a while before he was ready for big meals. Jason sat on his dad's lap, and they traded bites of waffle, dripping with syrup. One bite for Jason. One bite for Mike.

It was Friday, the second, and I was supposed to go to work. I decided to call in sick. Not a good move for first day at work in the New Year, but I knew I had my priorities straight.

The news of Mike's return had not broken. The CIA was putting together a cover story. The president would make an announcement at noon, Eastern. Mike needed to be back at the base later that morning for official photographs with the base commander and more debriefings.

After breakfast we lounged in the back yard. Jason showed Mike how well he could ride his tricycle. Mike sat on the chaise lounge, sipped coffee, and listened to the saga of my dilemmas while he was MIA.

I cuddled next to him and poured out all the emotions that had been pent up. "I was pretty optimistic for the first week. After that, it was tough. I felt your vibes, but thought maybe I was just crazy. I didn't want to tell anybody. I was struggling to keep the boys."

"Oh?" Mike jerked his head back.

"Yeah. Gestapo Sally came to visit on the day after your plane blew up. I disintegrated into a heap of jelly. She took the boys into protective custody. Paul helped me work that all out."

"You must have felt pretty alone, deserted."

"Mom and Dad came out. I wouldn't have made it without them."

"I was worried about you. I knew you were still not fully recovered from the psychosis," Mike said. "Did you go see that Falio guy again?"

"No. I have a new shrink. I like her a lot. She says I might have post traumatic stress disorder."

"Maybe I should go see her."

"She's just for women. But you could wear a wig."

"And heels?" Mike smiled.

It was good to see the spark in his eye. "Maybe not," I winked. "It helps to know that there are other women who've been through the same thing and recovered. I feel optimistic that I'm going to be okay, eventually. I have some new strategies that give me hope. It means a lot to know that you're willing to give me time to heal, that you'll be here to help take care of the boys."

* * *

After the president's press conference, the television crews returned. Jerome stationed a sergeant at our front door to keep them at bay. The Air Force released some footage of Mike stepping out of the tanker, and another shot of us hugging. The part where the rifles were aimed at Jason had been cut.

At work on Monday, I was greeted by cheers and a big banner in the front lobby. It read: "Welcome Home Mike Wahlberg."

I headed to the lab, mentally prepared to deal with Chuck's arrogance. To my surprise, the top of Chuck's desk had been cleared. The wall where his golf photos had hung was empty.

"Chuck's gone," a voice behind me said.

I turned. There stood Rosalyn. She extended a warm hand. "We heard the news. I'm so happy for you, Kate."

I stood there with my mouth open. Finally I stuttered, "Rosalyn, welcome."

"Sit down." She motioned to the chair behind the desk. I slid in.

"Fred decided to let Chuck go," she said.

"Fred, Francis, and I had a long chat after I met you and Chuck. The Boticellis don't want to lose you, but they didn't feel you were up to the challenges that will come with the expansion. Fred needed someone who could work overtime. I said I could get more work out of you in thirty hours than Chuck in fifty. Turns out that Fred didn't do enough checking before he hired Chuck. Your former colleague was let go from his last two jobs. Not an easy man to get along with, great with the brass, but condescending to his subordinates."

"So it wasn't just me."

"Definitely not. I told Fred that Campbell had initiated some flexible staffing in the past few years. It worked out well there, so we're going to try it at Marinara. Fred and I agreed that you can work part-time for now if you want. In six months we'll sit down and reevaluate."

Fred walked in and put his hand on my shoulder. "Staff meeting in fifteen minutes. We want you to sit in, while Rosalyn learns the ropes. The Boticelli family values your insights. We may still figure out a way to make you part of the leadership team."

I pinched myself, just to make sure I wasn't fantasizing.

78.

Mike came home that night from his debriefing. One of the SR-71 flight instructors was retiring in a month. Mike planned to apply for the job. Jerome had told him it was pretty much his for the asking. He would stay in the States, and still get to pilot his black mistress. No more TDYs, at least for the foreseeable future.

"One more thing. I delivered the letters. You'll never guess who the old pilot's girlfriend is."

It took me about three seconds to realize what he was saying. "Not The Colonel?"

Mike nodded. "The one you hate so much. Her lover saved my life."

I let this sink in. It had been convenient to blame everything on The Colonel. I was learning from Dr. Stone that many factors had contributed to the psychosis—my personality, the stress of bearing a critically ill child, the lack of a support system. My doctor was not to blame, but neither was I. It had all been the perfect storm.

We talked about my probation period with social services. Mike promised to arrange his schedule so that he'd be home to schmooze Sally. With Dr. Stone's help, and Mike home to shoulder the load, I felt capable of juggling career and family.

Mike suggested that we fly home to Kansas for Easter. There would be new baby chicks at the farm. He was looking forward to seeing his dad and his brother.

Jason crawled up on Mike's lap that night after his bath. "Dad, can we get a puppy?"

Mike looked at me.

I rolled my eyes and held my breath.

He tussled Jason's hair. "Give your mom and dad some time for things to settle down, maybe—six weeks—and then we'll talk about a puppy."

Postpartum Mental Health

by Teresa M. Twomey, JD,
Author of the book *Understanding Postpartum Psychosis:
A Temporary Madness* (Praeger)

Postpartum Mood Disorders Generally:
Mothers can experience a range of mood and anxiety disorders during pregnancy and/or the postpartum period. Postpartum symptoms may differ from our usual associations with these illnesses. *All postpartum/pregnancy mood disorders, including postpartum psychosis, can occur in women with NO history of mental illness.* It is important for a woman to know that if she does not "feel herself" she should seek help. All postpartum mood disorders are treatable. With adequate care, a woman will be herself again.

About Postpartum Psychosis:
When a woman experiences Postpartum Psychosis (which may include Postpartum Bipolar Disorder or Postpartum Depression with Psychotic Features) it may range from mild to severe—but the hallmark of the disorder is a psychotic break or "break with reality."
Some possible causes or contributing factors:

1) An underlying (but perhaps undiagnosed) bi-polar illness.

2) Incorrect medication. Some women who have a mild underlying bipolar illness may appear depressed and be prescribed an SSRI antidepressant. For those women an SSRI may cause a rebound mania so severe that the woman loses touch with reality (becomes psychotic).

3) Sleep deprivation. This can cause a psychotic break in an ordinary person. In addition, doctors often recommend rest and sleep for anyone who has had surgery or physical trauma so the body can repair itself. Therefore, it is vitally important that a woman have adequate rest postpartum. If a new mom is not sleeping well, she should seek immediate medical help.

4) Other causes and contributing factors exist. What is important to know is that *any* pregnant or postpartum woman COULD have postpartum psychosis—even if she has no underlying illness, receives adequate rest, and was fine after previous birthing experience(s).

Dangers of Postpartum Psychosis:

Postpartum Psychosis carries a risk of suicide and homicide (usually infanticide). Therefore, it is ALWAYS a **medical emergency.** Even a "nice" or "good" or "loving" mother may harm her child—she may even believe what she is doing is the BEST thing for the child, *even* if she knows it is illegal or will physically harm the child.

The vast majority of women with postpartum psychosis do not harm anyone. However, there is *no* way to predict who will or who will not, so families should always seek adequate help and educate themselves about this illness.

Women who have had this illness often struggle with "post-recovery recovery." After they no longer have symptoms of psychosis they generally return to their former selves but struggle emotionally with having had this illness. Even women who do not harm anyone may suffer severely. Untreated, this can last for decades. These women grapple with self-doubt, self-blame, fear of spontaneous recurrence, anger, grief, and other emotional issues.

Appearance of Postpartum Psychosis:

Postpartum psychosis is an "atypical" psychosis that does not always appear the same way. It may wax and wane, so a woman who appears fine one moment may appear psychotic moments later. Women have varying awareness of their own condition. Some may be able to initiate seeking help, others may not. A woman is more likely able to seek help if she is self-aware and knowledgeable about postpartum psychosis. However, the safety of all involved may depend on the partner and/or family (mother, siblings, in-laws) being able to recognize what is wrong and seek adequate help for the woman. (The family should be prepared to be active advocates for the woman—many tragedies have occurred after a woman or her family sought help.)

Symptoms of Postpartum Psychosis vary and a woman may not exhibit all of them (and because many of these rely on disclosure by the woman, the illness and the severity may not be obvious to an observer). Symptoms include: hallucinations (may include hearing things, seeing things, feeling things, or smelling things that are not there), agitation, bizarre thoughts, confusion, disorientation, cognitive impairment, paranoia, and delusions.

Postpartum Mental Health Resources

Websites:
Postpartum Support International   www.postpartum.net
   Resources include information about the various perinatal mood disorders, a warmline, and access to mental health providers and support groups.

National Suicide Prevention Lifeline   http://www.suicidepreventionlifeline.org/
   By calling 1-800-273-TALK (8255) you'll be connected to a skilled, trained counselor at a crisis center in your area, anytime 24/7.

Support For Military Families   http://www.postpartum.net/Get-Help/PSI-Support-for-Military-Families.aspx
   PSI has coordinators for each branch of the military, and there is a special report on Spousal Military Deployment and postpartum depression.

MotherWoman http://www.motherwoman.org/
   MotherWoman supports and empowers mothers to create personal and social change through support groups, facilitator training, professional training on perinatal emotional complications, and by teaching communities how to create community-based perinatal support.

Books:

Honikman, Jane, M.S. *I'm Listening: A Guide to Supporting Postpartum Families.* (portions included in this novel by permission of Jane Honikman) 2002

Twomey, Teresa M., JD. *Understanding Postpartum Psychosis: A Temporary Madness.* Praeger Publishers, 2009.

Feingold, Susan Benjamin, PsyD. *Happy Endings, New Beginnings: Navigating Postpartum Disorders.* New Horizon Press, 2013.

Sichel, Deborah and Driscoll, Jeanne Watson. *Women's Moods: What Every Woman Must Know About Hormones, the Brain, and Emotional Health.* William Morrow, 1999.

Akerman, Stacey, *Supermom.* iUniverse.com 2011.

Dunnewold, Ann L., Sanford, Diane G. *Life Will Never Be the Same: The Real Mom's Postpartum Survival Guide.* Real Moms Ink LLC, 2010.

Leung, Ivy Shih. *One Mom's Journey to Motherhood.* Abbott Press, 2011.

Moyer, Jennifer Hentz. *A Mother's Climb Out of Darkness.* Praeclarus Press, LLC. 2014.

Kleiman, Karen. *This Isn't What I Expected [2nd Edition]: Overcoming Postpartum Depression,* Da Capo Lifelong Books, 2013.

For a more complete list of books and resources
on maternal mental health topics, visit:
www.postpartum.net

Back In Six Weeks – Book Club Study Guide

1. Kate imagines that the Book of Revelation was written for her. How do Kate's strong religious beliefs create confusion for her? In what other ways might strong religious beliefs create confusion in the mind of someone who is mentally unstable?

2. Kate is admitted to the mental ward and medicated against her will. Do you think there are viable alternatives to medication? To hospitalization? Why or why not? How do you think women with postpartum psychosis should be treated?

3. What do you think might have happened if Kate had not received any mental health treatment?

4. In the opening scene, we learn that a nurse told Kate to go to sleep and quit bothering them, just moments before she gave birth. Do you know of cases where medical staff missed a diagnosis, or made a mistake in treatment? As the patient or family member, how did that make you feel?

5. Kate feels rejected because Robbie ends up as a bottle-fed baby. What role do you think breastfeeding plays in the emotional attachment between mother and child?

6. Do you believe that the report to social services was justified? Do you think that Robbie was in danger? If you knew a mother who was struggling with emotional issues and childrearing, how might you offer assistance or support? What signs or symptoms in a mother would prompt you to contact social services or call 911?

7. Compare Kate's three psychiatrists—Pointy Beard, Dr. Falio, and Dr. Stone. How do you think the gender of the psychiatrist might color the doctor/patient relationship?

8. What role do you think that sleep plays in mental health? Are all new moms sleep-deprived to some degree? How much sleep do you think a new mom needs to function properly? How long do you think a person could go without sleep before their cognitive ability is impaired?

9. Mike and Kate fight over Kate's going back to work. How have the expectations of working moms, as well as those of their spouses and employers, changed from 1980 to the present? How has your own perspective on the challenge of balancing career and family changed over the years?

10. Kate and Mike communicate about once a week via phone. Modern military families can communicate more frequently via email and SKYPE. What effect do you think frequent deployment has on military family life? What would it be like to have a baby when your spouse was half a world away?

11. Kate tries to hide her psychosis from friends and co-workers. Has the stigma of mental illness changed over the years? Is there a different stigma for depression than psychosis? Do you think it is possible that you have known someone who suffered from one of these, but hid it?

12. It takes Kate a long time to locate a psychiatrist that she trusts and who has experience with postpartum mental health. Does the internet make it easier to find support and resources? Do you use the internet as a resource for medical advice?

13. There's a scene where Kate puts her hand over Robbie's mouth to smother his cries. It's hard to imagine a mother harming her child. What factors would determine whether a mom who hurts her children should go to prison or a mental health facility?

14. Kate hides a lot from family, friends, and doctors. Do you think that individuals who are contemplating suicide leave clues, or does their act of desperation come as a shock to loved ones?

15. Has this book changed your perception of women who experience perinatal mood disorders, and in what ways?

Acknowledgements

The inspiration for writing this book came when I read *The Success Principles* by Jack Canfield. I started writing in May 2005, completed the first ugly draft in May 2006, and finished revising in May of 2014. Writing fiction has taken me down paths I would never have imagined, expanded my knowledge of women's mental health issues, and increased my appreciation for great literature.

First of all, I would like to thank Jonathan Maberry, who has informed and inspired so many authors. I was floundering with the process of writing my first novel when I enrolled in Jonathan's "Novel in Nine Months" class. Jonathan encouraged me to write under my real name rather than a pen name. His advice at the first class: You can do this. You'll want your real name on it. Go home and write.

Lots of people helped me to refine the craft of storytelling. At the Writers Room of Bucks County I met other budding novelists. Annette Hamilton led a great peer critique group in Bucks County. Toni Lopopolo conducted a writing salon on the nuances of writing fiction. Kathryn Craft is a great developmental editor. She analyzed my first version of the novel and encouraged me to revise my plot. Charol Messenger advised me to tighten the scenes. As the writing progressed, Deb McLeod helped to shape and refine the final manuscript.

I'd also like to thank the many volunteers at Greater Lehigh Valley Writers Group, Philadelphia Writers Conference, and Pikes Peak Writers Conference, who organize annual writing conferences. These have been a great source of inspiration and camaraderie. The Colorado Independent Publishers

Association gave me the courage to finally get the book published.

So many people have served as "first readers." I'd like to give heart-felt thanks to: Barbara Pearse, my very first reader, long-time friend, and supporter in this journey. Also to Nancy Jackson, Jennifer Gerdes, Kathy Scott, Donna Berry, Rose Schmidt, Sharlene Gardner, Audrey Schwery, Mary Jo Beug, Jeanne Kieffer, and Jerry Waxler for their suggestions and encouragement.

The book *Women's Moods* by Deborah Sichel and Jeanne Driscoll was a true revelation. It helped me understand the symptoms and personality traits of women with various perinatal mood disorders, and introduced me to the concept of Postpartum Post Traumatic Stress Disorder. Thanks to the members of Postpartum Support International who read my manuscript and/or provided suggestions and encouragement—Jane Honikman, Birdie Gunyon-Meyer, Susan Feingold, and Wendy Davis. Special recognition goes to Teresa Twomey, who helped me shape this final version. Heartfelt thanks to the many women I have met through PSI who shared their stories and insights on postpartum psychosis. Donna Farley Wade and Sarah Pearse helped brainstorm the role of social workers and child welfare. Korey Elger explained the nuances of child protective custody.

Joe Kinego's thoughtful review helped me understand the life of an SR-71 pilot as well as the inner workings of the 1st Reconnaissance Squadron. Richard Graham's book *SR-71 Revealed*, provided technical information about the schedule and attire of SR-71 pilots.

Special thanks go to Julia Vering and Cathy Bowers for the cover photography; Johnny Wilson for the author photo; and Angela Werner and Michael Höhne, my former bicycle buddies, for the excellent book and cover design.

Sharon Gerdes—Motivational Speaker

Sharon has presented around the globe. She speaks on food and nutrition topics, maternal mental health, and personal motivation. To schedule Sharon to speak to your book club or organization, visit her website:

www.SharonGerdes.com

At the website, you can also subscribe to her "Food and Mood Blog."

CPSIA information can be obtained at www.ICGtesting.com
Printed in the USA
LVOW04s0057051214

417160LV00001B/1/P